DREAMVINE

Book Three of the Harkentale Saga

by

Jeremy James Smith

Published by Harkentale Press

www.JeremyJamesSmith.com

Cover art by Desiree Harrison and Sheena Smith

This book is a work of fiction. Names, characters, places and incidents are products of the author's imagination or are used fictionally and are not to be construed as real. Any resemblance to actual events, locales, organizations, or persons, living or dead, is entirely coincidental.

Printed in the United States of America

10 9 8 7 6 5 4 3 2 1

First Edition

Acknowledgements and Dedication

For my oldest son, Coen.

Writing Dreamvine has overlapped your early teenage years, and I'm struck by your development as a person. Still the kind-hearted, happy, nerdy kid, but ever more the young man. Your transformation is akin to what the characters experience in the vine. The same person emerges, but with so much more; both apparent and hidden. I can't wait to see your next evolutions.

I'd like to acknowledge Sheena, my partner and literary enabler. You help this series happen in so many ways, and you make my days worthwhile. Thank you.

And Emily, who has kept me on task and helped make this book happen on a schedule.

And notably for this book, Robb - the person whom I picture when I write about the Ivon. Just physical appearance and mannerisms, of course; Robb is a truly good person. Thanks for lending your look - I'll make sure the executive producers of the film call you for the role.

Prologue

"I told them we could not save them,
I pled with them it was too late.
They looked, the one to the other,
And their bravery sealed their fate.

Two can ne'er o'ercome sixty,
Two is a number too small.
Two fought with deadly intens'ty,
And the two were the last two to fall.

I could not help with the battle,
My allies were too far away.
So I called with a rasp and a rattle,
A Dreamvine to Dream them awake.

The Dreamvine demanded a bargain,
Two Dreamings call for a high price.
So I promised if to me it harkened,
I'd offer a great sacrifice."

- Indaria lo Thenalah, The Song of Dreams Awakened

Chapter 1

What's in a Dream?

Dwarves do not belong in the woods. Angus was alone again in the elven forest, a day's ride southwest from his home. Not often prone to hatred, Angus hated this forest. By the mounting evidence of trauma on Angus' body, the feeling was mutual. And the forest was winning.

Somewhere along the way he'd been shot; a dozen arrows protruded from every vulnerable spot on his armor. The crude manufacture confused him; these arrows were not elven. Nor were they orcish. Those tended to be works of terrible art in their own way. While the dwarf would never admit it aloud, Angus respected orcs' ceremonial arrowcroft and their dedication to hunting and war.

These arrows were neither made to be beautiful nor brutal. *Mass production,* he thought, *can only mean one group: humans.* He saw none, nor any sign of habitation at all as he struggled, bleeding, through the mal-effluent mud. Rain encompassed everything. One of the arrows fell from his body. Blood spurted once and was stilled as if dressed with invisible gauze.

The perforated dwarf paused, considering, then fell as if tripped by a root rising from the soupy ground. A large rock, the first one he could remember seeing today, bypassed his raised visor, ridding Angus of useful consciousness.

----- -----

Johan marveled at the dwarf sitting at Patrick's forge. He sat astride two very large, very dead orcs. Smoking. Caked in layer upon layer of blood and bits, calmly enjoying his pipe. It was the single most amazing sight he'd beheld. He took copious mental notes for his later report to the Ivon. That the warrior came through the fight essentially undamaged was amazing.

He looked down at his own body, nearly ruined. The blood coating his body was his own, and it flowed from myriad wounds. Almost all injuries were from arrows, except for the two gut wounds from shortswords that Ivonian archers used. *Those orcs attacking the Sliver must have taken out a group of Ivonian archers to gain such weapons. But why bother using them? Orcish axes, maces, broadswords, and spears were all more effective weapons.*

----- -----

Angus tapped the back of the steel chisel with the small ball-peen hammer. One small chip at a time, never risking a crack. He'd been working on this small stone for days, progressing slowly but steadily. When it was finished, the stone would become one of a thousand in the wall of the expanded boar stye. Within a week, the excrement would build up, and not even the boars would see his work.

Remind me about how I should take pride in every stroke, how every stone matters, and how each action we take reverberates throughout millennia. This is ridiculous! Especially ridiculous given his wounded state. Angus did not remember being shot, but ten arrows protruded from his hips and armpits, all of the places that good plate might not cover.

He shook his head as an arrow evaporated from sight, leaving a deep hole that bled only for a few seconds. He felt no pain. As he observed his wounds, his hands still worked. That is, until a single missed stroke damaged the stone. *This is it,* he thought, *another week's work ruined. The master will surely send me down the road now.*

----- -----

Johan watched Ynghild dress from across the room. She was beautiful. Her youthful voluptuousness belied her highly athletic abilities. He allowed a remembrance of their recent activities, all the more amazing for the numerous arrows that should be rooting him to the spot. He bled from some of the wounds. His rudimentary knowledge of anatomy assured him of the mortal nature of his wounds. *She was my first and should be my last. Yet somehow, still I live. Perhaps I am immortal?*

----- -----

Angus glanced at his armor. Too far away. His weapons also sat out of range. The beautiful elven maiden read out a list of his crimes. She ended by asking if he knew what day it was. As he looked over his wounds, all he could say was:

"Thursday?"

The elf was not amused.

Angus was in pain. *How many times did they shoot me?* Held high by animated vines strung between two tall, red trees, the bleeding dwarf watched another green tendril snake itself around the shaft of an arrow that protruded from his right hip.

The world went white as the offshoot yanked the projectile from the dwarf's body. As another verdant runner pressed itself into the freshly opened wound, Angus felt himself slip back into unconsciousness.

Chapter 2

A Watchful Meeting

"Thursday?"[1] Indaria managed, in between fits of giggles. The elven princess laughed so hard now that the tears came. Hiding her face behind slender, flawless hands, her shoulders shook.

Bedwyn guffawed with her. He knew the joke from a previous telling, though the elf's rendition was a bit different. They sat on a wooden bench, a gift from Alene to Indaria and her unlikely tree. Indaria never left the spot, staying under the spreading branches of the ancient live oak as the weeks passed. Now the pair regaled each other with stories of Angus.

"At the time," she continued, "we discussed killing him. And that fell within the law, given the raw amount of damage he inflicted on the forest during his passage. One vote kept Angus alive. I was on that council…"

The dwarven king watched as her shoulders and body adjusted their shuddering cadence. Her mirth was replaced by sobs, and she buried her face in her hands. Bedwyn's hand rose awkwardly, hovering over her back. One did not touch royalty. Dwarves tried not to touch elves, as a rule. But he recognized this moment for what it was. A person, grieving, in need of comfort. He let his hand rest softly between her shoulders.

"You can't blame yourself."

"I can."

"Why? You didn't kill him."

"We nearly did. We should have."

---

[1] It is a long story, but important to the overarching tale. If you missed it, you'll find the original account in Holtgart, Book One of the Saga. Angus had become lost in the forest, bathed in a pool that turned out to be magical and a holy site to the elves, and been subsequently captured for his trespasses. It wasn't Angus' best day.

"But you didn't." The dwarf sighed. "Even if it was only by one vote, you did the right thing."

She looked at him, her cheeks slick with tears, fine eyebrows furrowed and creased.

"We didn't execute him. But only because of one vote. That vote, however you count it, was not mine." She dropped her head to his shoulder, bawling with renewed energy.

Bedwyn opened his mouth to speak, but nothing came out. As he patted her on the back with paternal concern, the old strategist regarded the parasitic vine that laced itself through the tree's branches. He could see no roots, but many-pointed leaves carpeted boughs where he expected gritty bark.

In the middle hung two giant, green sacks, looking like ten-foot-long peapods. Inside, he knew, lay Angus and Johan. He tried to imagine what they were experiencing, if anything. Indaria spoke as if sensing his unspoken question.

"I still do not know if it will succeed. The tree is very old, but the vine is much older. They are very rare. I only know of three on the Cyfandir." The elf took a moment to breathe deeply. "The vine craves dreams, and will go to great lengths to keep a person alive and dreaming. This one has been without a dreamer for decades and was - hungry - for more.

"So hungry it made two dreampods. Again, something incredibly rare. Neither Angus nor Johan were breathing when I gave them to it. They breathe now, and dream." Indaria spoke as she joined Bedwyn's gaze.

"And you say the tree brought it here?"

"I wouldn't call this a mere tree, but yes. I knew it was nearby, and I called it."

"Amazing."

"Not really." She wiped her eyes on a gossamer sleeve, no longer crying. "The calling is elementary. The fact that the being was nearby when needed, is what impresses me. I know of fortunate souls, but Angus' luck far exceeds any I've seen in my time."

"How long, I wonder, has your time been? You seem yet young." Regret at his rudeness crossed his face, even as he said the words.

“I am still young.” She gave the dwarf a considering look. “Yet I remember the tales of your tactical prowess when they were still news.”

They both chuckled at that and looked up at the newcomer, young Queen Alene. The Queen ventured alone and unguarded; whether out of overconfidence or a respect for Veynsian tradition, none could say. It was no secret whom she was here to visit.

“Don’t mind me,” the lithe young woman said, “I’ll be up here.” She stepped up onto one of the low, reaching branches and climbed the tree. Her climbing style appeared to be half dance, half outright risk. She jumped and swung from one to the next as she ascended in a rough spiral. She lit on a higher branch that allowed her access to both pods.

The old dwarf and young elf watched the freshly-adult woman as she laid an ear against each pod, listening for the breathing and heartbeat issuing steadily. The queen inspected Angus’ shorter and much wider pod with concern. Something much more than concern passed between her and Johan’s verdant cocoon. After whispering quiet words to the dreaming man, Alene dismounted the tree with a flourishing roll.

“Will they come out soon?” Her question was directed at the elf.

“It is possible and becomes more possible every day. They gain strength. If they do emerge, I suspect they will be somewhat different than when they entered. I would not expect the same people they were before the battle.”

“Battle changes a person.” Bedwyn’s tone was sagastic. “When you take a life, or spare one, something in your soul changes.”

“True, Bedwyn, but that is not the change I expect. They have been, well, *communing* with a Dreamvine for weeks. I have never experienced the process myself, and I never hoped to. In exchange for life, the vine extracts a price.”

Indaria paused, scanning the branches above and around her. “...and that price must always be paid. This vine has interacted with many generations of elves and men. The vine keeps a shadow of those it holds. Some portion of those shadows imprint those who survive its effects.”

The trio sat in silence for a while, waiting and hoping. A dwarf brought food around mid-morning—hearty sausages and potatoes for Bedwyn, and fruit and bread for Indaria. Alene enjoyed a share of both offerings. After the meal, Alene excused herself to sail back across the bay where she held court five days a week.

Bedwyn and Indaria kept vigil until after lunch when Bedwyn had a meeting with the merchants in town. He left her with guards at a respectable distance and a fresh platter of fruity foodstuffs.

When she was relatively alone, Indaria sang. She cantered elven prayers, chanted melodic stories of the long-forgotten past; and she sang love songs - always in elvish, and always directed at the long-healing dwarf whom she had once advocated killing.

Chapter 3

Running, Late

Alene's days became routine sooner than she'd hoped. Directing the budget of a city-state should have been enough, but being the ruler of the Veyns involved so much more. She took several hours early this morning to put some of the less public affairs in order before her daily visit to Johan's tree.

Now the young queen with curly golden hair sprinted from the docks to the central plaza, and right into the palace's main entrance. She didn't bother with her private staircase, hurtling instead up the grand stair in the center of the room that rose two stories, splitting and doubling back to the Cour Royale. One final kick and she approached her throne, sliding along the terrazzo floor until, at the very last instant, she pivoted and launched her body, pirouetting before landing seated on her throne.

The room, filled on either side with petitioners, clapped politely, although more than one glance brought her attention to the fact that she still wore her sailing pants. This wasn't the first time in her burgeoning reign that Alene eschewed fashion in favor of efficacy. Indeed, efficiency often won out over decorum when this Queen was involved.

"Good morning to you all," she intoned, to a rumbling set of responses. "I apologize for my tardiness. Let's get down to it, shall we?"

Piers, the beanpole of a court steward, took one step forward. "Gaufroi, Master of three merchant ships that fly the Veynsian standard, requests an audience."

"Of course! Master Gaufroi, I am familiar with your business. I'm particularly fond of the mangoes you import; they remind me of my childhood." This was true, although Alene suspected this would be another in a long list of petty merchants' squabbles.

"Ah, you like them! Excellent." Gaufroi was clearly uncomfortable. "I am glad because I face a choice, one that I am not fond of."

"And what choice might that be?"

"The choice of home port. The Ivon has declared that Veynsian-flagged ships may not sell their wares in any of the Ivon's ports. I have even heard rumors of Veynsian ships being burned for bounty by Ivonian privateers. I, however, have not witnessed any of these occurrences.

"The Ivon has invited any Veynsian ships that wish to fly Ivonia's flag and pay Ivonian taxes to become part of their merchant fleet. I do not desire that resolution. I stand proud of my Veynsian heritage. My only hope is that you can find a way to make this choice easy for me."

Alene sat silent, considering. *I wish Johan were here. He knows more about the Ivon than I ever will.* The simple act of anticipating what her Ivonian companion might suggest spurred a strategy in her mind.

"Ivonian taxes are somewhat steep, is that not so?"

"Quite. Nearly thirty percent, all tolled."

"What goods do you sell there?"

"The same as I do here: tropical fruits, woven reed baskets, and similar island fare."

"Business has been good, I take it?"

"Yes, Your Highness. Until now, we have been fortunate. But I fear the Veynsian market will not bear the same fruits, if you will, as the whole Ivonian nation."

"You are right, of course. Yet here is what I propose: You bring your wares to market here. Sell what the market will bear. Any unsold goods, I will purchase myself, at market value minus thirty percent. You will still pay our flat-rate tax, of course, but this way you can cut Ivonia out entirely without a loss."

The merchant considered, and the congregation tittered in discussions.

"Your Highness, that is an excellent solution! I would gladly accept!"

"Piers, I would like you to have this agreement drafted, and we will each sign tonight at the end-of-week feast on the plaza. Gaufroi, I will see you there, no?"

"You most certainly shall. My Queen, you are magnificent and generous!"

That proved to be the most popular subject of the day. How the Ivon bullied merchants, and how Alene would turn the tables. Fourteen more merchants approached with the same concerns, and fourteen times Alene offered a personal guarantee. By the end of the day, it was clear that she needed more warehouse space, and soon. She sent Piers with an invitation to the dwarves of the Pickled Marble Consortium for dinner that evening.

Chapter 4

A Community Re-formed

Bedwyn smiled as he entered the Crank and Whistle, a public room owned by an older dwarf, but geared toward the sensibilities of goblins - as far as he could tell. It was successful in that you could find men, dwarves, and goblins inside on any given evening. To the best of Bedwyn's knowledge, the pub was the first of its kind, anywhere.

He approached the table where several of the new players of what had been Veynsport - later Ivonsport, now Canolbwynt Masnach - sat drinking together. The goblin engineer Koksal alternated between snickers at the others' jokes and sipping at the black-as-midnight and steaming drink held in both hands. Bedwyn took the seat next to him and called for the server.

"Oh, your Majesty! Now what can I bring for you today?" The woman was large, somewhat gelatinous, and wore a confidently mischievous smile she knew made dwarves squirm. That fact may have landed her the job. "Koksal's got us serving that hot grease he likes, would you care to try some?" Neither the corners of her mouth nor her eyebrows could climb any higher on her face.

"Madam, as old and rusty as I may be, I still prefer a good stout for my social lubrication, thank you." The table positively erupted in laughter, and the serving woman left, nodding, swaying, and jiggling all at once.

The shrewd-looking man across from Bedwyn was Thodd, a farmer who spent most of his life on two hundred acres just north of town. He was here now representing the rural portion of Canolbwynt's population. As Bedwyn received his quart of dwarven stout, he raised his austere tankard in salute.

"Here, boys.[2] To a new way of doing things; to working together, and making something greater than before!" The table joined his toast, then went quiet as everyone lowered the level of their drinks.

When they returned their refreshments to the table, a new face drew their attention. Estelle. She always did grab attention. Even at fifty, her red hair and freckles were vibrant and full of fury; she exuded womanhood. Estelle was loud, and raucous, and did a very good job of representing the city-bound dock workers and related professions.

"Boys, is it? Perhaps I should send one of the boys from the docks to take my place…" She made to leave, and a chorus of "No!" and "Please stay!" brought her, smiling wryly, back to her seat at the head of the table. That was where she sat naturally, despite the presence of a bonafide king. Estelle was effectively in control of Canolbwynt, and 'the boys' liked it that way.

Graener Doublestein, the dwarven proprietor of the Crank and Whistle, took his place at the table, followed by refills for the whole group.

"All right, lads," Estelle started, "What do we have today?"

Koksal spoke first.

"Our move is going well. The dwarves left a solid water supply in the old Holt and a remarkable plumbing system. Once we pressurize the waste pipes, we'll be in business with a liveable space!"

"P-pressurize the waste pipes?" Bedwyn was incredulous. "Why would you want to do that? It sounds like a setup for a really big mess!"

"Nonsense! The pressure keeps the pipes clear, and the steam keeps the smell down. Trust me, it will be fine!"[3]

---

[2] Dwarves are an odd lot when it comes to pronouns. Dwarves are very private individuals when it comes to gender; in polite or working company, they feel it rude to address gender. In most situations, they default to the mundane masculine pronoun, only elevating to the more revered feminine when they give birth; and even then, it is only recognized when relevant. Dwarves, in general, don't like to brag.

[3] Goblins on the Cyfandir are very confident in their powered machines, whether steam, rocket, or otherwise. They will apply power to any problem, in the vein of "throw the spaghetti at the wall and see what sticks." In the case of pressurized sewage, most reasonable folks exhibit a healthy skepticism, because nobody really wants to see what sticks.

"Where have I heard that before?" muttered Bedwyn.

"I like the idea of keeping the smell down," Estelle said. "A long day of work gives our folk aroma enough."

"I'll say the supplies of provisions - foodstuffs, beer, you know - well, it's been a *lumpy* supply. I'd love a way to even the flow of imports out." Graener spoke for both the dwarves of the infant city, and its multiple pubs, inns, and restaurants.

"Any ideas?"

There was a moment as the folks around the table searched their brains. Try as they might, nothing good came out.

"All right then." Estelle moved things on. "We've torn down the last of the dangerous structures, and I believe we won't find any more dead left unburied. It has been a long and often sickening task, but I think we are past that part of our recovery."

Every eye looked downward, toward drinks or the table. Bedwyn looked up first.

"Every life lost in war is a tragedy. Even those of our enemies. I say this not as a platitude but as a leader of warriors for almost two millennia. The number of dwarven, human, goblin, and even elven lives lost under my command is something I would rather not calculate, but even so, I mourn them all - friend and foe, soldier and civilian." He raised his tankard again. "A salute to the men, women, children, dwarves, and goblins who lost their lives in this conflict. May your souls rest easy and your families remember you fondly!"

The company saluted after their individual customs, then drained their glasses. Estelle took the reins again.

"Thank you, King Bedwyn. It is an honor to have you among us. We relish your wisdom."

"To that point, my company and I will remove in the next few days to the Smaragdine Holt. We have business of our own to tend to. Your people have been very accommodating, and we will return soon."

After the thanks and niceties died down, they returned to business. Thodd reported on the state of crops and livestock in general. Estelle shared about the mood within the city. But it was what Graener learned that interested them the most.

"It is clear that we get on splendidly. But bartenders get to hear honest talk and deeply-held opinions, more the later it gets to be. We've been hearing about a bit of friction between groups.

Dwarves don't trust goblins, goblins don't trust men, and men don't trust dwarves. It is just talk at this point, but there are some genuine racists out there."

Koksal squinted his whole face and glanced at Bedwyn. "Is that true? Dwarves don't trust goblins?"

Bedwyn attempted to disguise his knowledge of the unsuccessful goblin attack on his Holt earlier this year. This was not the time or place to get into that particular twisted and muddy scenario.

"My dear engineer, dwarves don't even trust each other with knowledge of their gender. If a dwarf exists that doesn't trust a goblin, I'd chalk it up to a general skepticism about the outside world, not a personal grudge. And as for men not trusting dwarves, after the Ivon's recent campaign against Angus, I'm not surprised. There were handbills posted accusing Angus of all manner of evil; not one was accurate. Bad information is insidious. Once it is in the public eye, it comes up again and again in arguments.

"Let's keep listening, and please let me know if this grows out of proportion. If we put incorrect opinions in check, we can maintain balance. After all, without unpopular opinions, we cannot progress as a society."

Chapter 5

A Feast Fit for a Queen

Gertrude, much more than the small, middle-aged woman she presented, took good care of the dwarven stonemasters that inhabited Angus' villa. Her short stature allowed her easy use of a building specifically made for dwarves. More than that, Gertrude knew what dwarves needed from her and provided it without fail.

When she heard of a royal visit, the third in a month, she knew she had to make it special for the young woman who ruled the Veyns. Sausage, beer, potatoes, and beer[4] would simply not do for the Queen. So she went shopping.

The Veyns were an amazing place for buyers and sellers alike. Everything was imported, even the water. Every trip to the market was different. A fruit that you found every day for the last three weeks might not be available for months. Staples like flour and cheese varied wildly in price, too.

But Gertrude was skilled at running a household. Her children had grown tall and strong eating her offerings. Even her late husband often remarked on her creativity in the kitchen. Now that they were all gone, keeping house for a dozen grown dwarves held just the right amount of challenge. The woman flitted through the market plaza, lighting for a moment at one stall, buying from the next until she wore several baskets of fresh foodstuffs. Stalks and leaves projected in all directions, making her look like a miniature, marching garden as she returned to the dwarven villa.

The next several hours were a flurry of cooking, cleaning, and setting. Three times dwarven occupants dodged her as she hurtled down the hallway. Twice, they ran to her aid when a new mess was discovered. The woman, though employed by the dwarves to do so, ran the house with matronly authority.

---

[4] Standard fare for dwarves.

Her efforts paid dividends, obvious by the content and quality of her culinary offerings. The weather, not daring to offend Gertrude, contributed a picturesque sunset just after the Queen arrived.

----- -----

Alene smiled broadly as she exited the public gondola, climbing past layers of greetings as her feet carried her up three flights of stairs to the roof. Gertrude stood behind the table, beaming. Gertrude had become one of Alene's very favorite women, and she went out of her way for these visits partially to see the professional domestic; hoping to learn more about competence and effective attitude just by being around her.

"Good evening, Gertrude. This looks like a wonderful feast!"

"Thank you, Majesty. It is just something I threw together."

Clompy bootfalls preceded the third voice, this one dwarven.

"Now what have you gone and done, woman? Where's the roast? And what's this purple shite?" Gierman smiled as he spoke, apparently expecting to be cuffed.

"Shite?" Gertrude was upset. She picked up the purple root, cooked tender and bursting with flavor. "You call this shite? You should try it!" With that, she cast it with power at the dwarf's face. He raised his arm a moment too late, the still-hot tuber bursting on his cheek. His thick salt-and-pepper beard took the brunt of the impact. He chuckled for a moment, then stopped, noticing Alene for the first time.

"Your Majesty! I humbly apologize for the intrusion. If you'll excuse me -"

"I don't think I shall. Have a seat, Gierman. We have things to discuss, and my time is too valuable to wait for you to have a bath." Alene was trying on a mother's voice, as it seemed appropriate. "Especially not when you've mistreated this noble woman so. You should apologize."

Gierman stood, shocked. He wasn't used to decorum in general, and here he stood, guilty of transforming a meal cooked with care and craft into a crude dueling tool. If it weren't for the thick beard, his cheeks would have shown crimson embarrassment. He offered a bow towards Gertrude.

"I beg your pardon, madam. I have spoken ill of your efforts and that was wrong. Please accept my apology."

Gertrude pursed her lips and tapped a foot to indicate her continued displeasure.

"Don't let it happen again. You can go a day without overdosing on beef and pork."

"Yes, ma'am." He sat across from Alene and started to speak again when Flannan showed up. The smell of the pickling process rolled off of him, sour and pungent. Gertrude backed him up against the banister overhanging the courtyard.

"Flannan Elfblade, you will take yourself away and bathe, right this second! How dare you bring that stench to my table?" Gertrude's composure came apart at the seams.

Alene stood, taking a step toward the arguing pair, hoping to salvage the evening. But Gertrude was having none of it. Flannan's attitude, combative and flippant, did not help.

"It's been a long day, Gertie. Let me gather some food and I'll bathe later."

"NO!" She shouted. "You will bathe now!"

"I'd like to see you make me, woman." The young dwarf stuck his chest out, well-muscled, but a bit top-heavy. The short woman sank an inch, crouching, then burst upwards, slamming her shoulder into his chest, knocking him back.

Flannan tried to recover with a step back, but there was no space. Utter surprise painted his face as his feet came up. He fell, head-first and silent, over the third-story railing. Gierman jumped up with a gasp. Alene shrieked. Gertrude laughed.

A full second later they heard the splash. Gertrude was still laughing. Alene and Gierman leaned over the rail, seeing that his fall put him right into the watery slip, perfectly placed between the dwarven steamship and the stone quay. Alene turned to Gertrude, white-faced.

"You could've killed him! You are very lucky he fell where he did. If he'd died, I would have had no choice but to find you guilty of murder!"

"Lucky, you say?" Gertrude moved her hand from the railing, right where she had pushed Flannan. Two marks in the stone bracketed his last position. "I call it prepared. I found these marks while I was first cleaning the place up; it took me three weeks before I figured out what they were for. An old dwarven prank, I suspect. They mark the space where a fall can be survived. Or so I hoped."

Gierman studied the marks for a while. Alene took a close look, then started to laugh. The dwarf joined her, as did Gertrude. The only one not enjoying the moment was Flannan, climbing the ladder out of the brackish water. To the housewoman's credit, he smelled better already.

A short time later, the four sat around the table, enjoying some truly fine cooking in traditional Veynsian style. Before the third glass, Alene broached the subject of foundations.

"Gentledwarves, you have been very successful with the pickled marble business so far. Now I ask you to step up the pace. Recent developments require the Veyns to add several warehouses immediately."

"My Lady Queen, that may present a problem."

"And why is that?"

"We're out of marble."

Alene could not hide her shock. Her head flinched back as if someone had punched her in the face.

"What happened to it?"

"We've used what was here. Now we'll have to head back to the source and ferry more over. The pace of travel is the main limiter."

"Where is the source? Can the fleet help?"

"Heh. I wish." Gierman wagged his head. "The stones are heavy and awkward, and come from the Connemara Atoll to the south. Your ships can't traverse the entrance to the cave quarry where we obtain the stones."

"The Connemara Atoll, you say? Where? I've spent some time on the southern beaches." This was true. Her mother's tropical retreat lay there. Or used to.

"Ah. We are on the northern island. Where the craggy cliffs stand. It will take many trips back and forth -"

"Do it! And take me with you! You'll drop me at the southern island on one trip, and pick me up the next. I need to get away, and this may be my only chance for a while." Alene rose and proposed a toast. "To great deeds, great places, and great friends. When they all come together, great needs become simple chores."

She drained the glass, her third, in one draught. The others followed suit.

"I'll see you here at daybreak when we set sail." With that, she strode out, down three flights of still-wet stairs from Flannan's ascent. She ran home to pack, stopping only at the Hoot Owl to see Beatrice and issue an invitation.

----- -----

Gierman mused about Alene and her motherly ruling style.

"She acts like she owns the place. And like we are her children. Yet compared to us, she is the child. What an interesting world we live in."

"Agreed." Flannan was no longer upset about his fall after Gierman showed him the 'Go/No Go' runes on the banister. "And yet, she is pleasant. This one, however," he pointed at Gertrude, "has more than her fair share of spunk. How should we address that, do you think?"

"You can call me Ma'am." The woman smiled with seriousness. "Oh, and never address me as 'Gertie' again, eh? That's what we called our goat."

Chapter 6

Island Bound

Queen Alene knocked on the door to the dwarves' villa just before dawn, Beatrice in tow. Gertrude answered and took their light luggage to the quay. Bleary-eyed dwarves loaded meager supplies and plentiful coal onto the dwarven steamship *Aiseag Picil.* Conversation was sparse as they cast off and idled through the canals to the open ocean beyond.

Once clear of the city, a blazing ray of green shot up from the horizon on the port side. Every eye watched the phenomenon, which lasted only a few seconds. A beautiful yellowish-orange sunrise replaced the green, showing a largely cloudless sky. The wind was calm.

"A good omen. As strong as I've ever seen." Beatrice closed her eyes and tilted her head back, letting the morning sun kiss her neck. "This journey will yield knowledge."

Alene listened, then mimicked her mentor's pose. The young sun took the edge off the brisk morning's coolness. In the time Alene knew Beatrice, which amounted to most of her life, she learned that the elder's actions often made a moment more present. Indeed, an observer would note that much of the young queen's wisdom could be attributed to the owner of the Hoot Owl.

"I hope you are right about that, Beatrice. I never expected to be at war so early in my rule. I'd like to achieve some clarity."

Beatrice lowered her head, then turned to face Alene. Her eyes searched the queen's.

"May you find your clarity. I didn't think to return to the atoll, but I hope to find a bit of peace there myself."

----- -----

Gierman returned to his engineering duties, opening the throttles on both paddlewheels fully. The ocean offered perfect conditions for a steamship: flat, waveless waters and calm, cool air. The coal burned hot and the steam built fast.

"I think we'd outrun the *Hidden Queen* today, Dylaen. We'll have you at the atoll ready to cut stone in no time at all."

"I look forward to it. You've seen me twitching since our supply of pickled marble ran low last week."

"Aye, we've all noticed that." Flannan had his longsword out, with his prized whetstone, jeweler's rouge, and a polishing cloth working in turn. "I wasn't even a part of the battle at Veynsport, yet you don't see me twiddling my thumbs, do you?"

"No, we've smelled you down in the pickling pits. A few days away from that stench will do you good."

"True. I owe Bedwyn a barrel or two of aged Argentine brandy after he sent those interns. I'll be glad to cut back to a supervisory role in the marble pickling business."

Beatrice walked over and lay hands on the bulwark near Gierman's controls.

"If you tour the atoll, you'll find use for that sword of yours." Her back was turned, but her voice immediately held their attention.

"How so?" Flannan paused his polishing.

"Oh, did the Admiral not tell you? About the inhabitants of the Connemara Atoll?"

"No. The atoll is uninhabited. I've been there, remember?" Gierman tried to sound more confident than he felt.

"Oh, you have? Took a nice stroll on the beach, did you? Climbed the cliffs to get a better view?"

"Well, no. But I've circled the whole atoll and saw not one building or sign of civilization. It's devoid of any culture."

Beatrice laughed.

"When did I say anything about civilization?"

Gierman thought back. She hadn't.

"Make no mistake, however. There is a people there. And they have a culture, though very much unlike ours."

"The Admiral told us he was alone on the island; there were no people for company."

"So let us think this through." Beatrice looked on the edge of laughter again. She was enjoying this. "What kind of a people would an old dwarf not consider people?"

"Orcs, possibly? But no, they would have villages."

"Not orcs."

Gierman replayed his last circumnavigation of the atoll back in his head. The only things he noticed were cairns of the native marble, set in odd positions. No fires, no huts. No fishing nets. Nothing that said anyone had been there in a very long time. Then he was rocked by the realization.

"Trolls?"

"Trolls." Beatrice pointed to him, making a clicking noise at the same time. "Island trolls."

"I've never heard of such a thing."

"How much time have you spent on islands?"

"Touche."

----- -----

After noon, the clear sky and calm winds continued. The queen and the innkeeper lay back on the deck, heads propped on bedrolls facing south. The autumn sun felt wonderful. Alene could not have asked for a more comfortable ride or a more perfect day to have it.

"I haven't been back since we left," Alene spoke without opening her eyes.

"Neither have I, dear. I wonder if anything is left of our hut?"

"I kind of doubt it. Gierman isn't the most observant, but he claims to have seen nothing man-made from the water."

Beatrice laughed.

"Woman-made, I think you mean. We built everything there, remember?"

"How could I forget?"

"I just hope they remember us."

Alene opened her eyes, staring at nothing. They had to remember.

Chapter 7

The Rumor Schill

Leaning against a darkened wall between the marina and her next stop, the Hoot Owl, Allus adjusted her bodice to enhance her assets. Checking her polished silver pocket mirror, she collected a stray hair and set it in order, only to tousle one side a second later. Sure she looked good, but she wasn't looking for a companion tonight. She was looking for trust.

Common folk are more likely to trust a person with obvious imperfections.

She stood and strode purposefully towards the tavern. Just before the last corner, her stride adjusted. Her cadence varied, just a bit. The arrow-straight line she cut a moment before became a shallow wave with a hint of tilt. Allus grabbed the doorpost and paused, forcing a belch. She staggered into Beatrice's pub.

"Hey, good lookin'," she said, catching herself on the glossy oaken bar, "you got any Veynsian brandy back there?"

"Of course we do, my lovely." Luc didn't know the woman, but she looked to have had a few already. He prepared to cut her off at one. "Here. This should set you right."

"A thousand thanks!" Allus raised her glass high, intentionally swirling it too much. Her right arm was immediately drenched in aromatic alcohol. She took a swig, then staggered to a crowded table in the middle of the room. Standing behind two young dockworkers, she cleared her throat.

"Secuse me, boys. Can you make a little room for little old me?"

The men slid apart, leaving just enough space on the bench for her to squeeze into. Thighs pressed against thighs, and Allus' practiced smile rubbed everyone at the table the right way.

"OK, boys, whadder we talkin' 'bout?"

The men exchanged glances.

"I think we are talking about you, now!" He smiled.

"You are so cute! But I can't be the only woman here worth talking about. Tell me. Who was it?"

"All right, we were talking about the Queen. Alene."

"Oh, yes! Now she is pretty, isn't she?"

"Uh…"

"Well…"

"We'd never noticed. But now that you mention it…"

Allus smiled. This group would be easy, as they were already uncomfortable discussing the Queen as a woman.

"Heh, I'd hesitate, too, if half of what they say is true." She took a sip of her brandy and waited. Her tablemates were silent.

"Well, hell, I'll bite. What do they say, miss?" He was a grey-haired man, not graced with a preponderance of looks, health, or brains. Just what she needed.

"Oh, I didn't think it was a secret. They say she threw him off the building." The room did not go silent but was suddenly muted. Allus knew the attention was on her, but pretended not to notice.

"Yeah. I heard the Regent was tossed over the side. She may not have done it herself, but those stunty fellows maybe."

She listened as people buzzed. Her trap was set.

"Oh! 'Scuse me, boys. I need to find the privy. Watch my drink..." To alleviate any concern that she might not come back, she left her Veynsian brandy on the table. Sideways and laughing, she staggered to the back of the pub where the facilities lay and promptly bypassed them. Once out the back door, she straightened herself up.

Allus couldn't help but smile. This was too easy. Her training heavily emphasized the manipulation of minds. Start with a mildly compromised mind. Add a bit of metaphorical poison; rumors, hearsay, and outright lies. Watch as poisoned minds push against reasoned ones, spawning anger and discord. If peacemaking breaks out, groom points of contention. Stoke the fire.[5]

Ahead lay a dozen more public houses ripe for her to lay the groundwork. To sow the seeds of unrest and distrust. And, just possibly, depose a queen.

---

[5] If this sounds a little too familiar, a little too real, it is. Here we call it misinformation. Propaganda. Conspiracy theory. These are all variations on a theme of tools used by outside forces to manipulate a populace against itself. This will come up again later.

Chapter 8

No Problem Atoll

No spectacular green flash broke the sky on the second morning. Rather, the southern horizon was broken by the silhouette of the Connemara atoll. It was a very old island, formed when a volcano pushed the seafloor up around it. Dwarves knew this action to be the reason the pickled marble business worked; the combination of heat and pressure yielded a crystalline structure that held up to salty, tidal actions better than any other stone yet discovered.

Thousands of years passed while this miraculous substance languished in obscurity until a small town was formed by scuttling several dozen ships in the shallow sands of the Veyns. Even then, the Veyns persisted for several hundred years as a shanty town - half pirate, half trader. What began in chaos became an unlikely mix of libertarian values ruled by a feminine monarchy.

After sacrificing yet another of her ships to bolster the burgeoning town, one visionary pirate-queen reached out to the best stonemasons in the world - dwarves. A half-dozen answered the call from three Holts. They assessed the problem and gathered to discuss potential solutions.

One dwarf with a penchant for history had an idea. An old survey discussed a stone that would fit the bill, and it was found not too far away. Retrieval would be simple, and with a couple of quick techniques, the city could be built in a much more permanent manner.

With a workable solution in place, there was a bigger problem. How to maintain the knowledge as a trade secret? A pungent pickling process presented the answer. With a single mystical step added - one so offensive that nobody would try to emulate it - the secret was secured.

And so a young dwarf named Drailin, following notes cribbed in the margins of an old survey, led them here. This bespoke marble occurred all over the Connemara atoll; veins reached right up to the surface in more than one location. But the marble was useful to another people for far longer - the island trolls.

Trolls are a very curious creature. They are very strong, and covered in fast-twitch muscle. They specialize in short-duration, high-intensity activity with long periods of near-motionless waiting. A mature troll can sit completely still for weeks at a time waiting for the right prey to come along. Very few creatures can survive the spring of a hunting troll.

The most curious feature is their skin. Trolls express a sticky slime that covers their bodies entirely. To this skin, they attach native stone as armor and camouflage. To a casual observer, a sitting troll appears to be a cairn or somewhat orderly pile of rocks. The trolls did not appreciate Drailin's incursions to burgle their armory; so the dwarf needed to find another way.

The cliffs on the north side of the island proved to be the best approach. Trolls didn't use that general area, and it was very challenging to sail into. One natural fissure was widened over generations, leading to the current quarry. This is where Gierman, Dylaen, and Flannan would spend a portion of the next several weeks, harvesting and transporting marble blocks to restock the pickling pits.

As the *Aiseag Picil* chugged round to the southern arm of the atoll, Flannan spotted one of those piles of marble Gierman mentioned. Grabbing his clubs, he climbed the narrow ladder behind the pilot house. The dwarf licked a thumb and felt the wind with it. As he was selecting a flat-faced club with a deep head and addressing the ball, Gierman saw his intent and slowed the ship to a stable crawl outside the breakers.

Flannan wound up and smacked the ball with both style and power. It flew long and straight, rising above the breakers and descending just before reaching the beach. The ball collided with one of the larger stones at the top of the heap, ricocheting to land in the palm forest beyond.

The impact moved the top rock, which in turn seemed to destabilize the whole pile. It slid backward, multiple impacts cratering the dry sand. Then several of the stones rose, arcing over towards the stricken hunk of marble. The troll then stood - nine feet tall - facing the palm forest. Several of the upper stones swiveled as if surrounding a central, head-like structure.

After scanning the beach and forest several times, the troll stomped into the palm forest and out of sight. The watching dwarves broke into fits of laughter. They stopped when they noticed Alene and Beatrice watching them, telltale fists resting on hips with matching scowls.

“Ahem. Well, ladies, where would you like us to set you ashore?” Gierman dithered between amusement and shame.

“See that outcropping?” Beatrice pointed. “Just to the lee, there is a calm spot at the beach. We’ll land there. You can retrieve us at noon on whatever day you return.”

“You can’t seriously think you are going to land on an island with trolls, can you?” Flannan passed, dubious, and went straight for outrage. “Do you even know what they eat?”

“Yes, we do.” Alene crossed her arms and tapped her left foot, agitated. “We lived here for better than a decade, just the two of us. We… got along with them.”

“One does not simply ‘get along with’ trolls.” Dylaen, the best equipped to take on a stone troll with his pick and other stoneworking tools, had a point. “One is lucky to survive them.”

“Oh, pish-posh.” Beatrice developed a wicked grin. “This is a look I haven’t seen on dwarves yet - fear.”

“You are damned right we’re afraid, woman!” Gierman hit his breaking point. “If you are wrong about these trolls, we’ll be answering for your disappearance!”

“Don’t you worry, Gierman,” Alene said. “I’ve left a succession plan, and it doesn't look like we’ll have Angus or Johan back anytime soon, or possibly at all.” She put a hand to her head. “Just get us ashore with our crates and let us get to it, all right?”

Gierman nodded and made for the lee of the outcropping while Dylaen stoked the fires. In a matter of five minutes, they crashed over the breakers and pulled up to the beach. The flat prow dropped onto the sand, forming a ramp. Three dwarves and two women unloaded luggage and four crates in short order, then bid farewell to each other.

Gierman watched the women wave as he reversed both sidewheels and crashed through the small breakers, then chugged back around to the cavernous quarry on the north end of the atoll. The dwarves wasted no time in loading the already cut stones onto the *Picil.* Everyone wanted to get back to Alene and Beatrice as quickly as possible.

Chapter 9

Getting Ahead

King Bedwyn Foresight looked around the rustic room he'd called home in recent weeks. After packing his armor, weapons, papers, and clothes, he decided to give the place a thorough cleaning. It was now considerably cleaner than when he rented it; this was just a final check before relinquishing the keys to Graener. Satisfied, the old dwarf descended the two flights of stairs that led to the public room.

Sighting the dwarven proprietor, Bedwyn waved and approached. Graener wiped his hands on a dishtowel, then moved to embrace his elder.

"It's been good having you here, Bedwyn. Call me anytime. I'll follow you anywhere."

"Old friend, I know you would, and you already have. Here, your keys. The room was pleasant, as always."

"Can I get you one for the road?"

Bedwyn chuckled.

"Nay, thanks. I think I should be clear for this journey. I can't tell why, but something is up." He smiled, nodded, and turned for the door - but found his path blocked by a slender man in black. The smile left Bedwyn's face. He wasn't one to be surprised.

It was Ben, the man who had forsaken the Ivon to become a bounty hunter with a loose affiliation with Canolbwynt Masnach. His hands were behind his back.

"Your Majesty."

"Ben, you can dispense with the pleasantries. And don't sneak up on me like that! It is still possible that I might react somewhat violently." Bedwyn knew this was exceedingly unlikely these days, given his advancing age. Yet it was a reasonable request.

"My apologies, sire. I come with… *news* of our business arrangement."

Bedwyn thought for a moment. Weeks ago, he did put a bounty on DePet's[6] head. As realization dawned, Ben produced a small crate from behind him, roughly one-foot square. *One head square is more likely,* he thought.

"Ah. Is that what I think it is?"

Ben nodded.

"Then, ah, let us adjourn to the quay, if you don't mind. There is another issue I'd like to discuss with you."

Outside, they stepped to a little-trafficked spot. It was in the open, but not near any paths. An observer would have to go out of their way to overhear.

"Where did you find him?"

"In the woods north of Canolbwynt. Him and two domestics."

"They didn't come willingly, I expect?"

"No sir. But none of them were practiced fighters, and despite being outnumbered, I won the day. After retaining this," Ben indicated the crate, "I buried the rest in the woods. I can show you the grave if you like."

"Oh, I don't think that will be necessary. Let's see," said the older dwarf, stroking his beard. "I'd like to leave this to Estelle if you don't mind. Alene is unavailable, and my guarantee was on the other side of the coin. I'm on my way to the Smaragdine Holt, where I've got your thousand gold coins. I'm impressed that you found him so quickly. If you will accompany me there, I have another assignment for you that will be equally lucrative."

Ben considered his options.

"Yes, I think I shall come with you. Give me a quarter-hour, and I'll meet you… here?"

"I'd like to rendezvous at the entrance to the goblin's holt. Does that work?"

"Of course. I'll see you there in fifteen."

---

[6] Jean DePet had been the Mayor of Veynsport before negotiating a treaty with the Ivon to be annexed as East Ivonsport. DePet was Governor of the new state, until the Battle of East Ivonsport. DePet lost, as did everyone in the community. After DePet fled with a big chunk of the treasury, the remaining leaders set a bounty for his return. Ben, who had brokered the initial deal with the Ivon as 'Brennan', had everything 'in the bag' (literally) before the terms were set. See Pickled Marble (Book Two) for the whole story.

Bedwyn flagged a nearby dock worker and scrawled a quick note on the boards. The worker took the crate away to Estelle, with a silver coin for his trouble.

The dwarven king then took a walk around the docks to make his final goodbye to Angus and Indaria. What happened next, even the great Bedwyn Foresight could not have foreseen.

Chapter 10

Dead Air

"I haven't felt this young in ages," Black Zonka told the slack-jawed woman sitting behind her. "I've always wanted to ride a dragon. Now I aim to make it happen!"

The old woman left her mouth agape, but no sound came out. The ancient orc shaman continued unconcerned.

"I saw one once, you know. Flying off from the hills to my north. It was carrying something lumpy; about the size of a moose. I still wonder about that sometimes. It shined and looked heavy."

The human woman was about sixty, with the well-fed physique of a noble. Her stature was somewhat tall for a female; Zonka liked that about her. Similar size offered a common frame-of-reference for the unlikely pair.

"So long ago." The orc crone reminisced. "When was that, I wonder? Things were happening. The world was more active then, as it is becoming now. Wars and epic tales of heroism abounded. About a thousand years ago, I'd say. That's half my time, you know."

Zonka was not surprised when her ephemeral roommate didn't answer. She folded her trademark hoary rag cloak neatly and set it on the woman's dark blue bed linens. Opening the woman's glossy cherrywood wardrobe, she surveyed her options.

"White and blue, blue and white. So much blue! Have you people no imagination? No personality?"

The woman in the chair still didn't answer. Her fine sapphire and ivory smock was stained crimson with her own blood, the rug beneath the rocker soaked. Vacant eyes stared at the orc in now-perpetual horror. Zonka clicked her tongue in annoyance.

"White and blue it is, then." She layered the clothes on, selecting the deepest bonnet and covering that with a fine blue veil. Nightfall would complete her disguise.

"Are you hungry? I know I am." Zonka walked to the kitchen to forage. She wrinkled her nose more than once at dried spices she felt should only be used fresh, and at the gross preponderance of cheeses. After an hour a passable vegetable soup stood steaming on the table, and Zonka sat down to eat.

At least the old biddy had good taste in wine. A cellar stocked full of vintage Greenway reds - the best in the Cyfandir. Zonka didn't enjoy very many human products, but their wines were excellent. After her trip to the city, she planned to return here for a few more bottles before heading home.

She needed the concealing clothes of a stocky Ivonian noblewoman to allow her entrance to the library, where she would search the archives for old references to dragons. If the orc intended to ride a dragon, she'd need to find one first. The Ivonian archives would point the way.

As the sun set, Zonka stepped back to the old woman's bedroom. She regarded the corpse for a full minute, considering. No remorse or regret, just a vague respect.

"Well, my dear, thanks for your help. Big things are happening in the world, and you've just been a part. And a truly great listener! Rest well."

She stepped out into the dark streets, headed toward the city center. Layered blue garments indicated considerable status. Most Ivonians didn't rank highly enough to look her square in the eye, and those that outranked her would not likely be out this late. Those who were would still have to see through the layered chiffon veil she sported to discern her true nature.

She took in the grandeur of the city as she walked. It was an impressive place, but to an orc it felt superficial and forced. This was not the first time she enjoyed the beauty of the city, but if she was successful, it just might be her last. To that end, she noted any of the exposed timber structure and other flammable elements.

That's just what this place needs, Zonka mused; *a cleansing fire. It is unhealthy now - like a forest that has built up too much scrub and detritus. Flame is a great tool for renewal and rebirth - allowing new life to come to a corrupted place. Dragon's fire is even better.*

Chapter 11

Life's a Beach

Alene kicked her shoes off automatically, feeling the warm sand percolate between her toes. She took a deep breath, head tossed back, arms flung wide, and exhaled with a pronounced sigh.

"We're home, Bea."

The older woman still waved to the dwarven paddleboat, which grew smaller with increasing distance. When she could no longer make out individual dwarves, she stopped smiling and turned inland.

"There's work to do, girl. Let's get to it."

Alene issued a halting chuckle.

"It didn't take long for you to forget who I am."

"I haven't forgotten, dear." Beatrice dragged their luggage and supplies up the beach. "You are Alene, Queen of the Veyns. But we aren't in the Veyns, now are we?"

Alene put on a crooked smile and helped her mentor secure their belongings. Beatrice was right, of course. Getting loaded up into the treehouse before dark was crucial to their survival. The arrangement was very specific on that point.

Two hours later, the gear was stowed and debris from storms cleared from the porches. The two women took their fishing baskets and headed down to the exposed stone tidepools nearby. Slack tide exposed dozens of stone tidepools - far deeper than typical. Using their wide basket lids, the pair chased several large fish towards the open-mouthed baskets. In short order, they had enough fish for several meals, along with a few pounds of fresh kelp.

On their way back to the treehouse, the women waved at tell-tale piles of rocks along the way. Their greetings elicited no response. The trolls never responded directly. Slight movements in the rocks betrayed the hidden life within. Alene smiled again.

"I'm glad they are still here."

"Are you? Why is that?"

"I dunno. I guess I feel safe with them around."

"One is never safe when a troll is around, dear. And we've seen close to a dozen since we arrived."

They finished their trek in silence; cleaning the fish near their shelter. Beatrice took the cleaned catch and headed up the ladder.

"Be a good girl and fetch some firewood, will you?"

Firewood is somewhat of a misnomer on a small sandy island like this one. Palm trees will burn, but they take a very long time to regenerate. Driftwood burns nicely once dried; Palm fronds, coconut husks, and other detritus, rolled and bound into firewood-like shapes are more common in such environs. Alene set herself to these tasks for the next hour.

Of course, she saw more of the motionless trolls. Each time she offered a smile and friendly wave; the most reaction she received was a noise like two stones slipping against each other. These trolls wore a colorful mixture of smooth marble broken along natural fracture lines, as well as a mix of large seashells, punctuated by jagged sections of sharp and glassy volcanic rock.

Back at the treehouse, Alene built a fire while Beatrice finished preparing her fruit-and-fish meal. Using a beautiful triangular knife she drew from her belt, she sliced ginger root and crushed garlic brought from the Veyns. Adding a dash of salt and exotic pepper imported from lands she had yet to visit, she set the covered, cast-iron pan directly on the fire for a bit.

The pair reclined into hammocks. Beatrice puffed on a pipe. Alene closed her eyes and sighed into a lazy near-sleep. Ten minutes later, Beatrice rose to turn the fish and add a few finishing touches. Alene broke the silence as Beatrice sat back into her hammock.

"I can't go back, can I?" She spoke with eyes still closed. "Never again. It's gone."

"You'd better plan on going back, girl! I haven't spent decades getting you to the point you are for nothing!"

"No, Bea. I mean I can't go back to the way it was here. When it was just us and the old trolls. When I was a kid." Tears escaped her lidded eyes.

"Ah, that. No, my dear, we all become adults eventually. And once we do, we cannot return to childhood." She rose again and went about plating the meal. Beatrice was truly a culinary artist. Alene wept silently.

"And you, child, carry a greater burden than most. Even greater than a parent with a child. Even greater than a poor woman caring for several children all on her own. You, dear, must care for an entire city. At barely twenty years old. Your burden is real, and even a trip to a warm and beautiful place like this cannot more than dampen your stresses. And you are doing it on your own - it is incredible! You are incredible."

"You keep saying I'm doing this on my own - am I supposed to marry and share the burden?"

"Oh, heavens, no!" Beatrice set the small table with two chairs on the western balcony. She brought out one of the bottles of white wine and placed it on the table. "Come to the table, dear. Have some wine. No, I don't think you should marry Johan just yet."

Alene squawked in protest, but Beatrice cut her off.

"Oh, now don't pretend you don't know what I'm talking about. My children were grown before I came to work for your mother. The workings of the world and how it is peopled haven't changed that much since then. I know what you have with Johan. But you should not marry him now.

"In fact, don't marry him, not even soon. You must get through this war, and the rebuilding after, on your own. If you were to marry now, it would undermine your authority for the rest of your time on the throne."

They ate quietly, watching the sun go down over the water. Distant clouds created layers of oranges, reds, blues, and purples. Neither spoke for an hour, when the dregs of wine filled their glasses for the third time.

"I like him, you know." Beatrice didn't take her eyes off the growing starscape. "He's smart. Capable. Daring. And quite cute, for an Ivonian!" They both giggled at that.

"I can't say you're wrong. He's quite good at..." Alene paused, glancing at Beatrice, "...a lot of things. He makes me happy."

"That's about the most important thing, now isn't it?"

Chapter 12

Here Comes the Thunder

Metal-clad wheels clattered on cobblestones as the dwarven wagon rolled along the road towards the former Veynsport. Many years stood between this and the last time Mountain King Artemus left the Holt he led. Four of his dwarves were with him, along with Floin Thunderpick - Angus' father. Sober and silent, they approached.

This artificial jetty, built and rebuilt over the last several hundred years, was without a doubt man-made. A dwarf-made structure would have lasted for millennia after the first building. Still, a jumbled-stone breakwater like this had no soil to support such a grand live oak. To say that the tree did not belong here was an equally grand understatement.

Yet here it stood. Thick green leaves provided some cover for foot-wide branches that cantilevered out wider than the whole height of the tree, which itself rose as high as twenty dwarves standing one atop the other. A thick, striated vine wove itself up and around the branches, wide leaves filling open spots between the oak's plentiful foliage.

A bulbous green flower pulled the dwarves' attention. Nothing like this grew in the mountains they traveled from, nor had they encountered anything like between there and here. Next to this attractive flora perched a thing of such beauty that the scene might as well have not existed; Indaria stroked the giant flower's petals, humming sadly. To complete the otherworldly scene, two pea-pod-like appendages hung from the vine, just below the flower.

Symmetry escaped these elements; as one was tall and narrow, the other short and squat. They hovered five feet above the ground, right over the leveled gravel path the guards patrol along. The pods' skins undulated slightly, as forms inside contorted. As the dwarves arranged themselves in a semicircular line facing both the pods and the elf, Indaria spoke in that elegant singsong voice:

"Welcome, Artemus. I'm glad you are here. It is almost time for the Transition." She enunciated the word "transition" in a way that conveyed an almost ceremonial importance. As she spoke, she caressed the edges of the flower - almost massaging it. Tears marred her otherwise perfect appearance.

"We thank you, Princess." Artemus gave the higher honorific, though his status as a King was somewhat higher. "What is this? How did this tree come to be here? It cannot have grown in this brackish lagoon water."

"An astute observation for a hole-dweller. No, this tree did not grow here. Nor will he stay much longer; the 'soil' I prepared for him has been exhausted, and he longs to sink his roots deep into the mud to the north. He is ready to be back in his forest." She ran her left hand along the rough bark. "My influence over him is also near its end. Soon much will change; possibly forever."

"If I may, Princess," Floin advanced one step toward the elf. "I would ask after my son, Angus. I received word that he was under your care, here. Is that so?" He trailed off, exuding parental worry.

"You must be Floin Thunderpick. Angus told me so much about you during our journey here. You are a lucky father - his fondness for you is great, and his respect even greater." She paused and tilted her head. "And he is a lucky son; for I see that his respect is deserved. One day, I would like to hear about his mother. Angus had little to say on the matter. But for now, you need to know more about Angus' state.

"To say that Angus is under my care is inaccurate; that I arranged for his care would better describe the situation. This tree is one of the original live oaks - so-called for their consciousness and mobility. Very few remain, cut down by men for the most part while they slept.

"Even scarcer are live oaks with healthy dreamvines. I last encountered this one about six hundred years ago, living near coastal towns that no longer exist. He tells me that he has stayed near Veynsport as long as it existed; it makes sense for him to stay near.

"The dreamvine is the entity actually caring for your son Angus and his friend Johan. I made a pricey bargain to bring it here, so steep a price that I will not be able to help with the rest of the war.

"You must keep my terms with these beings if you wish to keep Angus alive. First, let the process come to fruition. If you interfere before Angus and Johan are both free, the oak may object and take action. No matter how fearsome you believe yourself, you will not survive a confrontation.

"Second, you must allow the tree and its dreamvine passenger free passage when it leaves. Do not molest it, no matter how concerned you may feel. This is crucial; you must help Angus and Johan to understand the same."

The dwarves nodded their assent. Floin, brow deeply furrowed, stepped even closer and reached a hand up towards the two pods.

"Which one… where is my son?"

Indaria's mask of respect dropped visibly. She responded through a sideways smirk.

"Do you really need to ask?" She looked pointedly at the rounder of the two.

Tension broken, the other dwarves burst into fits of laughter; Indaria's lilting titter joined in. Floin reached a palm to rest on the fuzzy green curve that cradled his son's body. The movement brought a memory of his wife's belly, heavily pregnant with their only son.

"Oh, my boy," Floin muttered, "come back to me whole."

"Don't worry, Floin." Indaria's tone returned to its normal perfection. "Angus was whole when he went in, just a bit perforated. He and Johan charged sixty Ivonian archers - alone. They killed every one of them, Angus' vorpal axe responsible for more than half. When they were through, I found them dying on the ground, each pierced with multiple arrows. I called this oak with its vine, and we were blessed it was so near. Mere moments later, and we would have lost them."

"Did you say sixty?" Artemus was flummoxed. "Two warriors charged sixty, alone? He's done it again."

"How long until he -" Floin began, then was cut off as the heavier of the two pods dropped to the ground at his feet. The elder dwarf fell backward in surprise, landing on his rear. He gasped as the husky seam burst, a single fibrous coil curling back and away.

Two armored hands burst through the fresh-breached vulvic carpel. Covered in clear, green slime, they pried the opening larger, until a wide-eyed Angus burst through. He lurched forward, still-armored torso clear of his sickbed prison. Falling forward, the dwarf choked and vomited more of the slimy substance, clearing his lungs. The remaining shell broke asunder, sending a gelatinous tidal wave that crashed into Floin.

The wave carried collateral items, like Angus' axe, now imbued with a greenish-blue tinge on the Blood Onyx, and many, many arrows. Some of the arrows were broken; some tips still held chunks of clothing and flesh. Each bore strange spiral marks.

"So many arrows." Artemus' shock increased. Never in his many years had he seen even half this number of arrows in a person - of any race. "How could he have lived?" His eyes stayed on the arrows.

"Dreamvines are very special," Indaria answered from above, "They are incredible healers, due to their natural drives. You see, we call them dreamvines because they thrive on dreams. In order to get all of the dreams a 'Dreamer' can provide, they became talented at keeping them alive.

"This vine has seen many Dreamers over its many millennia; dwarves, men, orcs, and goblins. Even a troll. But rarely has an elf strayed too near, and it desires nothing more than the dreams of an elf."

The dwarves had gathered around Angus, exchanging emotional greetings and embraces. The other pod dropped to the ground, Johan squirming aggressively inside. When the wiry midrib suture curled up and away, the man likewise fell out; retching and hacking the goo from his lungs.

After a moment of rejoicing reunion, some of the dwarves headed towards the water to clean the very organic slime off. From above, they heard a sound like a twig snapping. Angus and Johan looked up as one, and the smiles fell from their faces.

"Indaria! What are you doing?" Angus was already climbing the tree; struggling for grip with vine-greased hands. "Get out before it's too late!"

But the elven princess was already being closed up inside a newer, more delicate pod. Angus reached it just as the sides were sealed by green tendrils forming the suture. He caught her hand and eye for a second. Indaria used the moment for a few important words:

"It has to be this way, Angus. I made a bargain, and this is the price. Live well, My l-" The sound cut off as the pod sealed.

Angus leaned his head back and wailed his grief; a deep, warlike keening.

Angus was knocked from his perch by another branch, sweeping across the tangle like a tacking boom. Rolling out of the fall, he watched with the others as the ancient tree rose on dozens of large roots and ambulated away with aplomb. As it moved, it littered the trail with hundreds of red and white sticks and rocks.

Moving now at the speed of a trotting horse, the oak plunged into the nearby forest. The only sign of its continued passing was a rustling in the forest canopy, and even that faded soon enough. Artemus stooped to lift one of the sticks left behind.

"She said the evidence would be clear. It looks like that thing cleaned the bones of the archers you two slew." With an odd reverence, he replaced what looked like an arm bone on the ground. "What a terrible way to end."

Angus sank to his knees in shock, Indaria's sacrifice weighing heavily on his mind. At his feet, he found the small satchel she kept with her at all times. He took it, but only after cleaning himself up in the lagoon. His elven friend was fastidious when it came to cleanliness.

Chapter 13

One More Thing...

Ben hung over the side of Koksal's steam wagon, retching. He ran to the back as soon as he realized that the nausea would not pass until they were stopped. *It's so embarrassing*, he thought, *losing your lunch over a little rocking motion*. Even thinking of motion spurred him into another round of dry heaves.

They hurtled up a dirt trail next to a creek, winding up the valley towards a large mountain; the easternmost of the range. Ben tried to get past his sickness by looking at the defenses. Dwarves are known for subtle but effective earthworks that stymie armies. This valley would do just that.

Koksal's racing engine clipped branches and launched over hillocks, splashed through small creeks, and banged off the sides of trees. The path was barely wide enough for the train to snake through. Ben knew one thing for sure - he would not ride this thing again if he could avoid it.

When they did arrive, Ben sat on a bench for fifteen minutes before his world stopped rocking. He more than most could appreciate the need for fast travel; but the tradeoff of an emptied stomach and no desire to fill it was just too great. He sneered at the cooling engine as he walked into the Smaragdine Holt for the first time.

Very few humans entered the Smaragdine; certainly less than a dozen in the last century. So for a man like Ben, a spy without a nation, a warrior without a war, it stood out as remarkable. If the approach would be difficult, an assault on the gates would be suicidal.

Banks of mounted repeating crossbows - lever-operated and bigger than most men - lined rows of narrow slits in the walls. The gates themselves were granite four feet thick, with bolsters on all sides. King Bedwyn had nothing to fear.

"Ben!" The dwarven king approached as if bidden. "I'm afraid you got in without an escort. Here, let me give you the grand tour!"

Ben listened as Bedwyn showed him every obvious part of his defenses - leaving out anything that was not in plain sight. *Smart,* Ben thought, *his reputation is deserved.* He drank in every drop of new information.

They made their way through the common areas of Bedwyn's Holt. The king pointed out functional areas like the galleries of apartments, the boar sties, and even the gravity-operated sewage system. Ben soaked in the information and ideas Bedwyn offered. The intelligence on dwarven life he gained far surpassed the value of the bounty on DePet.

Eventually, the pair wound deeply into the tunnels, pausing in a wide, round chamber. At one end stood a wooden door with familiar, if not dwarven, markings. Around the outside of the chamber, a ledge about ten feet deep ran, with ramps connecting the ledge to the chamber floor. A thick layer of dust coated most of the surfaces, with very little evidence of recent use.

"What an interesting place," Ben offered, "is it ceremonial?"

"Ha!" Bedwyn chuckled. "Far from it. This is a trade and transfer station."

"What - in the center of the mountain? It took us an hour to get here. You can't expect to bring wagons down here to offload. It's too far from the front door to make sense." Ben looked at the markings on the door again, understanding where he had seen the like before.

Bedwyn simply raised his eyebrows with a smile and waited for Ben to connect the dots.

"Goblins?" The man pointed at the door. "There are goblins behind that?"

"There were. And there may yet be. But the dust should tell you why I'm not sure."

"It doesn't look as if you have traded with them in some time."

"Correct."

"But why not?"

"A good question. One I have not been able to discern the answer to. And yet, here we are. Here you are. Why?"

Ben paused for a moment to consider.

"You want me to find out. To spy on them for you."

"Isn't that what you do?"

"Of course not! I was a soldier, and am a bounty hunter now. I'm a simple man, Your Highness."

"Ben, I don't believe that schist for a second." Bedwyn's face wavered; magnanimous humor interspersed with confronting a devious person. "I never bought into your lie that you are a simple soldier. Honestly, you aren't good enough at it to be a leader of men."

"Begging your pardon, highness, but I never-"

"Stop. Don't give me that 'highness' crap. You were comfortable speaking with royalty from the moment we met. That puts you in one of several select groups. I know you were a spy. Yet I brought you here."

They sat in silence for several seconds. Ben broke the tension first.

"Bedwyn Foresight. You do see more than others, don't you?"

The old dwarf merely smiled and waited for Ben to continue.

"Is this going to be problematic in our relationship? You did appear to accept my renunciation of the Ivon - I meant that."

"I know you did. As did I, accepting your new path. A path that led us here. We have established your skillset and my need for such. Your Ivonian appearance absolves me of any wrongdoing if things go poorly. And so we arrive back where we started; will you investigate the Goblin city that lies at the end of this tunnel and report back to me? I'll double the reward that you've already earned with DePet's head."

Even if the gold alone weren't enough, Ben considered, *a close investigation of both a goblin city and a dwarven Holt puts me in very rarified company within the human intelligence community.*

"I will."

"I'm glad to hear that. And so are you. Thannon, come on out."

Ben followed Bedwyn's eyeline past his own shoulder, turning to see Thannon, one of Bedwyn's greatest heroes, step out of a shadow carrying a great crossbow. Once in the open, the armored dwarf made a show of de-cocking the weapon with a CRACKCRACKCRACK that resounded through the chamber. Ben turned back to Bedwyn.

"Well, that's not fair. You had me at any moment, but didn't let me know."

"I wanted you to feel comfortable. To feel free to be honest."

"You accomplished that."

Thannon pressed the pack he'd worn into Ben's arms.

"You'll need this. Food, water, and a bedroll. Candles, and a dwarven ember tin. I even included a simple knife, though I doubt you need it."

"Thanks?" Ben wasn't used to such attention. "I presume you'd like me to leave immediately?"

"If you are willing, yes." Bedwyn left little room for discussion. "I've been itching for a report for several months, but could not tip my hand. I'd prefer that you investigate as much as possible, and return the same way. If everything is as I expect, you won't be seen or accosted."

Thannon opened the old door, which creaked ominously on its hinges. As Ben peered down the long, dark shaft, Bedwyn fixed a headband with a reflector and glowing fungus onto the man's head. The light it gave was dim, but Ben knew it would be enough once his eyes adjusted. He took a few steps into the tunnel, looking back just in time to see the door shut behind him.

Trudging forward, the erstwhile spy shook his head in disbelief. *How did he do that? Bedwyn must be one of the greatest manipulators I've ever met, and I was trained by the best. And for Thannon to sneak up on me? It makes no sense. I'm never surprised!*

----- -----

Bedwyn smiled wide. "It worked."

"But can we trust him?" Thannon did not sound convinced.

"We can this time. Just like any addiction, the first one is always free. Spies will execute one or two assignments perfectly, just to gain trust, and get people like me addicted to great intelligence."

"But what about later? How will you be able to trust him in a year?"

Bedwyn waved for the other dwarven archers to reveal themselves.

"I don't intend to have that problem. You play Kings and Pawns, right?"

"Well, yes, but I don't play well. I can plan about three moves ahead."

"That sounds right. Ben, I suspect, can plan four moves ahead." Bedwyn smiled a sly and vicious smile. "I'm already seven moves out on this one."

Chapter 14

Have Gold, Will Travel

Back at the dead woman's house, Zonka finished her packing. She planned to play the part of an ancient aristocrat on tour as long as possible. This was, of course, necessary; no Captain in their right mind would grant passage to an orc. Much less carry an orc through uncharted waters infested with deadly myths and legends.

But such was her destination. The old orc's research in the Ivonian archives turned up a southerly continent that fit her needs perfectly. More than perfectly. Now to get passage.

She lifted two heavy chests onto the old woman's carriage and added her luggage. The horse no longer shied away from the crone after a week of feeding it apples and carrots. Zonka felt a vague sorrow at the thought of leaving the animal at the docks; she hadn't made friends with another being for a very, very long time.

An ovoid moon shone above, lighting the world the way an orc preferred. Zonka again locked the door to her dead host's home, hoping to remain undiscovered for a while longer. She climbed the buckboard's ladder to the cushioned-plank seat, and with a flick of the reigns was headed south towards the port.

The damp air kissed her exposed skin with a chill, while misty fog rolled in from the sea. The old mare's hooves clumped on the damp dirt ruts with a slow, regular beat. Wooden wheels splashing through occasional puddles began a cacophonous clatter when they reached the cobblestone streets of the town proper.

Zonka took her time with a long ride along the quay, observing each vessel. She must be as careful with this choice as she was in choosing the dead woman; a stray shout could undo her permanently. She needed a ship large enough to carry the sea - one in good repair. But it must also show a Captain in need of money.

Money she had - stolen from Ben, who stole it from DePet, who stole it from Veynsport's treasury. Two despicable men, in her view, and one gross group of bigoted people. She felt no remorse for how she would use her ill-gotten gains.

After an hour of consideration, she settled to observe one ship that piqued her interest. The *Mujer Astuta,* a stout brigantine, looked ready to set sail. She knew from her observations that it carried cloth and bushels of dried herbs and garlic, bulky yet not heavy. Its two thick masts spoke of strength. Stains on still-furled sails showed - possibly - age, as a sign that the captain may not have seen too much success recently.

The Captain was easy to identify; this man was tall and lanky, wearing a long, blue coat and tricorn hat. He strode from one end of the ship to the other, barking orders, pulling lines, and trying to set the place in order. She waited for him to disembark, as she suspected he would, to grab one last shoreside bite. Eventually, he obliged.

"Good evening." She spoke with a pleasant tone, edged with abruptness. It had the desired effect, that of a man caught off-guard.

"Eh, a good evening to you, madam." He paused long enough to lift his hat in salute, intent on continuing.

"That's a nice ship you have there. Good bones."

"Thank you, Madam." The Captain exuded discomfort. "That she does."

"It looks like a good cargo, too."

"Uh…yes, Madam. We loaded a number of items to take to the Veyns; not the rarest of cargos, but certainly it will turn a profit."

"Cloth? And bundles of common dried herbs? Not that profitable, going to the Veyns."

"Er, if you'll pardon me…"

"I will not pardon you, Captain." Zonka's tone was motherly - as of an agitated mother. "Suppose I wanted to go to a different port? One where the value of your goods would be treble what they are worth in the Veyns?"

"I'd say you were mistaken. There is no such port within a thousand miles, east or west."

"Then it is good I don't intend to go to the east or the west."

Blood drained from the Captain's face.

"South? You mean to go south?" His shock was obvious. "You cannot go south. Nothing good lives there. No amount of profit could be worth that risk."

She tossed an Ivonian coin, a heavy gold one, into his hands. He caught it and looked closely.

"Suppose I were to offer you a thousand of those for passage, reducing your risk. Would that be interesting?" She leaned in, smiling. Sharper-than-human teeth gleamed in the moonlight.

The Captain took almost three seconds to consider that offer.

"I'd say you had a deal."

Chapter 15

For Truth

Angus twiddled the lock of green that graced his otherwise red beard. He would re-braid it before leaving his villa, but for now, it stood out as a verdant reminder of the vine that saved him. More than a dozen new scars testified to the events on the jetty. But here was his armor, repaired and buffed to a mirror shine, and his axe, likewise polished. Swirls of green and red played in the stone - ever moving, twining, lacing - but never mixing.

He left those on their stands and walked up two flights to the rooftop dining veranda. There he met Floin and Gertrude. Artemus took his small company north to consult with Bedwyn, leaving just the family here at the only dwarven villa in the Veyns. At the end of the meal, Angus asked for Floin's analysis.

"Well, Da? What do you think?"

"Honestly, son? I'm having a hard time absorbing it all." Floin raised a glass in his son's direction. "But I can say this with no doubt or qualification - I'm proud of you!"

"Angus, I can see where you get it," Gertrude spoke through her smile, "or at least some of it. Master Floin, we are proud of your son, too. He's done a lot for our little kingdom."

"I can see that!"

"Da, I meant the city. What do you think of the Veyns?"

"Oh, that. S'wet. Beer is weak. And the sausages too salty." He looked at Gertrude. "No offense meant, Madam."

"It's the pickling process," she responded dryly, "generally perceived to be a good thing around here. It indicates care and quality, or is intended to at least."

Angus shot his father a meaningful glance - *don't spill the beans* - and drained his glass.

"And our little villa? It was made by dwarves, for dwarves, you know."

"Oh, yes. It's quite nice. A bit draftier than the tunnels, but the stonework is pleasant." He looked around and up. "I'm not sure I'd get used to eating out under the open sky like this. I feel so… exposed."

Gertrude stood and collected some of the plates.

"You know, Angus, he's got a point." The woman had a way of making a point while seeming absent. "Especially with what the rumors say."

"Rumors? Don't forget, I've been out of the Veyns for a spell. What rumors?"

"Oh, nothing much. Just that you and the other dwarves might have thrown Villeuse over the side of the palace instead of him jumping."

"What?" Angus nearly shouted. "I was the only dwarf there; the others didn't come for months!"

"Well, I know that. And you know that. But apparently the rumors don't." Gertrude, arms laden with empty plates and trays, started down the stairs. "I don't know what you should do about it, but perhaps something. The sentiment is spreading."

Angus and his father watched her descend to the floors below without words. Floin broke the silence.

"Well son, did you do it? Did you toss a man?"

"Da, that's no less offensive than when they say it about us. And no, I didn't. He jumped. Alene made it clear he was going to jail and indicated torture was forthcoming. I may have hefted my axe suggestively, but nothing more."

"I thought you were popular here. Lord Protector and all that."

"I am. I was."

"So what changed?"

"Good question." Angus searched his mind for an answer.

"So you don't know?" Floin grinned.

"I told you I have no idea - what's with the smile?"

"I'd say, son, that we need to get into the rumors. Take the pulse of the people. And there is only one way to do that. Well, only one good way."

Angus waited.

"My boy, now that you've learned to walk through life on your own, you'll learn to crawl with one of the best - your dear old Da."

Angus' confusion inflated. Floin waited to see if his son would catch on. He didn't.

"Boy, the best place to hear the truth is to go through the public houses and listen. It'll take fortitude and constitution; we must drink with these people and hear what they have to say. Set a few straight. Son, we're going on a pub crawl. A pub crawl for truth."

Angus was shocked. This wasn't the thing a father said to his child. But it was appropriate for peers - adult to adult. *My father is treating me as a grown dwarf!* As he reveled in the insignificant but poignant moment, Angus began to laugh. Deep, basso profundo belly laughs that moved his whole body. Floin joined him.

----- -----

They hit the ground at nightfall, laughing and joking incessantly. As their gondola let them off outside the Hoot Owl, they left the first big tip of the evening, with sincere thanks to the gondolier. Dressed in traditional dwarven party colors, they entered the bar. The typical press of men and women surrounded them, and it took five minutes before they found an available stretch of table to squeeze into.

"Dark ale and biscuits!" Shouted Angus to the server - an overworked young woman. Faces around the table showed disapproving frowns directed Angus' way. Seeing this, he adjusted his order. "For the table!"

It was as if the dwarves' tablemates had a heavy weight removed from their shoulders as a whole. Still no smiles, but these men rapidly approached a neutral outlook towards the short-yet-stout pair. Angus knew he had to make this moment last and better it.

"Where's Bea? I wanna introduce her to my Da!"

"She's out - on vacation!" The man looked and smelled the part of a fisherman. Ivonian by birth, most likely. Angus pressed.

"Beatrice? Vacation? Well, she probably deserves it. That woman works as hard as anyone I ever knew. Where'd she go?"

"She said she was visiting her old neighborhood. That it is a tough place. I don't get it."

"I do." Angus looked Floin in the eye. "There is always a draw from home. A person should remember where they come from."

About this time a man deserving the term giant approached from the back of the room. He finished his drink and smashed the ceramic flagon to the floor. He made a salute-like motion, thumb to his heart, and shouted.

"You must be at least this tall or be really pretty to drink here! Get out!" The burly worker pulled his belly up to the now-standing Angus. "Or would you rather I throw you out?"

Floin rose, placing a calming hand on Angus' shoulder. He looked squarely up at the big man and spoke calmly.

"No need to throw your weight around, friend. We can tell when we're not wanted. We can see our way out."

"No, Da. I can fight my own battles! I'd like to see him try to toss me out!"

A collective "oooooooooh" ran through the crowd, and Floin lifted his hand away from Angus and stepped to the side.

"Ah," said the elder dwarf, "I'll just stay low over here then. Toss him if you must. Careful, mind; he's a bit heavy."

"Wait, what?" Angus' head snapped to look at his father, but only until he felt the two largest hands he'd ever contacted grab him by the neck and nethers. Then his full attention was in the moment of being lifted up to contact the soot-stained ceiling.

Looking down on the crowd's heads, he saw a circular blur where Floin stood. Then he fell, straight down onto the giant's head. Standing again, Angus looked down at the now-unconscious pile of man at his feet. Floin shrugged.

"I told him you were heavy. Some people just can't take advice." Floin took the flagon from the server and drained it. Smiling, he handed it back to her and asked for another.

"I still don't get it." Angus laughed. "He said I had to be really pretty to drink here - did he think that all this wasn't pretty?" He indicated his beard and belly to the crowd, posing awkwardly.

The assembly erupted into raucous laughter and hoots, and the drinking and carousing resumed. Angus listened as the rumors were told, setting many half and un-truths straight. After an hour, they adjourned to another bar along the way and repeated the process. By the end of the night, they made their way back to the villa. Holding the walls to steady themselves, they chatted just inside the doors.

"Me son, you've proved something about yourself tonight."

"Yeah, Da? Whassat?"

"When it comes to drinking, ye don't come up short."

"Thanks, Da. Offensive, but true."

"Did you notice anything about those rumors?"

"Sure! They were all wrong. Wrong about me."

"More'n that, son. They were all the same."

"Yeah. What'd I say?"

"Verbatim. Like someone had given them points to talk about. All across the city, rich to poor, they all had the same specific points."

"Whass *yer* point?" Angus wrestled with sleep for control of his body.

"These weren't mere rumors." Floin sounded stone-cold sober considering how much he'd put away. "Angus, someone wanted to discredit you. And Alene."

Chapter 16

Dark Business

Ben longed to see the sun. Or the moon. Or any light greater than the dimly-glowing moss in his head-mounted lamp. He'd thought the silence would be the greater threat to his sanity, but silence never came.

Each footfall created noise - the immediate noise, then echoes of the same from each end of the tunnel, tortured auditory returns, always twisted and changed from the original. He splashed through puddles. Even when he sat still, his ears had tuned in to the ambient noise level. He perceived each breath as loud as a conversation.

He chose to walk mostly on the raised hump between two well-worn tracks in the stone. No doors. No life. No light. His mind twisted, replaying recent events.

He made a deal with an orc - that went south. When it came down to it, despite the worst things he'd done, he couldn't watch orcs tear into a civilian population. And that had been, he thought, his undoing. But now Bedwyn offered him a second chance. He'd continue here for a while, and gather intel on the goblins and dwarves. Then he would decide which master he should serve.

The passage climbed on as it had for hours now. The air changed. It wasn't as stale; it gained an acrid, smoky smell. Flavor pictures jumped into his mind as he ascended. Burned wood. Hot oil. A rubbish fire. A midden heap. Scorched meat. Rotting flesh. The first side passage revealed a long stair winding upwards. The air there was cleaner - it must lead outside.

Ben, successful in many circles, knew the value of a good escape route. The tunnel did lead to help, but an hours-long trip in the dark wasn't generally the best plan. He started up the stairs. Dark, ashy dust coated them for the first few flights; eventually

Ben found clean, well-worked stone. Light filtered down, rendering his glowing moss useless.

He stopped several times for water or snacks. The man had a well-developed constitution, but he'd been going for many hours without sleep. After four hundred and eighty-two steps, the sunlight hit him full in the face. It was mid-morning, and he stood on the northern side of the mountains.

Ben turned slowly in a full circle, scanning for threats. He saw none, just a couple of buildings worked into the slope, one with a long rail cantilevered out over a drop-off. Inhaling the clean air deeply, he searched them both. One was a workshop, with tools sitting out as if their owners left in the middle of their tasks. The other a small, smelly bunkhouse. The food there was long-rotten and desiccated, past the point that even scavengers would want it.

A wave of fatigue swept Ben's will away, and he set up his bedroll on one of the bunks. *I'll get a few hours of sleep*, he thought, *then check out the rest of the goblin holt.* Within three breaths of lying down, deep snores shook the little shelter for the first time in months.

Outwardly deep sleep masked vibrant and horrible dreams. Ben often dreamt of his deeds at Pentref. Murdering the occupants of an entire village just because they wanted to live free was the worst thing he'd ever done. In turn, those villagers tortured him every night since.

Ben exploded upwards, his head ricocheting off the upper bunk. Darkness surrounded him, both literally and metaphorically. *To do such a thing and see it fail. Pentref was meant as a warning, yet Gymdeithas Fasnach used it as a rallying cry. Nothing I could ever do would make it right. I never want to see such horror again.*

Rubbing furiously at the expanding lump on his forehead, he brought himself back to the present. Hundreds of feet below him, the goblin holt awaited his perusal. Now at least he was somewhat rested. Collecting his gear, he exited the small bunkhouse.

The moon was high in the sky; he'd slept much longer than he'd expected. His leg muscles ached from the previous day's exertion. The mountain air bit his skin with an autumn chill. Not too long, and this camp would be covered in snow. With a shiver, he ventured down the stairs. The way down was less tiring, but the impact of each downward tread built up.

Pausing at the doorway to the passage, he listened for any activity. He felt for differences - in the air, the temperature, the smells. Nothing. Assured of his continued solitude, Ben stalked around the first curve in the long and otherwise straight passage. Deep scars spiraled up from the floor along the outer wall. Dozens of pairs of parallel lines populated the wall. He followed.

The arced furrows cut off when the passage opened onto a large chamber. Ben stopped at the threshold and gasped audibly. A deep silence spoke louder than words, bearing witness that nothing lived here. Small skylights lent dim illumination to a scene of vast destruction. The air here smelled acrid, a sulfurous, toasty aroma that seared his sinuses.

The shattered, cratered stone floor testified to a tremendous explosion. White and grey streaks sliced the walls and ceiling; punctuated by sheets of twisted iron driven deep into the chamber walls. Row upon row of galleries collapsed into each other, lying like a tall forest after a windstorm. Nothing could have survived this catastrophe.

Back in Canolbwynt, Ben heard jokes and rumors of goblin machines gone wrong; the worst stories didn't approach the magnitude of this destruction. He stood in place for a quarter-hour, trying to piece together what had happened. When he could not see the events unfold, he ventured deeper into the ruined holt to see what else he could learn.

Fatigue from yesterday's climb drove him to explore this level and downwards first, a decision he soon regretted. An hour's combing passages and rooms here yielded nothing notable. He found a long passage that sloped downward and tried that. Within a hundred yards the light from his mossy headlamp was the only useful illumination. Two hundred yards down, and around a gentle turn, his feet splashed into water. A jumble of shapes lay in front of him, some moving gently after the water was disturbed - some of these shapes floated.

Retreating to dry ground, Ben rummaged through his pack for the candles and a firestarter. The shapes barely moved and made no sound. That little voice in the back of his head babbled something just out of earshot, but he was sure there was no physical danger. After a couple of minutes, he had a candle flame started. Standing, he removed a sheltering hand from the safely burning flame and looked at the shapes.

Bodies. Easily a hundred dead goblins floated in this passage, presumably having found their way upwards over the months between the apocalyptic event and now. The normally staid Ben stood frozen in shock and horror until one of the bodies vented some built-up gas and rolled, cloudy, bloated eyes staring at him. He dropped the candle and yelped. It rolled down to join the macabre scene, extinguishing as it met the water. Ben grabbed the pack and retreated up the passage to the larger chamber.

Back in the dim natural light, he sank to his knees and wept. Another unforgettable image would haunt him now, pushing him farther from sanity. He wrestled himself to a seiza position and forced himself to calmness. Regular deep breathing and imagining the flow of energy in and through the world around him helped. He visualized a round crystal that housed the sun and the sea; all of the sun and all of the sea in a crystal that fit between his palm.

The Ivonian stood, closer to calm. Here, alone, he had the opportunity to expand his exercise - he took it. He ran through the forms he learned as one of the Angels.[7] Realizing he hadn't practiced since the battle at Canolbwynt, the man poured his concentration into them. Ever-present was the crystal, reminding the practitioner to move like the sea, flexing around your opponent's strong points, and crushing them with power backed by floods of proper stance. To mind the sun - know what is visible, and what is concealed.

Ben flowed over broken, uneven ground as if it were glass-smooth. Hands and feet flashed through parries, blocks and strikes. Unseen opponents fell and flew. Dust rose from the floor as the middle-aged man danced through form after form. He stopped in the center of the chamber, under a dusty beam of light descending vertically from the noon-day sun above him.

Not since his meeting with Zonka had he felt this centered, this aware. Details he'd missed in his earlier scans unveiled themselves as he put information together. The sheets of iron were driven into the walls from a point near him. He straightened a few in his mind's eye and saw similarities with Koksal's steam wagon train. The scents became more discrete; he could identify several

---

[7] Ivonian Angels were a group of gymnastic actors and bards to the casual observer; they used their position of popularity and fame to gain trust in myriad places around the Cyfandir, where they would gather information and sow the seeds of change their master, the Ivon, wanted.

as smells he associated with fireworks. His eyes slipped from one detail to the next, until he translated the scratches in the tunnel wall. *So clear - how could I have missed that?*

The goblins had taken a train like Koksal's and loaded it with more explosives than Ben thought existed and set it into the tunnel aimed for the Smaragdine Holt. If it ran like Koksal's, it would crash right through the stone door at the other end. *But what would it have done on the other end? That's for Bedwyn to determine. It would not be good, under any circumstances.*

Exploration of the upper levels revealed nothing more than a thick, metal-bound journal in a language he could not read. After two days, he'd learned all he would. He left the way he came, leaving no mystery as to why the goblins abandoned this once-thriving city. It lay an empty shell; its highest and best use now as a tomb.

Chapter 17

News from the South

Alene shielded her eyes from the sun, staring out over the southern ocean. She could just make out a black speck on the horizon. Beatrice stepped back from the mounted spyglass and smiled.

"He saw it. They've turned north. Let's get our haul ready."

The women loaded raw mother-of-pearl and island fruit onto one litter and dragged it out to the beach. Alene added another bucket of seawater to the crack in the yellow-stained rocks, creating another plume of steam, visible for miles. The trolls were afraid of the hot spot; they treated it like an angry deity. It lined up with the best landing site on the southern arm of the atoll and offered the women a safe place to enjoy the beach. Only one man in the world knew why this worked; when he died, the secret would die with him.

They skidded a bucket of large, live clams to the rendezvous. Captain Lohani was always glad to trade clams for fruit - and the fruit of the Mahadesa was abnormally large, sweet, and flavorful. Growing up on this island, Alene looked forward to these visits with glee. Even now, with her greater station, wealth, and power, she struggled to suppress a child-like excitement.

"Do you think they'll have rambutan?"

"Not likely. While it is fall in the Cyfandir, the Mahadesa spring is just beginning."

Alene let her shoulders sag, moping.

"But I haven't had one in so long! I wonder what he will have."

"We'll just have to see, now won't we? I expect he'll have spices I've been running low on. That will make me happy. I'll be right back."

Beatrice retreated toward the treehouse. Alene sat down, warm sand conforming to her curves under her light garment. Modesty alone justified clothes here; the climate was heavenly. The light, multi-hued sand invited her to lay back; she surrendered and let her mind drowse. Her thoughts neared a dream state, dreams filled with rambutan fruit and other tastes she'd missed for far too long.

A clattering, clicking racket pulled her from sleep, and a shadow passed over her face. She opened her eyes to see two larger looking back at her, surrounded by pink-streaked marble and seashells. The mess of matter shifted and rearranged as it stared. Alene stayed perfectly still. The troll blinked, then took two big steps toward the clam barrel. It reached in with both hands, selecting two near the top, then strode back into the forest.

Alene breathed again. *Did that troll seem... concerned? It didn't eat me, either. It's been so long, I wasn't sure...* If the troll wanted to, it could have smashed the woman to a pulp in seconds. But it didn't; it seemed more interested in stealing clams. As valuable as they were in the trade, a couple of clams was a small price to pay for one's life.

She stood and looked around. No visible trolls, but neither Beatrice. As Alene looked for the older woman, she heard sounds of exertion coming down the trail. Investigating, she found Bea dragging a small but heavy chest towards the beach.

"Here, Bea, let me help you with that!"

"All right, but mind you don't hurt yourself."

"Oh, don't be silly. Ungh!" Alene pulled hard on the side handle, and the little chest moved just a little. "Good grief, what do you have in here, cannonballs?"

"Don't worry about what's in the box, Alene. It belongs to the captain."

"Ungh! Hrrrgh -" Alene struggled to move the chest. "Beatrice, my back says I should be worried. What do you have in here?"

"Something I promised to the Captain a long time ago. You are right, it is heavy; things just seem to get heavier each year I grow older. You know, Alene, I've been thinking..."

"UUNGH!"

"Don't hurt yourself. As I was saying, I've been thinking... of retiring."

"Hurrgh! Nope. Too young." Alene made halting but continued progress with the chest. "I'm not ready to lose you. I still need help."

"Hush. You won't ever lose me."

"No, I mean grab this, I need help pulling it!"

Progress was faster working together, and soon they were with the rest of their trading goods. At least those that hadn't been stolen by a troll.

"Bea, what would you do with yourself if you retired?"

"First, it isn't an 'if', more of a 'when'. I'd sell the Hoot Owl. Good time to do that, I think. Then rest. Maybe come back here."

"Fishing for your supper each day? Avoiding trolls? That doesn't sound like much of a retirement."

"Hmm." Beatrice looked out to sea.

The ship dropped anchor just past the wave line and lowered bundles into a longboat. Three shirtless, dark men boarded. Two rowed while one sat at the stern, guiding them in with the rudder.

"It's not fair, is it?" Beatrice said as she stared at the swarthy man giving the orders. His oiled skin accentuated the bundles of muscle that rippled beneath. "Some men just get more attractive with time."

"I suppose." Alene had known this man as a man her entire life; to her, he was more of an uncle. A man desirable as an ally, but nothing more. "I intend to stay young as long as possible."

Five minutes later the longboat's keel scrunched into the sand. Three sweaty men disembarked, all smiles. Each sported piles of dreadlocked hair tied stylishly, but the leader's bore dramatic embellishments of gold and red lacquer. His hair also bore gray in addition to a black similar to his men's. The captain smiled at Beatrice, a wide, toothy grin.

"It is so good to see you again, ladies. You look well, Alene. But I must apologize, this full-grown beauty still has my eye." He took Bea's hands.

"I'm full-grown!" Alene pouted, hurting her case.

"Zidane, it makes me happy to see you too. You look as strong as ever. A little more gray, perhaps."

"The gray increases only when we are apart. A time too long, I think. Come, let us walk. Warm sand calls to my soles."

"Alene, you can handle this, yes? We'll be back." Beatrice turned and walked away with Zidane, letting an alluring laugh roll over her shoulder.

I could have predicted that. Zidane appears, and I'm on my own with two handsome, burly, young men. Eh, it could be worse.

Alene watched as the two young men unloaded sacks and crates from their longboat.

"We bring goods," the taller man stated ceremonially, "and we see yours. Shall we trade?"

"My goods have value," Alene replied with a smile, "As do yours. Let us trade fairly."

The shorter man stepped in between them with an oar from the longboat. Extending it to one side, he dropped the tip to the sand. He spun in a smooth, practiced motion; dark locks flinging themselves dramatically as he drew a trading circle in the sand. He hopped out of the circle and added a serpentine line, dividing the circle into two equal parts.

"Trade well." He said and stood to the side.

Alene moved with purpose to the barrel of shellfish the troll had plundered. She tilted it towards herself, then rolled it into the circle. The tall man came to view her offering, then grabbed a large sack and added it to the circle. He opened the bag and arranged it to show off the exotic tropical fruit inside. Alene took a few moments to observe and added more to her side of the circle.

This process repeated until most of the goods each had brought were in the circle, and neither moved to add more. They walked around the circle opposite each other slowly, visibly appraising the proposed trade. After three times around, they locked eyes, smiled, then reached across the circle to grasp hands. Alene worked hard to maintain her balance with the long reach for her stature.

"Well traded." The shorter man stated, closing the ceremony. He immediately went to work loading the items Alene had offered into the longboat, while she brought her newly-acquired treasures higher onto the shore. Her mouth watered as she carried the fruit; especially the small bag of rambutan. She didn't get fruit of this quality in the Veyns.

----- -----

Beatrice laughed like a woman twenty years younger. Zidane's presence was as intoxicating as ever. They walked side by side until they were out of sight before they spoke with sobriety.

"The girl is different. No longer a girl." Zidane was serious.

"She is a queen. Alene has led troops in battle. She's lost friends who fought for her and her throne. That she is no longer a girl is making a gale out to be a breeze."

"Does she suspect?"

"No."

"How can you be sure?"

Beatrice tilted her head in irritation.

"How important is this? Every one of our long-woven plans relies on her not knowing."

"And the plan? Will our trade circle become a reality?"

"I'm working on it, my love." Beatrice sighed heavily. "The Cyfandric situation is more complex than I hoped. Veynsport was erased from the world; replaced with Alene's blessing by a new independent group. Independents are unpredictable. And these dwarves; they've added a wrinkle with their operation on the north end of the atoll. Don't worry; I'll work it out."

Zidane stopped and looked back along the beach, then at the sun.

"We should return. The trade will be complete."

"So soon? I had other plans."

"Beatrice, I would never disappoint you."

"You never have, Zidane. You never have."

Chapter 18

A Long Boat Story

"They won't go any farther, crone." The Captain was blunt. "I hid our destination for a while, but the crew have caught on. We'll have to turn back."

"I feared there might be a… lack of resolve at some point. So I've come prepared." Zonka, still hidden behind her veil and the dim light of her cabin, opened the lid to one of her chests. "We have good weather for a time, yes? Why don't we ply the boys with a party?"

A case of fine wine and liquor plundered from the old woman she shared a tailor with, gleamed in the dark room.

"Not usually the tack I'd take, but I see your meaning." The Captain had his eye on an unbelievably rare bottle; one worth more than Zonka's passage alone. "Let's see if this buys enough time to find your island!"

Zonka closed the chest and slid it over to the captain easily. He grunted as he dragged it into the hallway. After he closed the door, the old orc chuckled to herself. Men were so easy to manipulate.

Chapter 19

The Ivon's Wrath

Ynghild blinked away the tears and stood. Her cheek burned from another of the Ivon's vicious slaps. This time, she'd let the impact carry her to the ground, where she still knelt. No words would help her; so she let him rage on.

"Brennan fails me. Johan betrays me. I lose the Sliver to these upstarts. Ivonsport. And now the Greenway? I will tolerate this no longer!" The Ivon's crimsoned face contorted again in fury. He lifted Ynghild's map, letting his eyes slip across too much red - denoting lost territory.

"Begging your pardon Ivon, but you haven't been tolerating it. Yet Gymdiethas Fasnach grows while Ivonia wanes. Neither your disapproval nor your troops have slowed the movement." She considered her next words. "Your efforts, Ivon, have in fact played right into their hands."

"I DO NOT PLAY!" The Ivon screamed, throwing the map at Ynghild. It slid off her face and shoulder, clattering to the ground. They matched stares, furious to resolved, for minutes. Eventually, the Ivon broke the silence; his voice much more controlled.

"If my tactics will not work, then what will?"

"With respect, sir, I suggest you make peace with them. Establish trade. Then eventually, over the course of years, we can infiltrate them. Weaken them. Turn them against each other; until eventually they come begging for your leadership."

"Make peace with them?"

"Yes."

"Rescind all of my orders to the contrary?"

"That would be essential, yes."

"Establish trade and enrich them for their treachery?"

"Yes," stated Ynghild, "and no. You must do these things in a manner of friendship and trust. Using words like treachery will only work against you."

"You think that calling people who break their oaths and recant citizenship and their duty to me, their Ivon, treacherous might be offensive?"

Ynghild did not answer. The Ivon verged on another tantrum, and she hoped it would defuse on its own.

"You feel," he flicked his tongue as if the words tasted bitter, "that I might hurt their feelings? And why, my dear, should that affect me?"

Again, the young spy held her tongue. Patient silence was the only route away from the Ivon's fury.

"I have no patience," continued the Ivon, "for subversive disobedience. Your tactics have never worked. I hoped that you could fill the shoes of your predecessor, but that is not the case. You will return to the Greenway and resume gathering information, from your knees or back or whatever it is you do. I expect a report at the next full moon. It had better contain a new and effective solution to our problem."

Ynghild knelt before him, head down and arms spreading wide, upwards, and behind in the salute of the Angels; it was only ever used in the presence of the Ivon. After several seconds of that pose, she rose to her feet gracefully. As she gathered her map, the Ivon stopped her.

"Leave it."

Ynghild let weeks of work and sacrificed principles drop to the floor and walked out the door. *Why do I work for this stupid bastard? He says one thing, does another, and his moods change with the wind. Except for being offended - one who offends the Ivon never lives long.*

Outside, she walked to the Ivon's personal balcony and surveyed the city. From this vantage point, a designed view spread out. A marine layer showed only the highest spires of the city, the rest masked in a heavy fog. The Ivon's perspective was that of a shining city on a hill; blue-topped white towers rising like perfect toadstools from the mist.

The Ivon had no clue about the realities below the fog, while she existed to live there only. Her position was to gather information and influence events where she could. Ynghild took one last breath of the clean, cool air, then descended the many flights of stairs to the city below.

----- -----

Johan watched Ynghild leave. They were in school together, and later in a very special school. They were more than close. Yet once they became Angels - spies for the Ivon - their wefts and warps never wove again. That part of his life past, Johan let a tear fall to the floor. He recomposed himself and observed what transpired below.

The Ivon's ever-present, rarely seen servants appeared and diligently removed all traces of his outburst. Within the space of a minute, serenity oozed from every surface.

"Leave us." Domestic staff dressed all in white except for a blue sash, filed silently out of a secret door behind a curtain before completing the double entendre. "You may come down now, Johan."

Johan's eyes swelled momentarily in surprise. After a calming moment, he stood from the angled rafter he rested against and descended. Soft leather soles barely tapped against a stone ledge, then the top of a bookcase, and a dressing chair; landing in a shoulder-led roll. He completed his maneuver in the kneeling Angel-wing salute, two feet from the Ivon.

"Your Majesty."

"Johan, you disappeared. I had both Ynghild and Brennan looking for you. You haven't killed Brennan, have you?" The Ivon spoke dispassionately, as appropriate for the worldwide game of Pawns and Kings he played. "He's late as well."

"I haven't killed any of your Angelic brethren, Majesty. I have merely been in deep cover in the Veyns."

"Have you? I was led to believe you had joined Alene. Possibly in more than one way."

"As I said, Majesty; deep cover. Alene does rule the Veyns, but she is scarcely more than a girl."

"Shall I not be concerned with a girl Queen, then? One that attacked my men?"

"To be fair, Majesty, DePet was setting up an attack at the same time. Alene just got there first. And your cavalry was late. Add to that four cohorts from different parties all attacking at the same time, and the odds were never in your favor."

"Mmm. And how do you propose we correct that?"

"You don't. Ivonsport is gone."

"But I want it."

"With respect, Majesty, you don't."

"Who do you think you are to tell me what I do and don't want?"

The man is insufferable. How did I ever work for him?

"I merely suggest, your Majesty, that the town you knew as Ivonsport no longer exists. Canolbwynt, as the residents call it, does nothing to forward your principles or even basic Ivonian virtues. It is infested with dwarves and goblins. Chaos rules. Even the treasury was looted by DePet in his retreat. I reassert, sire, it is nothing you would want."

The Ivon turned his back to Johan, ostensibly arranging various items displayed on his mantlepiece. The two stood in silence for a time, only the faint scratch of porcelain on marble echoing through the chamber. The Ivon spoke after a time.

"Tell me what you know of this unrest in the mainland."

"I trust you are acquainted with Gymdeithas Fasnach?"

"Subversive troublemakers, seeking to manipulate my people for their personal gain, yes."

"It seems, sire, that they have transcended subversive and risen to become the de facto governing system. Not a body, as they have no central control."

"There is always someone in control. Who is the puppeteer that pulls their strings?"

I am that puppeteer, you arrogant ass, thought Johan, *but not for my gain. For theirs.* Johan had the presence of mind not to speak that last. Instead, he calmly stated:

"They are fully independent. If you would control them, befriend them. You cannot do it by force. Gymdeithas Fasnach is loosely organized, but incredibly reactive. Whether those lands once belonged to you or not, they are no longer yours. And those men and women will fight to the death for their perceived independence. You must work with them if you wish to gain anything."

"NO!" The Ivon's fury exploded. "The Sliver, Ivonsport, the Greenway; they are all mine! I will not stand idly by, much less reward traitors for their transgressions!"

Ivonian guards materialized as if from the air, blocking all exits - even the secret ones. Johan knew where this was going. He edged back towards the balcony, many stories above the courtyard. The Ivon recognized his intent and commended him.

"Yes, you have been a faithful servant in the past. I will allow your suicide. Do you have any last words before we part?"

Johan stood on the parapet and donned thick leather gloves as if it were part of a ceremony. Then he spoke.

"I do. These words are not my last. Nor is this the last time we will meet; but I promise you, our next meeting does not end well for you." With that, he stepped backward into thin air.

The Ivon stepped up and leaned over the parapet to watch Johan's doom. What he saw was the young man descending on two long ropes tied to each edge of the Ivon's banner. Smoke billowed off the surface of the gloves from the friction. With several rebounds using his feet to rappel, he was on the ground - and even from this distance, the Ivon could make out the rude gesture.

"After him!"

Several of the guards ran for the stairs, and two tried to repeat Johan's dramatic exit. But they did not know the secret of Johan's knot and fell screaming to their deaths. By the time their bodies splattered the courtyard floor, Johan had faded into the cityscape.

----- -----

Outside the palace gates, the city maintained its glamorous facade. Ynghild passed the Great Library, where the largest collection of information in the world gathered dust. Past the massive Gallery, where the Angels perform for state dinners. Past the towering homes of the powerful families of Ivonia.

At the bottom of the hill, she wound her way through alleyway markets and close-set brick homes with cracked plaster, a single trench down the middle of the cobblestone street that served as a sewer. After a dozen blocks, these masonry buildings gave way to wood, lath, and plaster constructs that mimicked a safe place to live, if somewhat poorly.

Then the muddy road north pointed her to the Greenway. She could have provisioned herself at her apartment, but she needed nothing more than what she carried on her back to fulfill her mission. She'd take a room in the Greenway and set up shop - a road-weary woman on foot making a more believable story than the truth - a well-off, well-educated spy who could live out her days comfortably without working if she so chose.

Because what she did choose was unbelievable.

Chapter 20

Ebbing Floin

Angus squirmed on the hard wooden bench of the wagon. Indaria had taken up no room at all when compared to his Da's retired, dwarvish breadth. *This will be a long trail, crammed together like jarred pickles. Oh, to travel with an elf again!*

"It's nice of you to take me back with you, son." Floin looked around as the wagon creaked along. "This should be a fantastic trip, if a bit cold."

"Of course, Da! If you were to wait for Artemus, it might be years before you returned." Both dwarves laughed. "And it will be good to spend some time together. I can't think of anything I'd rather be doing!"

"A kind thing to say, son. A kind of lie, but I'll take it." Floin chuckled. "Honestly, son, I'm keen to get back. You have no idea how much fun it is having a Hero for a son. I've learned so much about dwarven women! Things like -"

"Stop, Da! I don't want to hear about it!" It wasn't the first time Angus' father had embarrassed him, but this was as racy as it had ever been. They needled and joked with each other for two days, humor and irritation ebbing and flowing as happens with family.

The pair traveled along an east-west road towards the Greenway, camping and singing, laughing and drinking. And they both enjoyed it tremendously.

On the third morning, nearing the home of the old couple Angus had lunched with months ago, the dwarves were arguing again. They argued so often, over brews or battles, tricks or tools. They were arguing about how effective water would have been at extinguishing dragon's fire when Floin changed the subject urgently.

"Stop."

"What?"

"Stop here."

"Why?"

"Son, I can piss myself, or you can stop."

"We're on a bridge!"

"I don't care!" Floin grabbed his pick. "I've got about five seconds before this is happening. Your call."

Angus stopped the wagon. Floin disembarked quickly, flourishing his pick and using it as a cane. He stepped straight to the southern edge of the wooden bridge and released the floodgates. He tried, at least. Nothing happened. After thirty seconds, Angus piped up.

"Sounds like a real emergency."

"Quiet, boy."

Another thirty seconds passed.

"We certainly couldn't wait another ten seconds and cross the bridge, now could we?"

"Shush! I'm concentrating here!"

Angus hopped off the north side of the wagon and mirrored his father's efforts. Being merely ninety years old, his plumbing still worked very reliably. He was finished when he heard a staccato splish from his father's side of the bridge.

"Ha! I hit the column! And what a ridiculous thing; a giant, stacked stone column next to the middle of a short bridge."

Angus saw no such column on his side.

"Da, what are you talking about? This is a simple, timber, free-span bridge. Mounded dirt on either side. There is no column."

"Well, I'm pissing all over something."

Angus developed a tightness in his gut as he crossed the heavy, squared timbers to stand next to Floin. Sure enough, there was a pile of rocks on the south side. And it moved.

"Put that thing away and get your pick!"

Floin had his eyes closed, focusing on keeping the flow going. Feeling splashback, he opened them to see that he was wetting the granite-coated face of a gigantic stone troll. The urine stopped as he took two steps back, towards the wagon, floundering to get a better grip on his pick. Angus was no longer by his side.

The troll sprang straight up, shaking the bridge like an earthquake as it landed. Floin held its complete interest. Ten feet tall, this was a mature troll that had taken up residence under this bridge specifically to capture food. This troll presented as hungry and very offended. It took a heavy step towards Floin, who raised his pick in response.

The troll didn't care who this offensive little dwarf was; the fact that the dwarf might have a name never crossed his mind. To the troll, this dwarf was a morsel that needed to be eaten before it anointed him again. The troll should have cared.

Floin Thunderpick brought his namesake down on the largest of the stones that covered the troll's foot. That stone shattered, breaking several of the bones underneath. Floin's weapon continued down through the foot, securing it to the timbers of the bridge. He left the pick there and stumbled backward, jostling the pony.

The troll screamed in agony, then pounded both fists down onto the spot Floin had stood. Wood shattered, sending splinters out like a wave. Neither dwarf wore armor; they hadn't expected a fight.

"Da!" Angus shouted at his father, tossing him the blood-onyx axe. Floin caught it and looked at the troll. Angus clattered around in the back of the wagon. With a practiced twist, the axe spun in Floin's experienced hands; the pick faced the troll. His bits faced the troll, too, survival outweighing modesty.

If the troll noticed this compound slight, it gave no outward sign. It fumbled with the pick, trying to pull its foot free. Failing that, the troll thumped wildly with its stone-clad fists, damaging the bridge further. Sooner or later, the wood would fail, releasing the damaged and bleeding troll.

Floin was raising Angus' axe, pick-side first when he was stopped by a monstrous mechanical sound. CRACKCRACKCRACKCRACK rang out as Angus operated the ratcheting cocking mechanism on his siege bow. Resting the bow on the back of the bench, Angus took aim. The troll screamed and bashed the bridge again.

"Sooner rather than later, son."

A click-twang-pow resounded as Angus' first shot ricocheted off the side of the troll's head. It reeled, then raised its arms for a strike against the wagon. Angus pulled the second and third triggers at once, generally pointing at the troll's moving chest. The first bolt clattered off a round boulder, ricocheting over Floin's head. The last bolt struck the gap opened by its predecessor, disappearing into the troll.

The beast screamed again, this time with a gurgle added. It lurched towards Floin, falling over its still-trapped foot. Floin stepped aside as it fell, Angus' pick already arcing downward to the back of the troll's neck. Floin expertly threaded the needle, hitting a slight gap in the troll's rocky armor. The blow severed the spine just below the head, and the troll slumped onto the timbers, dead.

Floin finished his original task, laughing.

"Da, my axe!" Angus jumped onto the twitching corpse to retrieve his axe. It sizzled as he yanked it out. Trolls' strange chemistry corrodes many metals, including mithril. He pulled off his vest and used it to soak up the acidic fluids. The finish was damaged - again.

Floin put his personals away and kicked the troll's leg away from his pick. With a well-practiced twist, he created room around the point and gently retracted it. Its finish was significantly more scarred, having been inside the Troll's foot for longer. Floin used the same vest to clean his tool, but he smiled at the damage.

"This'll buy me drinks for years," he smiled, "and I know more than one ladydwarf who might enjoy a close look."

"Schist, Da, that's gross."

"What do we do with the troll, then?"

"Good question. It's ruined the bridge."

"That's true."

"I think we should tell someone." Angus thought that through. "I think I know just the folks."

They resettled their belongings and continued west - only after Floin chiseled his mark into the largest stone on the troll. He also took the pieces that his pick shattered from the foot. These he smiled at, playing with them as Angus drove down a country lane with low hedges towards a lonely old farmhouse.

It was owned by the couple that had traded a lunch and rest to Angus in exchange for some Argentine brandy at the beginning of summer. The old man was sitting peacefully on his porch when he spotted the dwarves' approach. He jumped up and ran inside, bringing his wife out again.

"Master Angus! We hoped we'd see you again!"

"Of course I'd come back! It's on the way home. Speaking of home, meet my Da, Floin."

"A pleasure to meet you, Master Floin," said the man, "I'm Timothy.

"A pleasure and an honor, sir," returned Floin. "My son tells me you were very hospitable on his last passage this way. I thank you for that."

"No thanks needed - he filled this snifter," Timothy said, indicating an empty blown-glass pitcher, "with some fine Argentine brandy. And that in return for some sandwiches! We are the ones who should be thankful. Here, let's sit together."

"I have something very different to share with you today, Tim." Angus' grim visage brought the mood down quickly. "You know the bridge a league or so east?"

The couple nodded with obvious concern.

"We were attacked there not long ago. By a troll."

Shocked expressions grasped the old farmers' faces.

"A troll," Tim nodded. "That may explain a few recent problems. Folk have disappeared now and then. Should I raise a posse in town to go after it? I hope it isn't overlarge."

"It was large enough. And yes, you could bring a crew to dispose of it. I'd say it wouldn't trouble you, but your bridge needs significant repairs now."

"Will you be collecting the bounty, then?" Tim's wife Marlene asked. "That bridge is right on the border of the Greenway and Ivonia. You could choose which to collect from. The Ivon offers a larger purse."

Angus did not attempt to mask his surprise.

"I thought the Greenway was a part of Ivonia. What changed?"

"Gymdeithas Fasnach," Tim offered. "The free-trade association has swept the farm and ranch communities south of the mountains. In truth, Ivonia is little more than the largest city I know of now, an insular city-state with nothing but grudging anger at our independence."

Angus traded a meaningful glance with Floin.

"And how far will this organization spread, Tim? Has it crossed the river to the west?"

"It might have done. I'm not sure. It moves fast, due to the very attractive terms."

Angus didn't hear much more of the conversation. He was processing the simple but important information he'd just received. *No wonder the Ivon hasn't committed a full attack against the Veyns - he's been busy here. Bedwyn needs to hear about this.*

"Tim," Angus said, interrupting the others, "I think you should collect on the bounty."

"But I didn't kill it."

"No, we did. On your behalf. I'll head into the Greenway now and let them know. Besides, I've some arrangements to make."

Within minutes the dwarves were on their way, Timothy and Marlene following behind on their buckboard. The humans' draft horse was no faster than Angus' pony over any distance. For this next segment, Angus would need speed. He hoped he could find it at the Greenway.

One long stretch of the road had two sets of wagon ruts, and the four drew abreast and talked as they rode.

"You know, Angus," Tim said, "this bounty will help considerably with our plans."

"Yeah? What plans are those?"

"We," piped Marlene in her high-pitched, bird-like voice, "are going to retire. Fifty years of farming everything from grain to children is enough. We're ready for warm sun and rest."

"No more fog and snow." Tim spit as he mentioned snow.

"There's seasons everywhere. If it isn't snow, it's rain." Floin was no world traveler, but he knew a good portion of the Cyfandir from five-hundred years of living. These folks likely never traveled more than fifty miles from their homes.

"Now that nice man from the southlands had something different to say." Marlene sounded almost offended at Floin's assertion. "He spoke of sand and coral, sunshine and pools of hot water that bubble up from the ground. My old bones could use some of that!"

"Hot water bubbling up from the ground?" Floin screwed up his face, searching for old memories. "That's a rare thing indeed. Where was this?"

"He said," offered Timothy, "that taking a ship directly south from Ivonia for a week would get us there. The storms that rage for much of the year would stop us; but he told us of a time when the storms settle for a few days, allowing safe transit."

"When was that?" Angus asked.

"I'm sorry, Angus," Tim responded, "but he swore me to secrecy."

"That's interesting. I wonder why?"

"His people, the Nyanjan, are honorable traders. We took him in for a month while his wounds healed. Since he had nothing to trade for that service, he traded information."

"We learned a lot from him." Marlene nodded vigorously as she talked. "The Jambeaux culture seems friendly and just. I never objected to the Ivon beyond taxes and my boy's conscription, and honestly, I like this Fasnach group. But I'm ready for a change. We're ready for a change. And thinking of a hot bath without an hour's labor to prepare it is very, very attractive."

"For my part," Tim offered, "I would be perfectly happy if I never threw another shovelful of snow again."

They laughed just as the two trails merged, and rode the rest of the way into town in tandem. An uneventful journey, one Angus would miss soon enough.

Chapter 21

Land Ho!

Black Zonka watched as the ship turned away from the craggy, black island chain. The crew had voted to set her adrift, keeping her coin and her bags. She'd convinced them to surrender one of their longboats, but only after killing the Captain, the first mate, and the first three that tried to toss her overboard. Breathing deeply, she put her back toward the nearest island and rowed.

"Humans are so predictable," she muttered to herself. "Afraid of everything, and only bent on gathering gold. You'd think they'd learn that, no matter how much gold and wealth you accumulate, you can't take it with you. And there is always somebody who can take it all away in one quick move."

Her distraction had worked, of course. Knowing there would be a fight, she set the fuse to the cargo of fireworks as long as she could. That gave her time to be noticed, accosted, and for a longboat lowered into the water before they found it.

"Any time now…"

Pops and booms echoed across the water. Whistles and showers of colorful sparks emanated from the gridded cover over the cargo bay. Several small fires erupted, including the main sail.

"Yep. That'll do." Zonka laid back into the oars, putting more distance between her and the ship. They couldn't fire on her; probably couldn't even see her in the moonless, dark night. But the crew of that ship was not her real concern. She swiveled her head from side to side, looking over her shoulders, and even over her head.

"Moment of truth, hag. Now we find out how accurate those old books were."

Zonka rowed, hard, for twenty minutes with no signs of the things she came here for. She'd started to doubt her decision when a patch of stars disappeared in the dark, returning to existence a moment later. With a deftness unusual in a bulky old orc like herself, she placed the oars in the boat and sat back, wrapped in her hoary rag cloak. In broad daylight, it would appear a boat adrift with a pile of fisherman's nets in the middle.

Now, Zonka watched.

The patch of darkness came nearer the ship, over, and back again. The crone was enthralled. Then a second, a third, and finally a fourth splotch of moving darkness joined the airspace above the trading vessel. A keen observer would have seen the pile of nets open a wide, toothy smile and issue a tittering giggle worthy of a twelve-year-old girl.

----- -----

The boatswain barked orders to the men, dropping sails and dipping buckets over the edge to gather seawater for firefighting. For a while, it seemed as if the crew could get the fire under control and save the ship, and their lives with it. He'd never expected to gain a command, much less advance several ranks in one night. But things happen fast on the ocean. That orc woman was one of them.

The sails fluttered several times, buffeted by inconsistent breezes. The headwind they'd just turned into was still steady and strong.

"Bring 'em down, boys. Let's get these fires out and then we'll get underway again!" He strode up to the wheel deck, grabbing the tiller more out of ceremony than function. Looking over the crew and foredeck, he was happy with the situation. Hours ago a boatswain, likely never to advance again, now de facto captain of the boat.

With a newfound bravado, a sudden gust buffeting him from behind, he whistled to the crew. Every set of eyes turned in his direction, wide with wonder and attention, and… fear? *This is it!* He thought, *A crew that fears me will certainly come together under my command. "Be a blacksmith like yer ol' pap," he'd said when I told him. "Naught but death on the seas," he said. Well, I've shown him, and in record time. Now to rally the men to follow me, while I have their attention.*

"Wel-AAAAAAAgh!" His voice was cut off by darkness, wet pressure, and pain shooting up from his shins. Suddenly surrounded by something fleshy, and his feet were in excruciating pain. His legs tilted up over his head, arms pinned to his sides. Light stormed in, jagged cracks in the darkness starting from his feet to his sides, and for a moment he was free, falling head first. He looked towards the ground, seeing a charred, pink fleshy hole opening. The perimeter of that flesh was lined with pointy, gleaming white teeth.

He barely had time to register he'd been eaten, and one of his last thoughts was the dreadful certainty that at least some of his men would follow him - follow him right into the gullet of this beast.

His very last thought?

I should have listened to my father.

----- -----

The doomed crew fully comprehended the hopelessness of their situations, as four dragons landed on the ship at once. The boatswain eaten first, another shattered the mast near the deck. If the cackles from the longboat reached the ship, they were drowned out by several minutes of screams. The dragons rent the ship to pieces physically after silencing the crew, then circled in flight a few minutes more, looking for survivors.

The old orc stayed silent and still for an hour before cautiously looking about. Convinced the coast was clear, she rowed for the smallest in this chain of islands. She reached the shore just before sunup. After skillfully stashing the longboat and its secret cargo above the high tide line, she found a spot to nap in the sun. Only now did the hard work begin. She wanted a dragon. But not just any dragon; The Dragon.

If the charts and books were right, she'd find it here.

Chapter 22

Harvesting News

Shadows grew eastward as they entered the Greenway. Timothy and Marlene bid their goodbyes and headed to the constable to discuss the troll, while Angus and Floin searched for a place to spend the night. Floin made the call.

"The Hustled Bustle - that sounds like a fun place. Let's try it!"

"Are you sure, Da? The people there are rather… loose."

"If you mean they drink and throw things, then I'm there! Let's go!"

Floin went in to arrange rooms while Angus stabled the pony and wagon. He got the same stall he'd had the last time. *But without Mr. Bloody Brightshirt here to announce me, I won't likely have the same problems this time.* Angus walked round to the main entrance and pushed the swinging doors aside. A lively tune lit the room from a stringed instrument; no words to this one. The attentive innkeeper turned his head away from the entertainment to see who had entered. A smile chased his mustache into his nose as he shouted a greeting.

"Master Grimbrow! Welcome! So good to see you again. Young Johnny's been singing your ballads again, and my how they've grown! Here, have a seat, I'll fetch some ale."

Angus, red-faced, settled down next to Floin, who fairly dripped amused pride over his son's welcome.

"Da, I'll have you know these people are easily impressed. All it took for me was to kill a few orcs at the Sliver…"

"Few indeed!" The busty, middle-aged woman chided him as she set down two tankards filled to overflowing with Greenway Stout. "I heard the count at thirty-five dead orcs when you were at the Sliver, to say nothing of the troll you left dead down the road!"

"Aha! The troll I blame on my father, Floin Thunderpick. He had both the first and the last strike of that fight, so it's his to claim. What do you say, Da? Shall we start calling you Floin Trollbane?"

"Trollbane!" Floin laughed hard for a few seconds. "Well, I suppose so. Of course, being a Trollbane is still a bit silly when your son is a Dragonbane."

Floin laughed harder and longer, thinking his an excellent joke. The rest of the tavern fell silent. Angus adopted a sheepish grin. The innkeeper was at his elbow.

"Is that true? There was a dragon? And you killed it?" The portly man stood awestruck. Angus gave a small nod. "When was this?"

"Oh," Angus replied, "back at the beginning of summer. At the Argentine Holt, two days north of the Sliver."

"How is it we did not hear of this before?" The music ceased, and the innkeeper glanced towards the stage. A young man in a bright red-and-yellow shirt approached them, eyes squinted from the smile that split his face.

"Because, sir," Johnny Brightshirt responded, "the Ivon banned the story. He was concerned both about the veracity and value of such a panic-causing event. If it was true, then the sole dragon had already been dealt with, and he saw no value in spreading such concerning news. If it wasn't true, then letting a false news article spread could only damage stability in the region. Either way, the story had no value to his kingdom."

Floin's face reddened as Johnny talked.

"That's the official story, is it?" Angus had regaled him at length about their escape from Ivonia over the last few days. As a father, he wasn't pleased by the news.

"Yes, Sir," replied the man, "that is the official story. Who knows what the real reason is? As a simple bard, I merely relate the great deeds of others. I can't imagine being in the company of Queens and Ivons, as Master Bloodaxe here has."

A sharp, snide laugh barked across the room as Johnny said this last. They looked to determine the source, but there was no clear indication of the laugher. It broke the spell for the innkeeper, who asked what else he could bring them and left. When he was gone, the three spoke conspiratorially.

"There's more to this story, I'll wager." Floin's cheeks still wore crimson.

"It is a long and complex story," said Johnny, "much larger than Johnny Brightshirt. I know a man who can explain more fully. I'll ask him to visit you before you leave." His wink was almost imperceptible.

A large chunk of slow-cooked beef showed up wearing a rich sauce charred into a tasty crust. The dwarves tore into the best food they'd eaten for days. They listened to the conversations around them as they ate.

"Are you ready for the Festival?"

"It's going to be epic. We've never had a harvest this good."

"Everyone I've talked to is planning to attend."

"Well, I wouldn't miss it for the world!"

"The way we shared work across communities made each job so easy. I don't mind that it means more days working."

"They're shipping in food and drink from all over!"

The Festival talk went on for hours, and the dwarves took it in deeply. When they'd had their fill of braised beast, beer, and banter, they retired to their rooms. Angus had enjoyed the meal so entirely that he missed the tell-tale squeaky step on the way up. He remembered nothing of the last time he stayed in this particular inn, months ago.

The dark figure that stalked him remembered. It knew what it was after, and was determined to achieve its goals this time.

Chapter 23

An Edgy Night

"Sleep well, Da." Angus closed the door to his father's room and crossed the hall to his own. It was the same room he'd slept in before, this time decorated with the traditional garlands of dill and fennel in recognition of a good harvest. Turning down his bed, he found a still-warm digestive biscuit wrapped in a coarse napkin.

Much better treatment than my last trip through, he thought. *These folks have had some lessons in manners from those high-and-mighty Ivonians.* He enjoyed the late-night snack while setting his things in order, tsking at the acid-etched mithril on the pick his father used to kill the troll.

After such a long day, Angus allowed himself only a few minutes of polishing before laying the axe next to his bundled armor and his small stash of gems and coins. He undressed and cleaned up with the cold water and basin, redressing in only his smallclothes. He tucked Indaria's small, white satchel back behind his beard, next to his heart.

The weary dwarf leaned back onto the soft bed, pulled the country quilt over him, and was asleep. This evening, Angus' dreams were relaxing and restful. At least for a little while.

----- -----

The floorboards outside his room were silent - the kind of silence that unsettles a dwarf. Then a muffled, nearly inaudible scritching invaded the room. Angus watched the scene from above and saw himself snoring loudly, mouth agape.

Great Stones, *he thought,* anyone could drop poison down my throat and I'd have no chance to defend myself!

A movement at the doorway grabbed Angus' focus; he watched in horror as the lock slid open a fraction at a time until, with a dull click, it freed the primitive yet functional latch. The lever eased upward, releasing the door to open. Swinging quietly inward, degree by degree, a dark-cloaked figure slunk in, closing but not locking the door.

Wake up, *Angus thought at his recumbent form.* You'll be robbed, kil't, or both! *The sleeping dwarf snorted but did not rouse. The shadowy interloper slithered with liquid grace, hovering over Angus' possessions. Long fingers caressed dwarven runes and bas-relief scenes on the mithril plate armor; stroked the deep black of the onyx axe with its bloodred undertones.*

Angus' horror intensified manifold at the realization that this sneak ignored the plentiful coin and pricey gems. The figure moved with intention, turning at last to Angus' sleeping form. It gently moved first one of his arms, then the other to the corner posts of the bed, securing them with firm knots. After Angus' feet were likewise bound, the entity leaned across his chest, approaching that gaping, bearded mouth.

Wake up, you fool! *Angus' perception rushed towards his head, under the looming, dreadful figure. He forced his way back into his head and opened his eyes -*

Angus saw nothing more than shapeless darkness above him, but it moved. Something slid across his belly, his chest, and behind his beard. *Indaria's satchel!* Angus reached for it but found his arms restrained. His feet, too. A soft voice whispered in his ear.

"Let it happen." The thing on his chest - that long-fingered hand? - slid back down his belly. He caught sight of a single lock of yellow hair, and felt two warm, soft masses lean onto his chest as the hand went - the shape was gone as the door opened.

"Angus!" Johan's voice broke into the room. "Wake up, I'm here to talk." The man lifted his lantern and placed it on the table, then looked at his friend. "Ha! Should I come back at a better time?"

A dark shape blurred toward him from behind the door. In an instant, the figure had a slim knife resting on Johan's jugular.

"You." The woman's voice struck a chord in Angus' memory.

"You?" Johan's echo stank of confusion.

"What the bloody hell is going on?" Angus shouted. "Why am I tied up?"

"You tied him up?"

"He got away last time."

"Still a naughty girl, I see." Johan's puzzled tone changed to mirth. "We seem to have each other in compromised positions."

"Oh, you are compromised," said the woman, sliding the blade just enough for Johan to feel it. "I have you where it counts. It's been a while. You've slowed faster than I thought you would."

"Have I?" Johan let his cold blade touch the woman's bare inner thigh, right where the artery is nearest the surface. Her sharp intake of breath showed that she felt it, and knew the equal danger she was in.

They stood there for what seemed an eternity to Angus.

"Hey, I'm getting cold over here. Would you two either kill each other or let me up? This is quite undignified."

Without taking his eyes or knife off the woman, Johan gave a chuckled reply.

"Angus, you were about to have a very interesting evening."

"So you don't find this to be interesting already?" Angus pulled at his bonds for emphasis. He saw the woman clearly for the first time. He could see that she was shapely under the dark, hooded robe she wore over… nothing else. Blonde hair framed freckled cheeks, which creased as she giggled at him. Her prodigious, practiced allure terrified the practical, proper dwarf.

"You, my dear little man, have no idea." She laughed, eyes still locked on Johan's. "Well, lover, it's time to decide. The proprietor is on his way up." The telltale step squeaked as she finished, confirming her statement.

Johan retracted his blade as she removed hers from his throat. She stepped to the little window and arranged her robe to cover more of, well, her. She didn't reveal her face to the portly innkeeper as he panted in the doorway.

"Is everything all right? I heard a ruckus…" He paused as he took in the untenable scene. Looking pointedly at anything but the mostly bare dwarf bound spread-eagle on one of his beds, he asked, "Master Angus, is there anything I can offer to make you more comfortable?"

"Yes, thank you. A bottle of whiskey and a heaping serving of discretion, if you don't mind. I'll pay triple for the drink." The host scurried gratefully down the stairs, shaking his head to clear the imagery.

"Three glasses, I think," Johan called after him. "Well, Ynghild, should we untie him?"

She turned and pouted, first at Johan then Angus.

"I was so looking forward to our time together, Angus."

"Ynghild is it? Have we met before?" He wasn't sure.

"You don't remember me? Dragonbane?"

"Enough, Yng," Johan said, "He doesn't deserve this."

"Neither did you," she shot back.

"Why are you here?" Johan sounded irritated. "You aren't into dwarves, as I recall."

"Neither were you." She smiled. "Yet here we are, three of us, in a room with a nude dwarf."

"I'm right here," Angus grunted with frustration, "and just as embarrassed. Please, for the love of all that is decent, free me!"

Johan moved to untie his wrists. After another momentary pout, Ynghild undid his feet. Angus jumped up and dressed, face out-redding his beard. Before he returned to sit on the edge of his bed, he retrieved his large belt knife and held it across his knees.

The innkeeper showed up again, carrying a tray bearing a bottle, three glasses, and a small pile of clean rags. Worry fell from his face when he saw Angus free and dressed. Ynghild had her back turned to him again. He didn't ask, but instead closed the door and retreated. Angus broke the silence.

"I think I deserve an explanation."

"Well, Angus, Ynghild here was one of the-"

"Hold, Johan. I can explain myself." She took a deep breath before continuing. "My name is Ynghild, and I was... associated... with Johan here somewhere south. I think my meaning is clear, yes?" The males nodded. "Here, however, I am known as Allus. I listen and learn about life in and through the Greenway. Much like Johan here, except that I enjoy my work." She looked at Angus mischievously again. "I truly enjoy it."

"Do all humans have multiple personalities? Or are you two just special?"

"Specially-trained, and mostly us and people in..." Johan searched for the words, "...similar lines of work."

"Ah," Angus grasped it, "Allus the Angel. I should have known you were on an assignment. That makes much more sense. You wouldn't be interested in a dwarf like me."

"Oh," she replied, "you'd be surprised. I enjoy new and different experiences. Things are so homogeneous and regular. It's nice to switch things up."

"Speaking of switching things up," Johan interjected, "What do you make of this Gymdeithas Fasnach group? Where did they come from? Do they have a chance?"

Ynghild's eyes narrowed with shrewd consideration.

"Do they have a chance? I would have said no, but here we are a season later, and they show no signs of stopping. I suspect the movement will be self-limiting. I just don't think you can have sixty thousand people operate as one without a common cause. The Ivon's cruelty is that uniting factor. Without him, I think the movement will fade, and Gymdeithas Fasnach will look for leadership. They may elect a king of their own."

"Don't you think a King goes against their pledge?" Angus asked.

"It most certainly does." A mocking smile grew across her face. "But this pledge isn't exactly carved in stone. As far as I can tell, it appeared just a few months ago in Pentref."

"How could you know that?" Johan asked. "The whole town was wiped off the map by the Ivon's forces."

"I know," she replied, "because I did my job. I tracked down the earliest meetings and talked closely with one of the junior councilmen. He claimed to be one of the framers and named the others. That earned him some special treatment, of course; but he got what he deserved when Brennan arrived."

"Brennan." Johan swirled his drink. "It makes sense he'd be involved. Our paths haven't crossed for many months. How is he these days?"

"Dead, I think." No grief crossed her face over that thought. "No one knows."

"Why do you think he's dead?"

"You really don't know?" Ynghild asked, giddy. "Well, I know a few facts, but they'll cost you."

Angus laughed. Johan sighed. Ynghild arched her finely-groomed eyebrows in expectation.

"What's your price?"

"You'll tell me about you - including your relationship status. Where did you disappear to?"

"I've been doing a lot of traveling, running my bard bit. Gathering information, specifically about this new political movement." Johan emptied his glass and passed it to Angus for a refill. "You may have noticed a theme in my song selections."

"I did," she confirmed, "It's more focused than it used to be."

"It helps start conversations in that vein."

"Tell me the rest." She stared him down.

"It's complicated. There is someone, but it can't be. You know how it goes."

"Pining over an unrequited love interest? I can't imagine that." She giggled, looking at the dwarf sitting next to her on the bed. "Except for this chubby bundle of love."

"Who are you calling," retorted Angus, "a 'bundle of love?' That's not me, you stealthy little tart!"

"That may be the nicest thing you've said to me, Angus. Thank you."

"We," interrupted Johan, "are getting off-track. I've told you mine, now you tell me yours. What happened with Brennan?"

"He botched several missions this spring and summer. Rumor has it he took the entire light cavalry east towards Ivonsport to support DePet, but every account I have shows the unit as essentially destroyed. No word on Brennan specifically. If he's not dead, he will be as soon as the Ivon catches him; so it's the same either way."

"Wow. Tough break."

"Yeah." She refilled her glass, and topped off the others'. "What's next? I honestly don't think brute force will work with these people."

"No, I don't think it will." Johan pondered. "I think he's got to give some ground and work with the populace instead of against it. Right now, he's just concerned about winning. If he worried more about the common good, everyone would advance. But it all comes back to him and his perceived supremacy."

"If only we knew someone with proven Royal blood."

"I'd settle for unproven." Johan threw back the last of his drink and rose. "I've got a long day's travel ahead. I mean to make the Sliver in time to book a gig tomorrow night. Would you two care to meet for breakfast? It'll be Johnny and Allus, of course."

"I," replied the dwarf, "have five conditions. The first three are bacon, eggs, and sausage. The fourth is my father. Finally, we never speak of this evening again, publicly or privately."

They agreed, and Johan left the room first. Ynghild paused at the door, turning and giving Angus an inviting smile. Angus returned a stern, unyielding visage, shaking his head as he pushed her out and closed the door. Locking it would not be enough - he slid the table in front and set several coins on edge to ensure he'd wake if anyone trespassed. After repeating the same for the window, he slept - fitfully.

Chapter 24

Dragonglass

The sun was high when Zonka started her search of the island. The coastline was much like any volcanic place, with ancient lava surrounded by a coral reef that swarmed with life. Just above the tidal line, where one might expect to find tropical plants and trees overflowing with fruit, there was just glass. Not clear glass like in windows, though some were transparent, nor like the colored glass in merchant's bottles. Most of this glass was black.

Black, however, was insufficient. Black Zonka got her name from her ritual costuming which usually made more use of black charcoal than clothing. Zonka was kind of an aficionado of the color black. But this was truly the absence of color. Nothing reflected from the black glass, even where sharp edges had knapped themselves as one giant piece clattered across another.

And giant doesn't adequately describe the size. Some pieces were smaller and graduated down to grains of warm, black sand. But some of the larger pieces were house-sized. Tower-sized. And at the center of the island, a single piece of glass the size of a small mountain.

In her long time on this planet, Zonka had seen many things, but this was new. As she walked, she looked not only for signs of her dragon but things to eat. No plants. Not even moss or fungus. When she spotted a raft of kelp stranded on the beach, she grabbed it and wrapped it around her shoulders like a shawl. She munched on the leaves and floats, and if needed, it made a bit of natural camouflage.

She clucked to herself as she searched. *This is going to take a while.*

After circling the island for several days to get the lay of the land, Zonka pressed inward. The immense obsidian shard that shot upwards from the center of the island appeared to have suffered a catastrophic failure near the peak at some point in the distant past. The old orc had identified openings here and there along the outer edge, most showing signs of fatigue and extreme age.

Extreme doesn't touch it. The records I found of this place were several thousand years old and spoke only of legends of the far past on the edge of memories of legend. Orcs have no records that far back, as most tend to seek study in areas that are relevant to the now. She sighed. *Which makes me different still. I was only interested in the 'now' over the course of my first few lifetimes. Now better than twenty lifetimes in, the 'now' loses meaning to the grander purpose - my people.*

She opened one of the urchins she'd caught in a glass tidepool on a vertical shard of obsidian glass, scooping out the insides with a bit of kelp leaf and munching it like a sandwich. Her unnaturally long life afforded her vastly more perspective than typical of her kind, and it hit her now.

Except for that dwarf. Every ounce of me says that ridding the world of him is the only way orcs can survive. And certainly, we saw him in action at the Aureate Holt and the battle of Veynsport. I wish I could remember more clearly what happened at my home. She chewed again, saltwater, saliva, and ichor dribbling down her chin.

That threat will end soon enough. I could not kill him with orcs or with trolls, but if I can achieve this dragon... My people will be saved.

She climbed for hours, careful with each step and handhold to stay silent. This island was an absolute terror. Nearly no safe surfaces. Few places to rest and fewer to hide. She'd studied as much as she could and had a semblance of a beginning of a plan. On this plan rested the sum total of the hopes of orcdom.

She went to grasp another handhold when it moved. She did not. She didn't breathe. As Zonka looked right and left, she discovered another thing she hadn't expected. This breathing creature in front of her - a dragon she presumed - was nearly indistinguishable from the glass topography that surrounded them. And it went on for a long way, in both directions.

Inspecting the scales, she learned more. First, there were organic scales underneath that resembled snake and lizard scales, and those she'd heard about on dragons on the Cyfandir. These had a directionality to them, like overlapping shingles. On top of this was the same black obsidian, somehow fused directly onto the living scale. And like the obsidian on the island, every scale's glass had been broken at some point in the past.

Some of the scales were missing, she noted. That lent credence to the idea that she had found an old dragon. Very old. She resisted the urge to touch the broken glass and deep-scarred scales.

Let sleeping dogs and dragons lie, she reminded herself. *But only for a while.*

She began a painstakingly slow crawl along the dragon's side in the direction she felt she'd find the head. It took hours. Zonka marveled at the scale of this enormous creature, several hundred feet long, with remnants of ornate glass decorations the whole length. When she reached shoulders and neck, Zonka mentally mapped out places she might be able to sit, should her plan succeed.

There had never been any doubt, of course. Hundreds of years had passed since she last failed to influence a living creature, given enough time. Surely this great dragon would be her greatest challenge, but Zonka remained confident. As the bulk of the dragon's head came into focus, the orc felt emotions she could barely remember. Awe. Respect. Honor. Fear.

Fear was the most familiar. Zonka experienced fear when she fled her hovel after the dwarven attack. It bothered her that the only detail she remembered was that dwarf's face, and how he seemed so at peace and unconcerned in her mind's eye. Almost as if he were asleep. Whatever magic he'd unleashed on her mind, it was the most concerning threat within her prodigious memory.

She pressed that fear deep down and out of sight. Concentrating again on the task at hand, she located a shard of obsidian about her size with a flat face at an angle to that of the dragon. She took cover and got her bucket of seawater ready.

----- -----

Uvrede the Deposed dreamt of odd smells and strange vibrations. A presence haunted her, one she did not know. Something new and old at once. Her anger grew at her disrupted slumber. Her mind stirred, then woke as salty water splashed the end of her wagon-sized maw.

"Wake up, sleepyhead," she heard. The accent was odd, but was certainly that common, vulgar language she remembered from eons past. There existed no entities on the planet who both used that language and were worthy of her time or respect.

"You've dozed long enough," the voice continued. "It is time."

Crust broke free of long-closed eyelids. Unused irises convulsed in the noonday sun. A blurry humanoid figure stood several yards in front of her face, waving. In one hand it held an empty, woven bucket, still dripping with water.

"Good morning," the figure continued. "Let me introduce myself. I'm-"

A thundering FOOOSH noise silenced the figure, melting it and the surrounding glass into bubbling puddles.

"...Dead, I know," Uvrede responded. "You can call me uninterested and sleepy." She closed her eyes again, returning to a deep slumber, if somewhat less peaceful.

Chapter 25

Ivon Control

The Ivon's slender hand traced the roads on the map before him, pausing at the points these men had just shown him.

"You say no one outside this room knows of this plan?"

"No one, sire. The intention is secure."

"How long do we have to prepare?"

"No time, sir. If we do this, we leave tonight, under cover of darkness."

"How many men do you want? I'm running short after Brennan's antics, and we've had too many desertions since these communities rebelled."

"Three groups of twenty men, sire. Two more two-man teams. All must be ready and able to camp. We'll need strong arms and backs."

The Ivon grabbed a sheaf of papers with figures, flipping through them, looking for the numbers he needed. When he found the required page, he set it down and wrote out some figures. He compared those to another page, nodding.

"Your plan is sound. Make it happen. My steward will make the arrangements with you. Succeed, and you'll each become landed gentry. If you fail, do not return to Ivonia."

The men retreated quietly, and the Ivon, the most powerful man in the Cyfandir, rested his hands on the northern balcony. It was a clear, bright day and he could see the Greenway clearly. Now into autumn, the grasses were yellow and cropped close. The harvest was nearly over. Soon, he would make his move. Soon, the rebels would beg him for mercy.

"As it should be," he said to himself, smiling wickedly.

Chapter 26

Top-Level Meeting

After her steamy saltwater bath, every inch of Alene's body felt clean and fresh. Her visit to Connemara, while restful, had been rather sweaty. The short sea voyage back had offered less-than-luxurious accommodations. The *Aiseag Picil* was a dwarven workship, and each amenity, each detail, reminded the passenger of that simple fact.

Being a Queen in her palace was a very different experience. While tradition kept Veynsian queens from being pompous or showy, life out of public view was much more than comfortable. Dwarven engineers designed the palace with air passages and water channels that allowed for precise control of temperature.

The surprise lay in her realization of becoming accustomed to luxury. Now that she knew how life could be easy and relaxing, the young ruler desired it; sought it out even. Life could be so easy…

Not this night. Alene eschewed her plush towel for the clothes laid out on her bed - simple peasants' style, with loose pants and a baggy blouse. More than simple - men's clothes. With her hair up and wrapped in the manner of Veynsian sailors, Alene easily passed for a teenage boy.

Dressed this way, she left via a back door designed for servants and wandered the city. In truth, this meandering route was one of several. By walking amongst the people in markets, cutting down alleyways, and strolling through parks, Alene felt the beating pulse of the Veyns. She heard the rumors firsthand, saw the problems and occasionally observed crime.

Bold strides tinged with an awkward swagger looked nothing like the practiced movements they were. After most of an hour, she wound her way towards the docks and into the Hoot Owl. She entered through the steamy kitchen, right up the back stairs normally reserved for staff. She didn't stop until she reached Beatrice's rooftop garden.

----- -----

Estelle chafed in her blue Ivonian garments. Sapphire head to toe - even her veil was blue - marked her as high up in Ivonian society. Her corset inflicted shortness of breath and bruised her lower ribcage. Platform shoes added four inches to her already tall stature, and they shortened her normally long strides by half.

How I drew the short straw, I'll never know. I can't wait to be out of this azure torture chamber! Twenty more agonizing paces brought her to the threshold of the tallest building in the Veyns, the Hoot Owl. Beatrice came right over and took her small bag.

"Right this way, M'Lady. We've been expecting you." The proprietor muffled her amusement; every eye in the tavern was turned on the out-of-place visitor. Beatrice led Estelle up the stairs, flight after painful flight. By the time they reached the roof, Estelle cursed each step with epithets of increasing offensiveness. Beatrice thought it was hilarious.

She laughed loudly as she descended four flights to the tavern.

----- -----

Goblins, as a rule, don't like water. Goblins don't swim, they don't splash - they don't even bathe. They certainly do not take boats across bodies of water. Koksal shook, a bundle of unrelieved stress, for the duration of the ferry crossing. He stood and held his riveted metal box of tools close, creating a one-goblin rhythm performance.

When he finally stepped off the ferry and onto the packed earth bounded by marble at the terminal, his heart filled with gratitude and relief. Shaking for the rest of the short walk to the tavern, he recited his lines under his breath.

"Where's the kitchen? I've come to fix the bellows. ...excuse me, but where can I find the kitchen? Pardon me, do you have any-QW-EH! Puuup-ooohn!" Tools skittered across cobbles in the dark as Koksal found himself on his hands and knees, vomiting. Seasickness. Eventually purged, he spat and collected his gear.

"I don't have the gearing for this." The brainy boffin said, dripping disgust, "This better not be a regular meeting."

The dining room boasted fifty men and women, dancing and singing, eating and drinking. Greasy pub fare presented a bouquet that puckered Koksal's limited palate. He stood in the doorway for a moment, wondering if he should find a better place to finish emptying his stomach. He opened his mouth, but the words merely fell out as malformed mumbling.

Beatrice, always on point, chugged over.

"I'm so glad you are here. We can't get the steak done right what with this machine broken. Right this way, master mechanic!" She escorted the queasy boffin into the kitchen, then up the stairs quietly to join the others.

----- -----

One hour, two loaves, three beers, and four sausages into his visit, Graener was in his element. Popular not only among dwarves, his stories kept the working-class folk that kept Beatrice in business enthralled. Each tale began with an improbable situation, introduced danger, nearly saw the hero dead, and then invariably ended with a hilarious, near-impossible punchline.

"My friends," he announced after another peal of laughter, "I need to let a beer out. Maybe more. I'll be back!" The crowd roared, and the dwarven bard ascended the stairs, ostensibly to fill a chamberpot. He paused at the door to his room, opening then slamming the door. He then continued the trip to the roof.

----- -----

Alene traced the lacquered inlay on the table before her. She chose the piece for several reasons. It was perfectly round, indicating that no one sitting was lesser or greater than the others. The art on the surface illustrated to the untrained eye a fantastic map of a fictional world, divided in half by a snaking line. The color scheme on either side of the line was inverted except for the water.

But most of all, the table had belonged to her mother. Placing it here in Beatrice's rooftop garden was a nod both to her birth mother and former Queen, and to the woman that raised her. Tonight, it provided a place to have a truly secret meeting with the leaders of the neighboring port town.

The motley crew could not be more mismatched if an orc sat amongst them. A middle-aged dwarf, red face betraying his level of lubrication, a proud, capable businesswoman, eminently uncomfortable playing dress-up in Ivonian finery, and the obvious goblin with his greasy tools and smock underpinning that over-large head like a confection-on-a-stick.

"You," Alene smiled, "constitute the leadership of Canolbwynt Masnach. Thank you so much for coming. We'll begin with you, Engineer. Were you successful?"

"I was, Majesty. Your cargo is safely stowed in our Holt."

"Was there any difficulty in the procurement?"

"Yes, but nothing of significance." Koksal offered a crooked smirk. "Simple superstition can often be overcome with extra coin, and this purchase was no different."

Alene nodded, took notes, and moved on.

"Thank you, Engineer. Estelle, my dear, tell me about the people's mood, will you?"

"Majesty, that is an excellent question." The middle-aged woman's green eyes narrowed. "We all remember and honor the way you and your soldiers helped to rid us of DePet. The fight was coming, one way or the other. Too many citizens died that night. Men, women, children. So many children." Emotion slammed visibly into her visage and echoed in the others' faces.

"Estelle, we-" Alene started, but Estelle cut her off.

"Wait. Hear this from me." Estelle's distress cleared with a deep breath, exhaled through pursed lips. Her experience as a midwife showed. "Many died in a battle that you brought to our shores. That cannot be denied. But the alternative…" The woman paused for effect.

"The alternative was that our troops were headed to the Veyns. Had they left on schedule, there would have been no one to effectively combat the orcs. We lost the majority of our people, but we could have lost them all."

After a respectful moment, Alene responded.

"Estelle, we speak plainly here. You should know that I intended to displace DePet. I had no idea orcs would be part of it. For that matter," the queen turned her gaze to the goblin, "I was completely unaware of Engineer Koksal or the Gymdeithas Fasnach contingent he carried."

"I was surprised, too," Koksal spoke. "I met those men in the course of a normal passage for King Bedwyn. If we'd been late or early, that chance meeting might well not have happened."

"Well," Graener added, "you may not have been aware, but I suspect Bedwyn knew. He always knows what will happen."

Estelle broke in.

"That may be. But I consider the intention to be less important than the result. We had the worst day in Veynsport's several-hundred-year history, but it could have been the last. For that, the men and women of Canolbwynt owe our thanks. But there is more.

"You came to remove DePet by force. This only months after Regent Villeuse's fall from power, and life. There are questions raised by this. Some see a pattern. I know - we know - the official story, that the Regent killed himself when he realized his plight. But rumors flow, and some say that you and Angus did more than merely speak that day. They say you threw him from the rooftop. They say it was murder; a bloody coup."

Emotions flashed uncontrolled across Alene's features: disbelief, confusion, realization, and anger.

"I see," she said, composed again with a Queen's comport, "and when did you first hear these rumors?"

"I suppose for months, but the story coalesced more in recent weeks." Estelle's face betrayed a realization of her own. "While you were at sea."

"Vipers," Graener spat. "Men are so devious. Starting disruptive rumors while you are absent and cannot defend yourself. Bastards."

Estelle emitted a low, mirthless chuckle.

"Men deserve the blame for most of the evil on the Cyfandir. But this time, I think not. There was a drunken trollop who came through the docks after dark, egging people on to exactly this story. I didn't think anything of it at the time, but it fits with your trip and the story gaining strength."

Graener, who had been leaning back in his chair, brought the front legs down onto the tar-coated timbers with a heavy clunk.

"You know, Estelle, you're right! I saw that girl and thought nothing of it. Lovely little thing, looked like she shouldn't walk the street alone?"

"That's her."

"That's just what I need," said Alene, "More rumors about my fitness to lead, or lack thereof. What else do I need to worry about?"

Koksal raised his hand.

"I have a concern. Several of my people have reported being treated like second-class citizens. Our inventions, while brilliant and useful, are regarded as dangerous and sketchy. Half the human population and most of the dwarves won't enter our stores. I've even heard complaints about flour that was produced using machines as if it were somehow poisoned through the processing. Imagine the ignorance!"

Alene looked over towards Estelle and Graener, who each studied their drinks.

"I thought you were working together to form a new society. Is any of this true?" She stared them down until Estelle broke.

"I have heard these things, yes. We have but two millers left in the county, the others killed in the orc raids at the outskirts of town. They may have started the rumor to protect their business interests."

"You think?" Koksal was visibly upset. Graener responded.

"Now we dwarves know that metal-milled flour is safe to eat, but we do prefer stone-ground flours. It has nothing to do with goblin tech."

Koksal looked hurt and bewildered. Alene came to his emotional rescue with a simple, "We'll talk later." Then she got to the real reason for this meeting.

"We can make Canolbwynt better as time goes on. Now, unfortunately, we have a problem. The Ivon is again massing troops and may come across the water or land-bound from the Greenway. After sleepless nights and endless consultations, I am left with only one clear choice. The time has come for the Ivon to fall."

Silence enveloped the four as realities and implications riffled through each mind. Several thoughtful seconds later, Alene continued.

"I have ideas to share about how to accomplish this, but first let's hear your thoughts. Graener?"

"I'd have to say yes. And no. I agree that the Ivon has overreached in a way that will only be cured by dint of his removal. But the dwarves in Canolbwynt are too busy and too few to contribute to an attack. We can be ready to defend the area, but we would not be effective attacking the Ivon."

Alene smiled an understanding smile.

"Estelle?"

"I'm against it. For your question, though, my opinion is not the only one that matters. As members of Gymdeithas Fasnach, we'd need to meet and discuss. I doubt you will see a significant force ready to strike until next spring. As Graener stated, there is simply too much to do."

"Koksal?"

"Well, you should know by now that goblins, as a rule, are not fighters. My people have moved twice this year, which is a traumatic enough fact. We struggle just to be accepted by humans. Uprooting to help men settle manly disputes is not in our future.

"That said, the errand you asked me to run was completed. I'm not sure what use it will be, but you'll have something to show for it."

Alene offered a smile. "Thank you, Engineer. It may seem a small thing to you, but your simple errand may prove critical in the coming winter. You have my gratitude."

The queen turned her attention to a dark space to the side, out of the eyeline of the others. She asked the shadow, "What of your people?"

Every one of the Canolbwynt contingent jumped when the answer came. The new voice was smooth, clear, and utterly controlled.

"We are still settling in. For the moment our goal is to blend."

"Has he been here the whole time?" Estelle was red and furious.

"Yes," replied the shadow, "blending. We live amongst you as productive members of society. To answer your question, Alene, I cannot answer. If we were to assist, it would never be known outside our circles."

"Wait," grumbled Graener, "who are you again?"

"Productive members of Canolbwynt's society."

Three sets of eyes stared into the shadow, swiveling as one to Alene.

"Blending." Alene showed no concern. "That may be the best option for now."

"I," stated Koksal, "have a hard time trusting someone I don't know or understand."

Alene held the goblin's gaze, head cocked as if waiting for more. Mental gears whirred nearly audibly as the boffin wrapped his head around the concept. One at a time, the three open leaders made the connections.

"Ah," Koksal allowed, "I am guilty of the crime I just accused others of. Alene, what can you tell me of our *arnyek baratom* - our obscured friend?"

"Obscured friend. Hm. That is accurate. Know that you should be pleased to have this person's - these people's - presence in Canolbwynt. They are powerful allies, and true to our collective causes. That, I'm afraid, must be enough."

"If this came from anyone else," Estelle said, "it would not be. I suppose I appreciate limited candor. I'll take what my sources share with me. You will be revealed at some point, and my people will get wind quickly."

For his part, Graener merely grunted through a sneer.

Chapter 27

A Dragon's Haunting Dreams

A dragon's dreams range vastly. Some are indistinguishable from reality, some a modified version; some are so far from reality as to be difficult to understand. Uvrede's dreams had trended unfathomable since she killed that smelly little interloper. *The nerve she'd shown! Of all the hundreds of invaders to break my exiled peace over the last* - she paused to do the math - *ten thousand years, not one ever dared wake me with a bucket of seawater.*

She sighed deeply, eyes still closed. The smell of that interloper remained, despite the incineration. *Odd,* she thought, *grease and sweat smells usually give way to ash and hot glass. Maybe I missed a bit.* She opened her eyes, tongue absently prepping the organs to mix the volatile chemicals that produce flame.

Apparently, she'd missed more than a bit. In fact, the whole orc sat there, cross-legged on a cooled lag-pile. Or was it cooled? She saw a slight red glow lingering in the glass. And the orc - the orc was smiling! But that wasn't all. She glowed, an aura-like effect, all greens and browns, movement leaving spectral tracks around her.

"Am I dreaming?" Uvrede asked.

"Almost." Replied Zonka. "I'm haunting you."

"I don't think so." But Uvrede was not sure.

"Call it what you want. You burned me to a crisp, yet here I am."

"Haunted."

"I'm afraid so, dear. If you think you are still dreaming, bite your tongue. If you feel pain, then you are awake."

Uvrede followed the orc's direction - *I never follow directions* - and bit her tongue. It hurt. She wrapped a lip around one of her fangs, drawing blood. She could taste the iron tang of it.

"All right, I can taste the blood, feel the pain. I can even smell the starlight on glass."[8]

"Well, if you can smell the starlight, you must certainly be awake," Zonka said. "Which means, unfortunately for you, that I am indeed haunting you."

The old dragon wiped chunks of salty sleep from her immense eyes, blinking and stretching to wake more fully. She still felt as if she was in a dream, but wondered if the disorientation and unbalanced feelings she experienced were simply symptoms of her advanced age. *Perhaps my time is near. I welcome the release, but I don't want to pass in the company of a smelly old orc, especially not the ghost of one.*

She stopped resisting. "Tell me, orc, who are you? Or who were you?"

"They call me Black Zonka. They called me Black Zonka." She smiled again.

"Black Zonka? Your hair is white, your skin is brown. You don't even wear black. Why the name?"

"Perhaps it has to do with my evil, black heart," Zonka chuckled. "Perhaps a slur against my people? Or maybe, in this case, the ceremonial garb I clothe myself in makes extensive use of charcoal and tar, upon which I add elements of the story I am telling, the message I wish to convey? The latter, I think, bears the most relevance to my personage. I love to bring people into my stories and make them feel a part. Immersion, a sharp young man once taught me, is a key to getting your audience to empathize with you."

She cackled then for a moment, leaning back. Uvrede saw sparks and stars fly from Zonka's mouth and eyes as she laughed. Surely this was no normal orc.

"He changed his tune when I immersed him in a cauldron of vinegar and spices," she managed through tears of laughter. "I told him not to worry, the scene would be done tastefully! Ah, haha! And taste good, he did. I learned a lot from that boy, both from a storytelling and a culinary direction!"

Mad, Uvrede thought. *Of course she is. Why me? Have I not suffered enough?* "Enough. Tell me what you want, so this

---

[8] You've heard the saying, "built different?" Dragons can do things like smell the starlight on glass because they, quite literally, are built differently than most creatures. It's a whole thing.

haunting can end. Are you looking for world domination? Do I need to kill another of my kind? Something brought you here, and telling stories wasn't it. What was worth dying for, crone?"

"That, my dear, is the right question." Zonka's normally sober voice of control was back in an instant. "I wish to dominate no one. I have never been wronged by a dragon - well, not before today. No, the thorn in my foot I came to ask you to remove is in the form of a particularly resilient dwarf."

"All right, how many dwarves disturb you and by extension me?"

"Just the one."

"No. No non-dragon could cause you to come so far, and lose so much. Why should I believe you? What danger could he possibly represent?"

"The answer, my dear, is in his name." She dribbled it out, like the last reagent in a volatile potion. "Angus Redbeard, the Dragonbane."

Dragonbane? Dwarves don't kill dragons. They can't. So either this will be an easy kill or the battle-borne release I've waited for all these years.

Uvrede chuffed in pleasure for the first time in an Age. "I'll do it. Where is he?"

Chapter 28

Dwarven Shortcuts

Angus guided the wagon north across the smoothest set of ruts. He did this with one hand; the other lay across his snoring father's shoulders. Floin wasn't used to this much travel, and last night's festivities echoed in this morning's headache. Still, they had a schedule to keep.

By noon the Sliver gleamed above them, reflecting the high sun from myriad steel shields hung from every battlement. To the unaware, an army of armed and armored men stood watch. Angus was more than aware.

Ivonian invasion remained Patrick's biggest concern. The subject dominated Angus' last visit with the smith, who also held the most senior position on the Sliver's council. Among their discussions was this very idea, a constant show of force. But things are not always as they appear.

Patrick manufactured dozens of imperfect steel shields and polished each to a mirror shine. Dents, dings, and irregularities enhanced the effect of the sunshine. Once coupled with flexible leather straps to mount them, an illusion of life and movement manifested. It seemed to work; Angus heard no stories of troops advancing on the Sliver since that night with the orcs.

Angus woke Floin as they started the long, switchbacked route into the bottleneck fortress that divided the north and south for hundreds of miles in each direction. They rode for the most part in silence, studying the massive stone walls that rose far above their heads.

The stonework testified to a long and storied history. The lower, foundational stones spoke of dwarven stonemasons. The stone was imported granite, fitted with such precision that water could not percolate through the gaps. Natural patterns in the stone were fitted to each other to draw the eye upwards.

Most of the upper reaches showed upward expansion, delineated clearly by the switch to native sandstone. Water stains betrayed gaps here; dark, organic slime marring surfaces new and old. The newer, weaker stone told more tales of wear and damage than the established dwarven masonry.

A new gate guard allowed them to pay the toll and pass without incident or fanfare. Floin disembarked and walked alongside the wagon. Stopping now and then, his head almost always pointed at the eastern heights, studying the space beyond the buildings they passed. When they reached the Elvish Respite, Floin looked over, around, and through the inn before announcing, "We've arrived."

"Really?" Angus said. "The only elvish place in town, and that's where you want to stop?"

"Yes. Besides," replied the old dwarf with a wink and a smile, "this place isn't elvish. Go in and get us a room. I'll take care of the wagon."

"Sounds good, Da. I'll have a pint ready for you inside."

Angus made his way into the tavern under the inn proper. Just inside the door, he paused, remembering Indaria's songs. Tears surged against his eyelids, and he was glad for his full beard as it hid contortions of grief.

"Angus!" The voice belonged to a councilman, younger and bigger than Patrick, "You can't come in here!"

Pulled fully from his memory, Angus looked the man square in the face. He didn't want to fight, but Angus wasn't above a barroom brawl. *I could do with a fracas right about now. All I wanted was a couple of pints.* The large man advanced.

"Like I said," he continued, grabbing a quart of ale from a passing server, "You can't come in here without us buying you a drink!" He extended the drink to Angus, froth sloshing over his wrist as he took it.

"I like the way you think, big man." Angus raised the drink and shouted, "To the Sliver!" Drinks and fists were elevated and the cry echoed, followed by laughs and draughts. Angus drained his and ordered a pint for his father.

An hour and four quarts later, Angus looked at his father's beer. The froth was gone, the brown liquid still and flat. He'd not arrived during the introductory celebration. Angus left some coin and took his fresh quart and his father's pint, venturing out into the later afternoon warmth. He found Floin outside, between the inn and the hillside. The old dwarf appeared flustered.

"Are y'allright, Da? Here, I brought your drink."

Floin stopped tracing lines in the dirt with his boot and regarded the drinks. "Why's yours bigger than mine?"

"I guess I don't take after you in every way, Da." Angus laughed.

"Funny boy. I suppose half a beer is better than none." He looked closer. "Half a flat beer."

"Well, Da, you've been out here a long while. What gives?"

Floin gazed at one hill, then the other. Then at the wall to their north.

"I'm trying to line up that peak with that one. Then with the highest balanced rock down the valley. Then I do some geometry, and...," he traced a triangle in the dirt as he spoke. That finished, he ran a line from the westernmost point east, crossing the eastern line and making a perfect right angle. He followed that line to the cliff-like mountain, examining the sandstone closely.

"...the door should be here."

"There's no door here. This sandstone is heavily worn. Even I know it'd be useless for a dwarven door."

"You're right."

"I've seen that shape you drew before when I was young."

"You are young, Angus. But I haven't shown this to you since you were a child." Floin drew back his left sleeve, revealing a tattoo that mirrored his drawing perfectly.

"It's a map."

"Yes, son."

"A map to what?"

"I just told you, didn't I? It's a map to a door that should be here."

They thought for a while, circling and facing each direction, until Angus asked his father another question.

"That balanced rock must be beyond the wall. Can you show it to me?"

"It's just beyond the second crenellation."

"Humor me?"

"All right," conceded Floin, "but bring a couple coins."

They made their way to the northern gate, where they met a solitary guard. Angus and Richard recognized each other right away.

"Master Bloodaxe! How are you this evening?"

"I'm well, Richard. I wonder if you would indulge us for a moment? We're heading north tomorrow and wanted to look north to see what we can expect. May we-"

"Climb the tower to look? Certainly, Master Bloodaxe! Anything for you, sir."

Moments later, they were at the top of the stubby tower, layers of pink and blue haze dropping into the distance.

"Now where was this balanced rock?" Angus asked.

"Up there on the western end of the valley, opposite the course of the road. To be honest, my memory had it above the road, over there, but the stone was set by our people and it would take one of our people to move it."

Angus adopted a sheepish grin and looked at his father. Floin squinted, considering, then traced the road with his eyes. One segment of the old dwarvish stonework had been replaced recently by a timber span. Marks on the hillside told a tale Angus had not. The remains of the peak that once held a massive boulder still standing.[9] Tsking repeatedly, Floin made a new chalk mark on the southern edge of the crenellations, then descended. Angus followed.

"Once we're safely away, I'll thank you to tell me that tale."

"Yes sir." Angus stifled a chuckle at his father's frustration.

Back behind the inn, a re-drawn triangle pointed straight at Angus' wagon. More accurately, the stable. The two dwarves entered, proceeding straight to the back wall, built against the hillside. This hillside was not sandstone, but a gigantic granite erratic laid down eons ago. Men had recently - within a few hundred years - added shackle points to secure animals and gear. Several of the iron rings bore Patrick's touchmark.

Floin closed the doors as Angus cleared a haystack that partially obscured the granite face.

"You think this is it?" Angus asked.

---

[9] During Angus' first adventure, in Holtgart, he delayed an entire orcish army from ascending this road. He had dislodged the boulder with the very same siegebow, and the boulder crashed down, putting a large gap in the old road. He had no clue his action would bring his father's wrath.

"It looks right, for the most part. Let me see if I can find the latch…" Floin felt the stone, caressing each feature and seeking the hidden release. After thirty minutes, Angus stepped out, returning with a couple of oil lamps, plus beer and sausages. They took a break, ate, and considered.

If a dwarven door were to be built here, this stone made sense. Strong and distinctive, yet nothing of note to non-dwarves. Their meal finished, Floin addressed the stone.

"I remember a three-point release, but I see no holes where I thought they should be. Any help would be welcome here, boy."

Angus looked again at the wall. *The rings. They are too irregular for men to have placed them; they must have used existing holes. If some of those holes house latch mechanisms…* He located several that mimicked Floin's tattoo. One hole remained, too low to be useful to men. He knelt and examined it closely with the lamp.

A lone spider evacuated when Angus blew gathered detritus from the crevice. Then he reached in with three fingers and heard a 'click', followed by a short-lived, deep rumble. He remembered that this was the last of four latches, and he needed to press them in a different order - *what? I've never been here before. How could I know that?*

----- -----

Angus reached slender, shapely, dark-skinned hands into the four cleverly disguised crevices. The water-powered door quietly sank into the mountain, revealing a triangular tunnel. He looked back at the lush, wet forest as the door closed in behind his limber elven shape.

----- -----

Still on the ground, Angus jerked his hand free of the crevice. He rolled back and looked at his father, who laughed.

"Looks like you found something. Why didn't it open?"

Angus gave no reply, rising to stand and gaze at the wall. Three of the rings were in the secret release holes. *Humans are such creatures of convenience. If something fits in a hole, they just shove it in. These look like screws…*

He grabbed the first ring, twisting it. It crept out with a series of scritchy squeaks. Once removed, it revealed a hole like the lower. The dwarf repeated the process until all four were clear, then addressed his father.

"Be ready, Da. I think I see how this goes." He touched each latch in turn, and the door scrugged open, releasing centuries of dust and detritus. A single step up, and both dwarves were inside. They watched as the perfectly triangular door obscured the dusty stable that obscured it. *How things change*, thought Angus.

Darkness flooded in until their dwarven eyes adjusted to the trickle of light provided by patches of luminescent moss. These Floin wet with a splash from his canteen as they passed; hydrated, the moss increased its light output. He did this, of course, in observance of tunnel tradition so ancient that no written record of its origins could be found.

"Our kin built this tunnel, long ago." Floin reached up to splash another moss-filled cove. "So long ago the world was different. I think our kin may have been a bit taller than us."

Angus remained silent. *I've hated elves my whole life. Now I've got elven memories stuck in my head? That won't do. There's a lot of brandy in my future.* Snippets of memory flashed through his head as they proceeded. He knew where they were going.

"Urg," Floin said, "here come the stairs. I'm glad we had a meal."

Angus grunted and led on. *Why do I know there are no traps? Why do I know we won't encounter anyone? Why do I know how many steps there are?* The stairs wound upwards in a wide, oblong spiral that took them into the mountain as much as upwards. No evidence of water damage or animal life showed. The stonework was marvelous; granite throughout. Each stone must have been relocated from a faraway quarry. *Whatever is up here must be important.*

"Let's pick up the pace, Da. We've got another hour at least." Angus' urgency flowed through his voice.

"Son," Floin panted, "I thought I was showing you an interesting heirloom. You seem to be on a mission. What happened?"

"I don't know, Da. Somehow I remember this place. I know I've never been." He paused, waiting for Floin to catch up. "What do you know about it?"

"Not much, to be honest." Floin exposed his tattoo again. "My grandfather brought me here when I was a wee lad. We looked around, and then he put this tattoo on my arm and told me I should do the same with my grandchild. As restless as you seem to be, I may never have a grandchild, so I figured we should take the chance while we were near."

"Why this place?"

"There is an old spot at the summit - so old the runes have weatherworn from the stones. I think it was a meeting place, but even my grandpap had no idea. He said our kin helped build it, so we should remember it was here."

They turned and climbed for a while, panting instead of talking. They marked time with the count, a habit dwarves trained as soon as they could walk. Each second was noted throughout the day and night, even while sleeping. Because of the Count, Angus knew the sun would be low when they emerged from another stone door at the summit, which was likewise in excellent order.

The door closed behind them silently after they passed, appearing to most observers as a large boulder. No outward trace of the passage was visible. After a short moment of dwarven appreciation for the stonework, they turned.

Before them lay three concentric stone circles in a dished bowl. The moss-covered ground made the place look purposeful. The dwarves walked toward the large stone slab at the center. The heavily-weathered granite slab was stained with a brown residue. As they drew near they saw that the big stone was likewise dished; whatever brown liquid was slopped over the side had pooled here.

Angus drew his knife and scraped a bit of the powdery coating off. He sniffed it, worked it to a fine powder between his fingers, then sniffed again. He took another sample and offered it to his father.

"What do you make of this?"

"Blood. Not enough iron to be dwarvish. Human?"

Looks of revulsion crossed their faces as they surveyed the rest of the scene. Eleven stones surrounded the slab, evenly spaced. Each was granite or marble from a different locale; reds, blacks, greys, and greens betraying the sites' broad genesis. Behind the eleven were twenty-two stones, closer-spaced but still allowing for a dwarf to sit comfortably. Thirty-three backed the twenty-two, each making a six-stone triangle pointed at the bloody, central monolith.

The mossy carpet must be tended each season to keep this level of organization, and the center-most aisle showed signs of disturbance - but no shoe marks save their own.

"Look here, Da. I think a group of barefoot people held some sort of ritual here."

"Yes, and it looks like orcish work." Floin held up a defleshed upper arm bone without humor. "Look at the tooth marks here. Sharp, but not from any four-legged predator I know."

The sun flashed beyond Angus, casting a dramatic beam on one side of the stone. He did a little mental math, looking around the site at intermittent tall standing stones on the periphery.

"Solstice. I think this was used for a solstice ceremony, and this," Angus indicated the bone and blood, "is all that remains of a hapless victim. Ugh." Turning his attention to the stone, he saw something remarkable.

"This set of stones has the same granitic pattern as the Aureate unless I'm off. I see nothing of the Smaragdine or Argentine." Another six stones keyed a memory of his time at the pool of Sara Tholah. He sat on the lead stone stool.

----- -----

Thick, lush moss cushioned his fat-free frame. He watched the amber rings move on his fingers as he gestured; each created from petrified sap of a different species of tree his people tended. They served as a reminder to consider all angles at these meetings; to look for the organic victory that served all equally, after the forest way.

The Severance indicated lasting change; never again would this council look to the Mirekkans for guidance and justice. The Cyfandric Cycle had begun, and no amount of fond reminiscence could alter that fact. Two centuries dominated by darkness, ash, and famine strained every race. So many dead, and more to die.

He remembered when his daughter passed away in his arms, her unborn child too far from birth to save. *Her death alone was unbearably tragic. Yet it was such a familiar story it is no longer worth telling.* The tears welled up, but he forced his visage to display adamant stoicism.

Elves do not cry. Kings must lead by example. As both, this was his only choice.

----- -----

Angus stood and took several brusque steps away from the old stone stool. "Did you see that? Tell me you saw that, Da."

"I did see, son," Floin retorted, "I saw you move in ways no dwarf ever should. What's the point of flicking your hands around like that?"

Angus could not hide his confustication if he'd wanted to. *An elf! I was an elf! I know I'm a dwarf, I've always been a dwarf, and by the old strata, should always be a dwarf. But how did I see what I saw?*

Angus' body pantomimed his flailing mind, leaving him reeling backward towards another set of stones. He came to rest on a shorter one that was coated in rust. He felt the sick ascending.

----- -----

After she retched the remains of her partially digested food onto the grass, she wiped the spittle from her gray lips with her greasy sleeve. *It's always like this. I am not fit to be on this council! If only there were more of us… left.* She coughed. *I feel so useless. We only need six because of the old ways. Since the old ways failed us, I question whether they were right to begin with.*

She took in the meeting around her, nine groups of six waiting nervously. Every soul was emaciated to some degree or other. All hungry, all dying slowly. One group of men no longer attended; their seats stood empty. Had they all died?

The dragons rarely come anymore; they are hungry, too. Nobody wants a hungry Dragon at their meetings. If I never meet another, that would be fine. Yes, yes. The old ways keep Dragons from eating people, but the old ways fade as we dwindle.

Her overlarge eyes noted a new movement amongst the assemblage. Every eye raked southward, looking at a common sight. She swiveled her heavy head on her half-starved neck to see for herself.

Dragons approached. Not the six prescribed by tradition, either. Three dragons dropped from above, using an unusual vector to join the council. Unlike the council members - or the vast majority of the population - these dragons appeared to be well-fed.

Strong, vibrant musculature rippled under tough dragonskin. These were young and powerful beings. As they approached, the young goblin noted an unfamiliar expression painting three faces - maniacal glee.

The lead dragon opened his maw, laughing. His crimson eyes fixed on a target; the young goblin knew at once it was her. She screamed as the gaping mouth enveloped her and blackness embraced -

----- -----

Angus stopped screaming as his father, Floin, shook him hard by the shoulders.

"Get hold of yourself, boy!"

Angus panted, obviously winded. *I was a goblin! A gobleen[10], more precisely! I think that bothers me more than being eaten by a dragon.*

"Angus," Floin tried, "come back!"

Angus squeezed his eyes shut, chasing the images away. Floin, concerned by Angus' relative lack of response, pulled his middle finger back with his thumb, then released it to flick Angus right between his bushy, red, furrowed eyebrows. Angus blinked.

"What was that for?" He yelped. "Are ye daft, Da?"

"Ah, yer back," Floin sighed, "where were you, son? You are acting strangely."

"Strange doesn't begin to cover it, Da. I'm not sure I should say anything, for fear you might think I've lost my marbles."

"Try me."

Angus pulled his flask from behind his beard and took a long slug. He took another. Very deliberately and slowly, he replaced the lid and tucked the flask safely behind his beard. His very dwarven beard. He rose from the ground to find a seat but thought better of it and sat back down on the mossy ground.

"I never 'went' anywhere, Da. I was right here. What might be a better question would be *when* I was. And *who.*

"Who? I saw you the whole time, boy. You were Angus and ne'er anything else."

"Well, you could have fooled me. I was sure I was an elven king at first. Then a gobleen. It felt like part memory and part

---

[10] A gobleen is a young goblin female. This dwarven term is rarely used, as gender references are offensive to the eminently practical and fluid goblin people.

dream. But I *was* those people. Not watching them but in their skin. Feeling what they felt."

Both dwarves paused, taking in that information and processing it thoroughly. This took some time, with both dwarves attempting to continue the conversation, but rethinking their choice of words before speaking. Eventually, Floin mustered the right combination.

"So, this felt real to you in the moment, right?"

"Aye."

"And you say you saw through their eyes and felt what they felt."

"Aye."

"Son, did you know what they knew?"

Realization vaulted into Angus' consciousness.

"Aye. At least a part." He paused as he quantified what he'd 'learned' in the momentary transmogrifications. "Perhaps what was relevant to the situation. I'm not sure. But I know the significance of the amber rings the Elven King was wearing, without having heard words to know."

"And the other bit you mentioned. *When* you were. What do you mean by that?"

"Oh, well, I assume that I was seeing this place, yet as it was a long time ago. I can't say how long. But long enough that-" he trailed off, gesturing to the southernmost slice of this circular pie, the wedge where Dragons roosted in these meetings.

"Well, that's an impossible chasm bridged. Da, what do you know about dragons?"

"I know enough, son. I know that they are greedy, hungry bullies who like to eat dwarves and take their gold. That they are a menace to be eliminated. What more could be relevant?"

"Hold that thought, Da. How long have we, as dwarves, known this?"

"For our collective history, I suppose. Our records go back eight thousand years. As far as I know, that's all of it."

"I think it isn't."

"I'm listening."

"Well, let me ask you this. You brought me up here to this place. Why?"

"Because our kin helped build it. It's a simple matter of the family connection."

"Why did they build it?"

Floin stared back blankly. After a few long moments of searching for memories, he realized, "I don't know."

"This is a council chamber. Dwarves sat here and here. Men sat here, here and here. Goblins here. Orcs there and over there - the two clans could not stand each other. Those wider stones? Trolls. Elves sat there. Here," Angus paused, trying to remember, "I'm not sure. I couldn't see who occupied these areas. But it was a council for sure."

"Did you hit your head, son? You aren't making any sense. That council could never happen. The peoples you talk about are too different from each other."

"You haven't heard the most impossible part." Angus rose, walking to stand on the extended flat wedge at the southern edge of the circle. It was wider and deeper than the others, by a considerable margin. "Da, who do you think sat here?"

Floin walked over, observed, and considered. "No one. This was likely either a space to view the mainland - see, there's Ivonia - or a space reserved for deities. There are no stones, and no indication there ever were stones to sit on. I think this space sat empty."

"Look at this." Angus kicked moss and detritus out of a series of grooves with his toe; chaotic groupings of parallel lines cut into the rock. It took a while since there were many such lines. "What do those remind you of?"

Floin, already knelt and inspecting the damaged rock, shied away suddenly. "Dragons. And not just one. How terrifying! These people had no chance!"

"But they did, Da. The dragons were on the council. They were part and parcel of the interspecies society that we began as before the ash fell, taking our societies with it." Angus stepped north to stand at the great, central slab. "This was merely a focal point, a place to lay symbols of their discussion. It was never meant to be a sacrificial altar."

He leaned heavily on the slab.

----- -----

Floin Thunderpick watched as his son, a confirmed dwarf, roared. Sounds came out of his mouth that people could not make. Points of froth formed at the corners of his beard, tinted with blood.

Whatever illness had befallen his son, he would not have it. Floin tackled his son, pulling him clear of this area where he claimed the dragons roosted.

Leaning up against one of the surrounding outcroppings of natural rock, the old dwarf cradled his catatonic son's head and shoulders. They sat like that for some time.

Chapter 29

Unlikely Companions

Uvrede was a great dragon. Eighteen thousand years old, she matched the bulk of several merchant ships. Now most of that bulk displaced many thousands of gallons of seawater as she floated along. Her massive wings acted as oars, pulling herself and the ghostly Zonka through the oceans, taking a northeasterly heading.

"Somehow," Zonka ventured, "I figured we'd fly to Ivonia." She shifted her foot to avoid the water from her perch on Uvrede's long, powerful neck.

The dragon chuffed again. "I'm not as young as I used to be. And I have been sleeping a long, long time. I suspect I can still fly, but I haven't tried in so long. Give me some time to get my sea wings first."

"At this rate, we'll have some days to reach our destination. Shall we talk in the meantime?"

"Exactly what," the dragon began, "did you think we've been doing for days?"

"Small talk."

"Small talk indeed. What would you like to speak about?"

"I'd like to learn more about you. Do you have a mate? Children?"

SWISH went the wings, pulling hard before another long glide.

"I'll tell you, but I want your story in return. You start."

"Ah, well. I had a mate. Sulga. He was fantastic. Tall, strong, powerful, and respectful, and he treated me like a queen. And when we were intimate -" Zonka shuddered in remembrance of activities long past, dormant desires. "He was something special. He did not live as long as I did. I watched my love grow old, and become weak; he faded slowly. I would not trade a moment of our time together.

"We had children, of course. Quite a few. I raised them, taught them the Ways, saw them have children of their own, and fade just like Sulga. After several generations, I started to see all orcs as distant relatives. I can't tell you who is related to me or not now; I suspect every orc on the Cyfandir carries at least a few drops of my blood in them.

"They are my greatest pride and my deepest tragedy. And not one of them was gifted with my long life." Zonka shook her head. "What a gift. And at the same time, what a curse."

Uvrede took a deep breath, absorbing. "I was a queen. The Queen, leader of the Drakhons - the nation of dragons. You may have realized by now, that the creatures you may have encountered on your Cyfandir are different than myself. You have not met the best of us, only the slag; the imperfect dross discarded by the true, pure dragons that thrived in my rule.

"You may be under the impression that dragonkind is greedy, stealing and hoarding gold just to own it. That would be a mistake. We use superheated glass to coat and grow our young in their eggs. We make that glass from *shurakhen,* the blood of the earth; it cannot be replicated away from our homelands. And yet those that live elsewhere must find other ways to raise their young. Gold is a passable substitute.

"So a male dragon, in order to attract a mate, often gathers up as much golden treasure as he can. He would take this treasure from men or dwarves, usually by force. Elves, and orcs, as you are aware, have little value for gold, being more tied to the earth and living things. Men rarely amass great wealth in their paltry lifespans, but dwarves? Dwarves hoard gold. I do not understand why. I never have.

"Also, dragons like me, real dragons, use that same glass to create our cities. Vast, transcendent spaces with aeries, halls, museums, and temples. They are truly spectacular. Mine was the greatest ever built, grown on the foundations of a thousand generations of dragon cities. But other dragons have no access and must find other places to live.

"Forests and cities burn too easily to make good dragonhomes. Caves and caverns are more suitable. Again, most dwarves live in underground tunnels, often epic in scale and decor. The perfect place for new societies, from a dragon's point of view."

"I'd like to see your city," Zonka said, somewhere between respect and awe.

"You cannot." Uvrede hung her head. SWISH went her wings, building speed again.

"Why not?" Zonka asked. "I'm dead, aren't I?"

"There is so much more than that. Things that happened. Things I've tried for millennia to avoid thinking about. Things that we did. Things that I ordered." She swam on in silence for a while.

"Shurakhame," said the dragon. "That is what we called it. The bloodhome. I ruled as the queen of all dragons for seven thousand years. It was a time of worldwide peace. I can't take credit for that, but some of my predecessors were part of the founding of the peace. Every people of the world worked together with the common goal of improving each other.

"Shurakhame grew over millennia to cover the entire island. The tallest towers stood as tall as the highest mountains. It was home to fifteen thousand of my kind, and they all looked to me for guidance. Life was good."

They swam on in silence for a time, pondering and absorbing. Zonka had the first question.

"Worldwide peace, you say? Do you mean that all dragons were at peace with each other, despite differences in lifestyle and belief?"

Uvrede craned her neck over her shoulder, trying to gain eye contact with the orc, who sat cross-legged between the dragon's shoulders and the base of her neck.

"Getting all dragons to be at peace with each other was a tremendous accomplishment, to be sure. My great-granddam deserves the credit for that. And peace describes, at best, the vast majority of dragonkind. There are always outliers. Troublemakers, some call them. Others say visionaries. Still others, revolutionaries.

"But outliers are essential to a healthy society. With no concerns, a society can become weak. Without dissent, there can be no change. Without change, no growth. So, yes, all dragons were at peace, but there were outliers.

"A mighty feat," Zonka stated. "I have found that the best way to unite my people is to show them a common enemy. I suppose you had others, perhaps humans, that you worked against?"

"Oh, my dear Zonka, you still have a lot to learn. When I say worldwide peace, I mean across races and continents. We had great councils every year, where representatives of each people gathered to discuss world events, deciding as a group how to proceed."

"That," Zonka stammered, "that sounds impossible! How did you manage it? How did you keep one group from being dominant?"

A deep vibration started from Uvrede's diaphragm, through her lungs, and up her long, muscular neck, emerging from her massive, toothy maw.

"Ah, I thank you, little orc-ghost. I cannot recall how long it has been since I've laughed. How did we prevent any one group from being dominant? Why would we want to do that? Dragons brought peace to the world. We taught men and elves and dwarves many things. Dragons, my dear, are the naturally dominant group. My mother knew that when she set up the councils.

"And those outliers we discussed? Some of them merely appeared to be outliers. A loyal dragon will do anything to please her Queen."

"So these dragons that attacked dwarves were rogue agents or outliers?" Zonka asked.

"For the most part, outliers. Dwarves never bothered much with the balance of power outside of their tunnels. Orcs are self-limiting, as you know. Elves have become more and more reclusive in recent years. Goblins were secretive and distrustful and kept to themselves. Humans, however, require more corrections than most. For thousands of years, humans were the most destructive force on the planet. Until…" She trailed off.

"Humans are still destructive, especially concerning my people. Dwarves left us alone until recently. I've never had any problem with elves or goblins." Zonka tilted her head. "Until I met you, I'd never had any direct contact with Dragons. They caused local problems, but never fought over anything more than an old dwarven holt, to my memory. I suspect you've been the least destructive race over the eons."

Uvrede raised her head straight up in the air. Clear liquid fell from just behind her eyes. She dashed her face underwater and raised it again, shaking most of the water off, and drenching Zonka.

"If only that were true." The tears still flowed, masked by her wet face. "Zonka, let me tell you why you cannot see the Shurakhame I knew. Better yet, let me try to show you. Will you try to join my *dream*?"

"Of course," Zonka replied. "What have I got left to lose?"

"Hm. Yes, I do believe I killed you already, and yet I can sense the heaviness of your presence still. I can almost feel your weight. Let us try to *dreamshare*. It is an old way, and I have never tried to use it with an orc. I have not shared my *dream* with anyone for millennia. But you feel... different. So close your eyes and listen. Then *listen.* Then *see.*"

Zonka checked the security of her perch before complying. Then mere moments after closing her eyes, Zonka stood, surrounded by fog, next to the disembodied head of Uvrede. Nothing besides the two of them was visible. The dragon's head swiveled to look the orc square in the face, analyzing.

"How do you feel, Black Zonka?"

"Fine. I am listening, but I don't see anything beyond us."

"Fascinating. I am pleasantly surprised at your ability to accept the *dreamshare.* In the past, I have *shared* with some of the most powerful mages - elder elves, mostly - and they all have a moment of adjustment. The fog enables a… calibration period. You seem aloof and aware. Ready. Not what I expected from an orc."

"I've shared already that I am not an entirely normal orc." Zonka smiled. "And this is hardly my first experience with an altered reality. It used to be a specialty of mine. But I suspect you brought me here to *share* more than a fog."

"True." Uvrede turned away from Zonka, blowing the fog away as if releasing the seeds from a flowering dandelion, revealing that they flew, side-by-side, above an island chain. The nearest island, below them, looked familiar to Zonka. "Behold the old city. That field of broken glass, shattered crystals and black sand is where we met. It is so old, so long abandoned, that we have no record of who built it or what it was called. It has even been lost in our *dreamshared* memories. This is where I was sent to spend the rest of my days after I was rightfully deposed.

"It takes a particularly heinous crime for dragons to wish someone to spend the rest of eternity forsaken and forgotten, yet this is where you find me."

"I did find you. But you were not forgotten entirely. I found an ancient record in the bowels of the great library of Ivonia that mentioned you, your name, and where you would be found. Uvrede the Deposed, it said, was one of the most powerful dragons in history. That she would be alone and angry. Those reasons led me to believe that you might help me."

"Did the record indicate why they deposed me?" Sadness tinged Uvrede's voice.

"No. It was only mentioned in the form of this being a place to avoid and you a dragon to avoid." Zonka chuckled wryly. "The expectation was that anyone who found you would die a fiery death. That part they got right."

"Oh. Yes. Sorry about that. Let us move east in location, and back in time. My memory of Shurakhame is as it was before the *khart,* the land-wound. I will show you that, first. And in so doing, you will be the first in ten thousand years to witness its greatness."

The pair flew on to the east, over several smaller islands. These had smaller quantities of broken glass and more black sand. In the distance, growing fast, was a much larger island. The sun set behind them and then accelerated unnaturally. Moon and stars erupted, in slightly different places than Zonka expected them. Before she could track the differences, the sun burst across the horizon from behind the massive, black mass of the largest island. Water sprayed up beside and behind them, as they flew at great speed over the sea, waves crashing on huge, colorful coral reefs that surrounded the - fortress? Every inch of this island seemed to be formed or grown into palaces of spiky black glass and crystal. Zonka saw hundreds - perhaps thousands - of dragons everywhere she looked.

Some dove into the sea, recovering large sea creatures. Some formed the constructs with fire, wielded with deft skill. One group surrounded a clutch of many large egg-shaped black-glass objects, moving and communicating.

"Those were my last brood. I was sure they would go on to accomplish so much more than me. They had the best teachers, as you can see."

Uvrede did not tarry in one place long. The next had a military feel; black glass like the rest, but with great granaries filled with powders of different types. Yellow, white, and black. Adjacent were several hundred dragons ingesting some of these powders.

Stacks of glass teardrops dozens of feet across lined the tops of nearby walls.

They banked left, soaring above thc center of the island. Zonka caught an orange glow for the first time, highlighting the bottoms of puffy clouds. A tall, conical volcano stood thousands of feet above the landscape. Lava flowed over one edge at the peak, flowing downhill in a spiral trough. Glass-encrusted dragons stood at intervals, gazing intently at the orange-red and molten lava.

"This," Uvrede shared, "is how it was when I ascended to power. How it always should have stayed. Shurakh." The pair circled closer to the draconic mining operation. "Here, the black glass you see us using in so many aspects of dragonlife is harvested, straight from the earth's blood. There, yellowstone. Over there, essential minerals. The mother feeds us from her eternal teat, as it were, everything that we need as dragons."

Zonka was amazed at how anything could work with molten materials with no more than rudimentary tools. "It all looks so hot. How do they keep from being incinerated?"

"There is more to dragons than meets the eye," Uvrede smiled toothily. "The glass offers some protection from stray particles. Natural effects allow for momentary contact; but the extended manipulation you see there, for instance," she indicated a dragon directing a flow of superheated glass from one crucible to another, apparently shaping the laminar flow with his hands, "has a supernatural element. Some dragons can manipulate molten solids with psychic manipulation. Not all, not even most. I have no idea if any can, now.

"But that is in the past. You can see, I think, that this island chain is somewhat unique. The constant supply of shurakhen was what drew my ancestry here, and we have developed in tandem with that supply. It is essential to every aspect of true dragonlife. You can imagine my consternation when this happened."

The world around Zonka sped up to a blur, the outline of the mountain with its spiral lava flow the only static and consistent objects in range of her perception. Cloud formations swept through, mighty storms, bright, sunny moments; the old orc could feel the passage of time advancing faster than thought. Suddenly time stopped, and she could see something changed - the lava flow was gone. Nothing glowed, nothing indicated the moving source of metals and glass.

"The world stopped bleeding for the first time in history, in any memory of memories past. I wondered for a time if this were the first. Our learned scholars studied the histories and islands to the west. The island we met upon, for instance, was the center of dragonlife long ago, so many thousands of years past we do not understand. It features a dry khart and the ruined glass from a city as large as Shurakhame. We do not know why the khart died, but we believe that there was an extended period where dragons left the islands.

"We believe that most died, weak, alone, and waiting for something to save them. Dragons are strongest together, as a society. I could not let our kind face extinction again. Not on my watch."

Fog once again filled Zonka's perception, save for Uvrede's disembodied visage. Huge, glass-encrusted eyes squeezed closed, opened, and the dragon blew the fog away gently. This revealed a circle of dragons, resplendent in black-glass raiments that tinkled and glinted as they moved in the moonlight. Each sat on an obsidian pedestal, formed into individual thrones after a distinctively draconic style.

After a moment, Zonka could tell that the largest was a much younger Uvrede. Not the deposed, but the mighty queen of a mighty people. The gathering was at once fantastic, awe-inducing, and somberly sorrowful. Young Uvrede addressed those surrounding her.

"The Shurakh flows. It has always flowed. It must always flow. Without it, we shall dwindle. Without abundant Shurakh, our lives will change. Our position in the world will inevitably lessen. We will become… vulnerable."

She stepped into the center of the circle, turning slowly to gaze into the eyes of each. "The. Shurakh. Must. Flow. The scab forming over the khart is yet thin. We must reopen the wound to keep the khart flowing."

"Impossible."

"It cannot be done."

"How?"

Uvrede nodded at each objection. "You are all correct. It cannot be done - safely. It cannot be reopened - without sacrifice. Yet if we do nothing, we will inevitably sacrifice everything we know."

Fog transitioned them once again before parting to reveal the empty, dead volcanic cone. A lone dragon flew above, throat unnaturally thickened; as if it had tried to eat something too big for its neck. It arced gracefully higher, flipping into a super-speed dive straight toward the crater. All of the same dragon council surrounded the mount, flying in place. They keened, high and low notes overlapping, in honor of the impending sacrifice.

The descending dragon breathed fire as it entered the crater, bright colors and concussion following the explosion. Uvrede moved them to see a mere crack in the solidified crust that separated them from the Shurakh - which in turn appeared to recede even further.

Another fogbank moved them to the next attempt, where half a dozen of Uvrede's people gave their bodies and lives to the effort. The crusty surface disappeared, and some of the crater walls collapsed inwards. The lava did not return to prominence.

Uvrede's disembodied head turned to Zonka. "So it went, with ever larger groups, always more impossibly engorged with the elements of dragonfire, never bringing back the Shurakh; always teasing that, if we would just sacrifice a little more, it would be enough. Until finally, we sent - I sent - two hundred dragons to give their lives to the fire in one beautiful display of self-sacrifice. I thought we would be heard by the powers. The Shurakh would flow again."

She hung her head. "In a way, I was right. The Shurakh flowed, with a ferocity I did not know it could." She blew the fog away again.

Chapter 30

Lighting up the Festival

Zain darted behind the largest of the haystacks, holding his youthful giggles in. He'd just turned twelve and felt honored to be trusted with watching over the harvest while everyone else was at the festival. Of course, since everyone else *was* at the festival, there were very few things to look out for. So he and Willim played a game of hide and chase in the otherwise abandoned yard.

It had been a good year in the Greenway; such that with the granaries filled and every farmer's barrels stocked with grain, the last wagon loads still sat here, laden to overflowing with winnowed grain, carefully tarped. The boys avoided those wagons, of course; grain on the ground would expose their fun.

Long shadows stretched eastward, and soon enough, the boys would settle down and make a fire for the night.

----- -----

Allus laughed and men noticed. Somehow she managed to add a lilt and allure to everything that came out of her mouth. Each movement was practiced and perfected for the sole purpose of gaining men's trust and breaking down their emotional barriers. More than once, she played on a vague hopefulness that men donned as they spoke with her.

It may have been her training, but this pointed flirtatiousness came naturally now. Allus had a very hard time turning it off. Besides, she didn't want to turn it off. She liked to be liked. She wanted to be wanted. *What girl doesn't?* She asked herself as she whirled from one dance partner to the next. She laughed again.

Greenway's harvest festival was in full swing as the sun went down. Men and women from surrounding communities assembled here and traded stories, money, and sometimes relatives. The Festival stood out every year as the time and place most likely to lead to a new marriage, with young adults and old all recovering from and celebrating the new level of wealth.

It was such a good harvest. While the totals had not been fully tabulated, this year stood out as the single most productive in the entire length of the Greenway's recorded history. If there was ever a year to get hitched, this was it. Even Allus had been swept up in the copulative mood.

The stony armor of the troll Angus and Floin slew had been stacked triumphantly in the town square. The cairn served as a reminder of the strength of the few. Vocal members of Gymdeithas Fasnach used it as a touchstone for resistance to the Ivon. And in truth, the Greenway was free. Patrick Smith, de facto leader of the new people, climbed the grisly pile to deliver a speech to the festival-goers:

"Good people of the Greenway, Sliver, and surrounding communities, I bid you a happy festival! You have so many reasons to be proud and are surely aware of them. Yet let us enumerate them, and keep the reasons for our celebrations at the front of our minds, the tip of our tongues, and hold them deep in our hearts as we go home tomorrow.

Most obviously, we enjoy the finest harvest in many years. Our larders and granaries flow over. This will be a winter of plenty, thanks to all of our hard work and no small amount of divine providence. Let's thank the Creator for great weather and plenty of water!

No less significant is our successful secession from Ivonia. No longer will we give the best of our sons and daughters to do the Ivon's dirty work. No longer will the best of our crops be reserved for his private use. From this year onwards, our destiny is our own!

Our best is just that - ours. And as we share in this bountiful harvest, let us share our families and set up the next generation to cultivate and enjoy our land of plenty. Enough talk! Bring on the weddings!"

Everyone cheered for Patrick, the applause lasting for a full minute. Then the traditional social fare: toasts, proposals, weddings, and naming ceremonies commenced. It was a party for the ages. Forty-three couples were married that night, and another fifty-eight proposals were given. More than sixty young children were named, too.

Patrick watched it all, smiling and laughing so much that his face hurt by the end of the evening. This was what he had dreamt of. The land was healthy, the people strong, and the winter would be secure. He fought the feeling in the back of his head that said it would never be that easy.

For the moment, everything was free and loose. When Allus looped her arm through his, carrying him onto the dancing round with her momentum, he let himself enjoy the moment. They danced, as did a thousand others throughout the night. The revelers reveled until it was time to part and find a warm place to sleep.

It was during their parting that a woman called out from the third-story window of The Hustled Bustle. "What's that light?"

The next shouts came from all directions, an overlapping staccato of horrified realizations.

"I see it - over there!"

"Is it a fire?"

"Is it the granary?"

"Let's go!"

The flood of humanity was swift, carrying every person in the Greenway along. As they drew near the granary on the outskirts of town, it became ever more clear that this was indeed a fire. It was already heavily involved, but they organized a bucket brigade to the creek that powered the mill and started fighting the fire in earnest.

"Willim!" A woman shouted for her child. "Willim, where are you?"

"Zain," shouted another, "where is my boy?"

A few minutes of dousing and searching went on like this, until a man's voice called from near the burning haystacks, "Over here! I see them! They… Oh no…"

"Patrick," Allus' face was white with horror. "Where are the wagons? The wagons holding the excess grain?"

"The tracks lead south," he replied, in between handing off buckets, "South to Ivonia, I suspect. He's gutted us. The Ivon has gutted us."

Chapter 31

Recovering

Floin led Angus down the long tunnel back to the Sliver. When they emerged from the secret door, the night was full above them, and the town was largely quiet. Floin took some time to re-set the secret, then they went indoors. Angus walked but barely spoke. He shied away from touching things; and hesitated to sit in the chair in the tavern.

Only the innkeeper was awake, and he made no issue of Angus' clear discomfort. He warmed sausage and delivered bread to the table, along with three dark beers.

"You look as though you've seen a ghost." Noulish was an odd fit for the Sliver; his features unusual and dark. Floin would guess he was an immigrant, but he had no idea where from. Angus offered no answer but drank deeply.

"That," Floin interjected, "is interesting. I completely agree with that sentiment."

When Angus started in on the food without speaking, the others conversed.

"You were outside for some time," Noulish observed. "No one knew where to find you. You did not pass through the gates. And the Sliver is not a large place."

"We went for a hike." After guarding this family secret for well over a century, he wasn't about to start advertising it.

"Interesting. Which direction did you go?"

"East."

"So you went for a climb. The mountain runs on our eastern border from the northern to the southern gate." Noulish was getting at something. He'd left little room for Floin to wriggle out of this situation.

"A lot of the path was upwards. It's an old dwarven trail."

"Very interesting. I was expecting that you found the secret passage behind my stables." Noulish wore a perfect poker face.

"You have a secret passage?"

"I think you know I do."

Floin looked at the man, thinking. *What good does this secret do for me, or any dwarves? If he knows already, does it matter if we talk?* He looked at Angus for help. Angus chewed with a steady, measured pace, offering no real communication. *Thanks, son. That's helpful.* Floin chose to go in the interrogative offensive.

"Tell me about your secret passage."

"Of course. I have nothing to hide. It resides in my stables, behind a cleverly hidden stone door. One only needs to know the correct sequence of hidden levers to gain passage to the… passage." A moment of embarrassment passed over Noulish's face at his literary faux pas but was gone quickly.

"I see. Where does it lead?"

"Eastward. And upwards, I think."

"You think?"

"It is, of course, conjecture. My father knew. He even took me along the tunnel once, but I was too young to remember the trick of entering. And my father passed early and suddenly. So I don't really know." Noulish looked at Floin squarely. "I was hoping you would share some information with me."

"I'm sorry, but no." Floin heard the way his Granpap would have responded, even as he said it. "If I did know of a dwarven tunnel, I could only tell another dwarf, and even then only royalty or a blood relative of mine."

Noulish was crestfallen. "Master Floin, I beg you. My father was sent to care for this entrance, and he has been gone for many years. I know that it is important, but not how. I've waited my entire adult life to witness someone using the passage, and now that I do, they won't talk. Please, tell me what *you* know."

"What did you witness?"

"When you did not return to use the rooms Angus hired, I came out to be sure you were alright. I found the plates and tankards he brought out, and I noted things out of place. When I looked very closely, I found where your tracks disappeared into the mountain where I knew the passage door lay. I've found several levers there over the years, but I must be missing a step or two."

"Well then, you know as much as I do about the door. It was Angus here who figured out the order of operations and opened the door. Angus," Floin shook his son by the shoulder, "Can you fill in the gaps?"

Angus' eyes moved to fixate on Floin's, then Noulish's. He raised his empty tankard with a meaningful gesture to the dark man, indicating the need for more. Noulish quickly filled the tankard and returned it.

"Thank you," said Angus, working quickly to ingest the frothy, dark beer. He said no more.

"Really?" Noulish was incensed. "You have no information for me?"

"It isn't mine to give."

Floin nodded. "Noulish, it's been a long day. My boy and I need to retire. We'll leave in the morning. And we will discuss what we might be able to share with you when one or both of us come back through the Sliver. For now, Angus needs some rest, and I do, too."

----- -----

Angus felt more himself when he awoke. His dreams were unsettling and often unbelievable. Thankfully, he didn't remember many of them, and those that left memories faded as his waking brain made sense of the more mundane realities around him.

The short shadows were among those. He'd slept through to midday. If they wanted to make it home in one day, that meant heading through Indaria's forest again. *It's Endaria's forest; he's the Speaker and she is merely his daughter. But for once I'm not afraid of the forest. Endaria is another matter. How do you tell a father that his daughter sacrificed herself so you could survive?*

Three sharp raps on the door preceded Floin's entrance by only a second. "Are ye up, boy? It's time. Past time."

"Yeah, Da. Thanks. I'll be down shortly."

"Never tell short jokes to a dwarf, son. It's insensitive."

"I think you are the uppity one here."

"Don't talk down to me, boy."

"Sorry, I've been feeling a bit under the weather."

Floin laughed. "It seems to me you're alright. You had me worried yesterday."

"I was worried myself. But those odd waking dreams - or whatever they were - have subsided. If they never come back, it'll be too soon."

They packed and walked out the back door, hoping to slip away from Noulish. The man was there, setting the dwarves' pony and wagon in order.

"Good morning," said Noulish, "I have fed and watered your pony, and he is ready to go."

"Thank you, sir," said Angus, fumbling with a purse to offer a silver argent as a tip.

"No, no. No money needed here. We share a secret, and money shall never pass between us again. Secrets draw the people who hold them together, like a family. Now you are family to me. And I yours.

"I respect your wish to tell me what you will when you will. I've waited decades, and I can wait for decades more. See that bundle? That will serve as breakfast for you."

Angus exchanged a glance with Floin. Then he moved to embrace Noulish.

"Thank you, brother. I'll be back, and we will have much to talk about."

"That we shall, brother. Travel safe."

Within minutes, the dwarves were through the northern gate and headed down to the valley floor. They ate as they rode, talking a bit about meaningless subjects; but never spoke about Angus' experience at the stone circle. By the late afternoon, they passed Zonka's hovel and continued without pause into Endaria's forest.

Floin offered a flask to Angus as they entered, which the younger dwarf curtly refused.

"Thanks, Da, but I'll be stone-cold sober for this bit. This forest is more than it seems."

"How so?"

"You wouldn't believe me if I told you."

"I've seen a lot in my time, boy. Try me."

"No sir. If I'm right, you'll see a lot more by nightfall."

"Care to place a wager on that?"

"Ha. Sure, ten argents. Ten argents say you'll be surprised before nightfall."

"Make it a hundred."

"Done."

For a while, the ride was far from surprising. The road was clear and flat, with long, meandering curves. The sun soared lazily above, sending warm, filtered light through the tall trees. Small songbirds offered lilted bursts of musical tittering,

"Astounding," teased Floin, an hour into the forest. "I've never seen danger and intrigue like this before."

"Give it time."

Floin chuckled and lit a pipe. After puffing a while, he goaded Angus again.

"Truly we are on the verge of certain doom."

"Shh. The sun's not down yet."

"It's well on the way, boy."

Something rustled the bushes ahead of them, just off to the side of the road. Without slowing the steady plod of his pony, Angus wrapped his fingers around the haft of his axe. When they passed the bush that housed the rustler, Angus leapt to stand on the seat and raised his axe above his head with a grunt. The bush exploded.

Instead of the troll Angus expected, a tall, white hart bounded across the road, disappearing once again into the forest. Angus hefted the axe a few times, turning in place to search the woods around him. Floin began to laugh.

"You're letting your imagination get the better of you, boy. Here, you sit down, I'll drive for a while. That'll give you the time you need… to count out a hundred argents."

"The sun's not down yet, Da. This place tries to lull you into a false sense of security with all its pretty birds and trees, and then WHAM! It gets you. Mark my words."

"Sure, son. And I have marked them. If I'm not surprised by the forest, you'll owe me a hundred argents. Good words, those."

Angus sat back down and tried to calm his nerves as Floin drove the pony on. He managed to close his eyes for a while, slipping into a nap-like state. There he stayed, experiencing fitful dreams of bounding trolls, ambushing bandits, and worse - sentient trees. He slept until something sharp jabbed him in the ribs.

"Sun's down. Pay up!" Floin laughed and jabbed him again. The sun was down, twilight well underway; and the road continued its sinuous course through the woods, winding back and forth.

"Come now, boy. You may as well start the count."

Angus sighed, looked around once more, then complied. The road was so smooth, that he found himself counting out piles of ten coins next to each other, arranged in a circle around his cloth purse on the bench. The pattern was roughly familiar, leaving a large space at the rear of the bench - the southern end, at the moment.

----- -----

They sweat together, working as one toward a common goal. This arrangement would work here as it had on the other continents, a grand council of disparate tribes and species, keeping peace, adjudicating legal concerns, and promoting the greater good while keeping each people appropriately represented.

While each group provided their own stones, it was left to him and his crew of dwarven stonemasons to arrange and secure them to last beyond millennia. This month was spent carving adequate drainage into the stone bed the circle sat on. Water being a prime agent of erosion, must be controlled before a lasting work is finished.

The earth jostled, and the central stones flew in the air and scattered. An old dwarf yelled something incoherent-

----- -----

"-real world calling Angus! Pay attention, boy!" Floin hauled hard on the reins, urging the pony to stop. The road was no longer smooth, the wagon felt as if it were descending a stone staircase at an angle.

The neat stacks of coin had scattered across the buckboard, and Angus' purse was gone. He looked back expecting to see glints of silver on the road behind but saw only dense forest closing in, blotting out the last vestiges of twilight. He looked forward to see the same image ahead, right in front of them. If not for dwarven infravision, they'd be completely in the dark. As it was, faint traces of heat in the trees showed them they were caught. No room for the wagon between trees, nor a pony, nor dwarves.

Angus shot his father a look, clearly visible so close.

"Shall I bother counting out the wager?"

"Er, no. That's fine. Color me surprised. Is this normal?"

"Mild in my experience. We're uninjured, so that's something. I should have known. We were due to pass through before dark; yet here we are, as deep as ever. I got caught napping."

"Snoring," said a new voice. "If you'd stayed awake, we might not have stopped you. But that snore is distinctly offensive. It identified you instantly, Dragonbane."

A firefly ambled near, followed by another, then more, until the assembly was lit from above by a veritable cloud of luminescent creatures. Angus and Floin were surrounded by seven elves. The one facing them held an extra power, palpable even to the non-magical dwarves.

"Endaria lo Thenalah," said Angus. "Angus Dragonbane, son of Floin Thunderpick, who accompanies me. We are at your service."

"Yes, you are, Angus Dragonbane. When last we met, you agreed to escort my daughter to the Argentine Holt. From there she had other missions. We were under the impression that young King Artemus sent you along to introduce her to Alene and Bedwyn. Is that impression correct?"

"Yes, Speaker, it certainly is."

"And were you successful in your mission?"

"Yes," answered Angus, with considerable hesitation, "...and no. Strictly speaking sir, I accompanied Indaria to Veynsport, where we saw Alene and Bedwyn. I was not able at that moment to introduce them, but they soon came to know each other."

"Angus," stated Endaria flatly, "do not play games with me. You are neither intelligent enough nor skilled enough to engage in wordplay with me. Tell me plainly; what happened at Veynsport?"

The young dwarf took a few moments to consider his words.

"Well, sir, we traveled safely from the Sliver to Veynsport, aside from a troll-"

"No, not safely then. How did you encounter a troll? Is she all right?"

"Oh, sir. Until we met that stone-clad creature, I worked under the impression I was there to protect your daughter. When she slew a large troll with ease, I knew that she was the one protecting me. Your daughter is impressive."

Angus laughed nervously. The elven leader was not amused.

"Elven princesses do not take part in melee, dwarf. Explain to me how you prevailed."

"Oh. Well, I took a swing - and I hit, mind you - but the thing knocked me out of the fight. Then she-" Angus glanced at his father, not sure if he'd believe it, "-she called the roots of nearby trees, and the troll was pulled underground."

Endaria waited. Angus continued.

"She broke the troll's neck with an animated tree root."

"Mmm." Endaria was still not amused. "So what happened at Veynsport?"

"Well, we arrived at the ferry to the Veyns after dark, only to find the ferry's guideline had been cut."

"Why would anyone do that?"

"Stay with me, please. The ferry station was abandoned, and as we approached the marina, we heard a hue and cry not too far off. A battle raged, with men and dwarves. We could not see the whole of it, but we quickly noted queen Alene on a dock with a small company of men, cut off from the rest by a conflagration."

"So you stayed concealed with my daughter until the battle was over, of course."

"Not exactly. We crept closer for a better look, approaching the long, stone seawall to the south. That's when we noted a company of sixty Ivonian archers flanking Alene to take up position on the jetty." Angus saw the question on Endaria's face. "They did not see us as they passed." The elven leader did not try to hide his relief.

"Unfortunately, sir, those archers started to loose their arrows on Alene's trapped company. They were doomed."

"Alas," Endaria said with empathy, "so run the short-lived fortunes of men. Who, I wonder, is in power now?"

"Alene, of course."

"Except that you related her demise."

"It was close, for sure. But Johan and I couldn't let that happen."

"Johan?"

"Yes, he's an Ivonian noble and a friend. And quite taken with Alene."

"I see. So Johan recalled the troops to save Alene?"

"No. Johan was undercover as a bard, unable to take command of these troops. Add in the fact that it was very dark and the terrain uneven; it made more sense to charge them.

"Two against sixty? Surely that is impossible."

Floin chuckled. "You don't know my son, do you? Anything is possible. Did he tell you he slew a dragon on his own?" He laughed the laugh of a proud father defending his son. Seeing Angus' distressed look, he added, "...Speaker."

Endaria looked back to Angus, who went on.

"In a flat battle, all things equal, I would agree with you. But Johan is no ordinary human. He was one of the Ivon's Angels and one of the best. His agility and skill with a sword are equally legendary. My skills are not inconsequential, and you have seen my armor, which I was wearing. They were all lightly-armed archers, unarmored, in the dark, on unsure footing. It was a battle, but we slew them all."

"You should not be standing."

"Neither of us could stand at the end. We were each mortally wounded. And again, your daughter proved her power and worth. She called an entity that took us in, literally, and healed us."

"A Dreamvine." Endaria pointed to the green lock in Angus' beard. "You have the mark. I know not how I missed it."

"Mark?" Angus touched the green whiskers absently. "I took this for a stain."

"She did not explain it to you? Odd. She was probably too busy with Alene. Was Indaria able to meet with Bedwyn?"

"They held considerable conference whilst Johan and I were in the vine. We heard some of it, though none that I could specifically relate."

"There were two vines? I've never heard of such a thing. They stay far, far away from each other."

"I think it was the same vine."

"Dreamvines take one dreamer at a time - otherwise the dreams can cross, which causes...problems."

"Indaria seems to have made a special arrangement with the vine - one she did not get to fully explain."

Endaria pondered this for a moment. "So this Johan must still be Dreaming, then? Dreamvines take years to harvest a person's memories."

"Er, no. Johan is healed, and travels the southern end of the continent as a bard."

The Speaker glared at Angus, obvious fury rising.

"Angus. Where. Is. My. Daughter."

"I'm sorry sir, but she entered the dreamvine as I was released. I saw her long enough to hear her tell me that she was paying a price. I tried to save her, but that aptly named live oak host knocked me to the ground and then trundled into the forests north of Veynsport. We searched, but could not find it. She saved us, and sacrificed herself." Angus' eyes brimmed over with tears.

Endaria lo Thenalah wailed a keening, grief-laden cry that echoed through the forest, and probably the next forest, too. He fell to his knees and wept for his daughter.

Floin put a hand on Angus' shoulder; when Angus looked he saw his father crying along with the rest of them. They stayed like that, weeping, for some time.

A long, resigned sigh emitted from the elf, his head and shoulders sinking deeply with the sound. When he raised his head, he stood again the proud and stoic leader; not a trace of sadness or concern remained. He looked Angus over, and let his eyes slide across the wagon.

"Did she say anything to you when she… did she give you anything?"

Angus recalled that devastating moment. *She had said something, and she had left her satchel, but would telling her father help the situation? No,* he resolved, and gave an abbreviated version.

"She said there was always a price. She said the vine desired the dreams of an elf; that it had been a long time since it held an elf. The very last thing she said," he lied, "was that it had to be this way." Angus was sure she had finished with "my love," but he just could not bring himself to say it.

The Speaker nodded.

"She is right, of course. My daughter has a deep connection with flora and fauna. If she felt that was her only choice, I'm sure she saw reason. But tell me, did she give you anything?"

"No, sir." *She didn't give it to me, she left it on the ground.* "She gave me nothing - beyond my life. For that, I am forever grateful."

"Very well. You will dine with us tonight, and camp under the stars."

Angus nodded to the elf as Floin whispered close, "That didn't sound like an invitation."

"Thank you," Angus stated to Endaria, "we appreciate the help."

----- -----

In the morning the dwarves woke to find their camp just next to the road beyond the northern borders of the elven forest. With little ceremony, they packed and climbed aboard their wagon and started north. They traveled in silence, except when the occasional snicker escaped Floin's lips. Several miles and more snickers in, Angus lost his composure.

"Oh, for the ardent love of silver, Da! What is your most major malfunction?"

Floin paused, pursing his lips - indeed, his entire face - in thought before completely losing it, laughing long and deep. When he regained a modicum of control, he said simply, "Those elves are a lot more fun than I thought they'd be. Are they always so polite?"

"No, Da. Remember, they strung me up naked by a vine."

"Hadn't you just desecrated their holiest site? You can hardly blame them." He laughed again.

"I do blame them. I can't stand Endaria any more than he can stand me. But for his daughter's sake, we both try."

"Hm. What'll you do with that, then? How will you save her?"

"I don't think I can." Angus sighed deeply. "I don't think anyone can."

----- -----

Hours later they arrived at the Holt. Everyone was happy to see them, laughing especially when they greeted Angus. The mirth was short-lived, as Mountain King Artemus called Angus into his chambers to talk.

"Angus, I'd love to welcome you home to stay. You've proven yourself in many ways over the last year; against all odds, you have become our hero. Well done."

"Thank you, your majesty. It is good to be-"

"I wasn't finished. I've had word from Bedwyn about a coming battle in Ivonia, and we're sending a contingent to help. We need your help, Angus."

"I'm not ready to lead - I have no experience."

"Of course you aren't ready to lead! That's why the contingent will be headed by Kelly Siegebreaker. He has the required experience."

"So what do you need my help with?" Angus asked sheepishly, "I don't think Kelly has forgiven me yet."

"Oh, he hasn't forgiven you, boy. Neither have I. But we both recognize the currency of your contacts and knowledge of the outside world. You will consult for Kelly, and open any doors he may need opened. Can you handle that, young Dragonbane?"

"Yes sire. Of course." Angus turned to leave, but Artemus placed a hand across his chest.

"Angus, either you are in love, or you've lost your mind. Either way, lose the flowers, will you? Your presentation as a dwarf reflects on us all."

Angus grabbed a silver platter and scraped the food from it, looking at his reflection. There, in the green strands of his otherwise red beard, were a dozen small, white, trefoil blooms. His free palm found his face.

"Not again. Those devious elves set me up. And my Da went along with it! That's why he was laughing all day long. Oh, but I'll have to dream up some good retribution."

The contingent left before sunrise, loaded on a dozen wagons. Each wagon sported a full team, dried provisions, and a dozen armed and armored dwarves. They carried cheerful faces with grim undertones, raucous jokes, and uncomfortable laughter, yet absolutely no strong drink. The wagons sped straight toward the Sliver, making better time than Angus usually managed. Just before the forest, Angus signaled for a stop.

"I'm going ahead to check on the road. Let's break for a meal and a short rest." He took three steps south before turning back. "No fires, mind. And clean up after yourselves! Let's leave this place better than when we found it!"

Several of the younger dwarves got a laugh out of Angus' odd display, but they accepted it. The request had come from the Dragonbane, after all. Undaunted, Angus walked into the forest several dozen yards before calling out.

"I know you are watching. We come in peace, and ask only for passage through to the Sliver." Angus waited.

Something akin to a wind in the trees moved branches on the eastern side of the road. Angus watched as branches twisted inward along a straight line, reaching as if to grab something from the other end of that vector. Several seconds later, the farther trees swiveled back to their natural positions, one after the next. When the commotion came within a dozen yards, Angus saw that they carried something.

The Speaker.

And then he was there, Endaria lo Thenalah, standing in front of Angus. His demeanor was stern, his scepter threatening. Angus took a half-step back without thought.

"Greetings, Dragonbane. Why do you stand at the doorstep of my forest with an army?"

"Your Majesty, this is not an army - merely a relief for the coming battle."

"Seven score dwarves is more than relief. What battle is this you speak of?"

"The battle for control of Ivonia and the Greenway."

"South of the mountains - hardly my business."

"The world is changing, Endaria. This is all our business."

"No!" The Speaker's fury rang out; even the forest shied away. "Their world is changing. Ours stays the same. It always has. It always will."

Stunned by Endaria's outburst, Angus allowed a few quiet moments to pass before responding.

"As you say, Speaker, this is no battle of yours." *Even if it should be*. "I beg your indulgence in letting us pass through on our way to the Sliver. If the way stays as straight as it seems, we should be past in a few hours."

The forest master looked past Angus at dozens of dwarves, all happily snacking and stretching limbs. They showed no trace of menace. He returned his gaze to Angus.

"Have you, by chance, found my daughter's lost belongings?"

Angus shook his head to indicate the negative answer.

"Very well," allowed Endaria, "yet you and the rest will be in peril of being shot every step of the way. For each live twig broken, a dwarf loses a finger. Major damage to the forest will result in like damage to your dwarven 'force'. Nothing is to be taken from the forest, and no trace left."

"Thank you, Speaker. I believe we have an understanding."

Angus returned to the company, and, after a brief briefing, they were underway. The road was wider than Angus remembered it, and smoother. Trees and bushes leaned away from the passing dwarves, and the leaves around them rustled constantly. Branches whipped around here and there as if blown by a tremendous gale.

Yet there was no wind. Aside from the constant rustling, the dwarves heard no sound. Not a bird, deer, or coyote to be seen.

As it appeared on this day, this supposedly lively forest wasn't as barren as the high desert. None of the company felt comfortable here, save Angus.

The dwarven company was through in the space of less than three hours, skirting the wonderful mossy mound that was Zonka's hovel with barely a word. They climbed the Slivern road at double time, too; yet it was not enough. Darkness engulfed the Sliver entirely by the time they arrived.

Chapter 32

Waymaking

Miles of travel accumulated faster than a mounted courier on an express run, and this with a small army aboard. *The red paint...* Bedwyn smiled for a moment at the thought, then frowned at the extension. He turned to Ben.

"It seems like a great idea at first blush. But this road of military technology leads only to sorrow."

"How could moving troops faster possibly lead to sorrow?" Ben asked, incredulity nearly frothing his words. "A faster response is a more effective response."

"In any given circumstance, technology is often a betterment. But overall," Bedwyn took a deep, thoughtful breath, "over the long run, thousands of years, technology in war means more fighting. More fighting means more death."

"I disagree." Ben's tone pushed the upper boundaries of assertiveness. "Sometimes a little death avoids the greater. The end goal, of course, justifies the means."

Bedwyn gathered his considerable beard in both hands, shaping it thoughtfully. His eyes remained on Ben the whole time. After a protracted pensive pause, he spoke again.

"Have you been following the development of Gymdeithas Fasnach, Ben?"

"Closely, yes."

"Are you aware of the events at Pentref?"

"Ah, Pentref." Ben's voice caught. "Yes, I understand the depth of evil that passed there."

"The Ivon feels as you do; that the ends justify the means."

"Yes, he does."

"He felt that killing everyone at Pentref would avoid a war."

"There was an argument for that view."

"Yet this war - the battle we approach - is largely because of Pentref. Agreed?"

"Of course. Obviously, it didn't work out the way the Ivon planned. Bedwyn, things don't always work out the way we planned them."

"But you think there was a chance the attack on Pentref could have worked?"

"Absolutely. If those farmers hadn't stumbled on the Ivonian company camped in the woods and taken them by surprise, successive forays would have rendered a result."

Bedwyn leaned over the side of the open wagon, wind whipping his beard violently. They proceeded at the pace of a galloping horse. A short bridge lay ahead, crossing a small river, large stones bounding each bank. The dwarf stepped back in and crouched down.

"My bootlaces have come undone." he said, "Loose ends are always a problem in battle." He felt the car angle upwards as it climbed the approach to the bridge, and grabbed Ben's ankles. He heaved them upwards, tossing the man over the side and into the river.

Ben's surprised scream faded immediately. Three dwarves nearby rushed to Bedwyn's side. One asked the question the rest wondered:

"Why?"

"He knew a detail that very few do; it placed him at the scene. According to Patrick, no Ivonians survived that night; but they never found a ranking officer."

"You think Ben was that officer?"

"I do. We know he was an officer in the Ivonian army, and his slip-of-the-tongue makes me confident of that fact. He might have betrayed us, something I can't allow in the coming battle."

"Huh." The inquisitive dwarf glanced over the side at the bridge, now receding into the distance. "Nice move, General."

"Experience and treachery will defeat youth and enthusiasm every time."

"I'm not sure the man knew that expression."

"He does now."

----- -----

Alene traced the complex curves of the figurehead with a fingertip. Shipboard carvings were her favorite art form; gilded, painted forms depicting the best and worst parts of naval life. This one in particular haunted her, showing a young woman, with fierce determination and interminable resolve reflected in her burning green eyes. And burn they did, formed with glass illuminated from behind.

Alene's hand moved across the figure's cheek, her temple, and then over the hair to the slim crown. Such a simple, delicate thing, yet it defined her personality perfectly. Dramatic power contained in a lithe package; plain, approachable, and yet so regal at once. She never expected to become comfortable with the role she was born for - yet here she was.

"Are you going to lie about all day, child?" The motherly voice came from the bow, yet on deck. "There is lunch to be eaten, and business to resolve."

Alene rolled to the edge of the bobstay netting she'd been lying on as the ship carved its way through the ocean. She giggled at Beatrice's gasp - Alene knew there was no danger. She stood, and grabbing the elbow jutting out from the figurehead, vaulted onto the deck of the ship.

"No dolphins today," she pouted. "I really wanted to see them jump with us."

"Now every day can't be filled with dolphins and debutantes. Come, let's eat before the business."

They walked towards Alene's quarters, housed in the stern where a captain would normally stay in relative luxury. This being the royal yacht meant a special suite of rooms made for a queen. An office, bedroom, attendant's room (Beatrice stayed here, as Alene kept few retainers) and a private bath flanked the large, window-lined salon. The room was dominated by an ovoid table of equally spaced and shaped chairs - no Veynsian standing above another, the queen only slightly elevated to signify executive power.

The table was set with Alene's favorite fresh fruits and fish, prepared with the savory and sometimes heated spices the Veyns were famous for. The women sat to eat, Alene eschewing the raised chair for a normal one. Within a minute they were joined by two men, each in the long, burgundy, hooded, oiled-canvas coats that signified their rank. Each offered a curt bow toward Alene and a nod to Beatrice.

"Good afternoon, gentlemen," Alene began, "do you think this glorious weather will hold?"

The younger of the two - a perceptive-looking man with more wrinkles than hair, known as Captain Pol Sterix - answered.

"I sincerely hope not. I would prefer to arrive under cover of the morning fog."

"Or darkness," added the older man. Fan Zindel was the admiral of the Veynsian Royal Navy and one of the few holdovers from the time of Regent Villeuse. Alene had kept him without question since he had been appointed by her mother twenty-five years earlier. "One way or the other, we need to have some cover or we'll be greeted by enough soldiers to make our trip useless. Surprise is our only hope."

"I certainly understand your desires, and I even share them." Alene regarded the men sternly. "Do you think the weather will hold?"

"Without a foggy morning, we would do better to flee." The admiral's voice wavered slightly. "If they get a good look at us before we have unloaded, we'll be done for."

"I made a promise to be there." Alene's palms spread, facing up and away in a sign of resigned determination. "We will be there, for better or for worse."

Chapter 33

Landed Gentry

"Well done, gentlemen," the words oozed from the Ivon's mouth, thick and syrupy, "although I feel you weren't gentle in your manner."

"My lord, you have the grain we promised. Your silos overflow." The man's indignance showed through his groveling. "The Greenway will have a tough winter. They will call upon you to save them in their time of greatest need. We did what you asked. All we wish in return is for you to hold up your end of the bargain."

The Ivon replaced the book he'd been flipping through on the shelf. His hand lingered on the spine, tracing the gilded inscription on the hardwood cover, which he read.

"Te whakahaere i te ngakau, te whakahaere i nga hinengaro. Do you know it?"

"No."

"Which don't you know - the book, or the saying?"

"My lord, I could not even tell you what language it is."

"Could you not? I thought more of you. No matter. The rough translation is this: *Control the heart to control the mind.* Your actions certainly created an intellectually proveable crisis, and allow me to provide a solution. But those are real problems that a strong mind can address in different ways.

"If this were simply the case, then hearts would lean into the need for food."

"Starvation," chuckled the thief, "is a powerful motivator."

"Indeed it is. Very few things motivate men above the need to feed their families. Men are protective of their families, especially their children, above all else."

The Ivon looked at the men before him, watching as the blood drained from their faces in terror. They followed his prompt onto the balcony, high above the city. He directed them to look over the buildings to the north, a slender hand on the back of each man's neck.

"Regard the Greenway. They are hungry and desperate. Their community is in pain, pain I intended to cause." The Ivon stepped towards the precipice, pushing the men so they stopped with their knees touching the railing. "I can help them. I may be the only one who can help them. And yet they muster against me. Why?"

Neither man answered.

"Here is a clue. They have a new phrase that appears in everything from poems and songs to battle cries. Have you heard it?"

If they did, neither gave an outward sign. Both looked concerned that they might fall over the edge.

"Willim. Zain. These names figure strongly in the zeitgeist of Gymdeithas Fasnach. My spies tell me that these were the names of two children, natives of Greenway itself. They tell me these children were set on a largely ceremonial duty to guard the harvest during the festival. Now that sounds sweet, doesn't it?"

The men nodded, their heads resting lower in apparent shame. The Ivon's hands still rested lightly on their napes.

"And yet, these children were slain at their posts, their bodies burned. This happened while their families reveled. Try to imagine what that community feels. What does their collective heart get out of this separation of child from parent?

"This does not stop at one or two families - the whole town would normally be swept away in a shared tragedy like this. Yet due to the timing of the harvest, this devastating and motivating sentiment was shared by thousands of families. Thousands!

"You fools have given them a rallying cause more powerful than any other. By killing these children, you negated any of the heart-felt fear of a hard, hungry winter and replaced it with righteous, consuming rage. Now they won't come to me for relief and succor.

"They come for revenge."

"My lord," began the older of the two, "We never intended for that to happen. We only ever strove to fulfill our agreement."

"Well then." The Ivon smiled cruelly. "Let me fulfill my part. Landed gentry, I believe the reward was? I have already recognized you as gentlemen. Congratulations, you are both gentry recognized by royalty. Now as for the rest -"

The Ivon bent his knees, dropping his weight as he pushed the two men over the railing in one smooth motion. He watched for the several seconds of screaming, helpless freefall. He did not smile and only spoke when it was finished.

"And now, gentlemen, you are officially landed gentry."

Chapter 34

Breaking Point

Patrick looked over the assembled men and women, forcing himself not to cry at the tragic end they all neared. Centuries of tradition dictated that when men went to war, the women stayed back to protect the children and keep the home fires burning. From his rooftop vantage, he watched women work alongside the men to find their best roles. He half-spoke, half-muttered his feelings to the two councilmen next to him.

"Women in combat. I don't like it. We stand to lose so much already. Why add them to the equation?"

"This isn't your doing, Patrick," said Noah, the older man to his right. Noah's still-dark hair quivered in a dubious architectural feat of disguise when he shook his balding head. "Nor is it your choice. No man chose this. They demanded to participate."

"He's right, you know." Jack inserted. A lean, lanky man in his early thirties with a voice to match, Jack was the junior member of this trio. "It was the Ivon what brought them into it. Hadn't they kilt them boys, we'd be only ourselves, only men doin' the fightin'."

"I believe you," replied Patrick. "Women are the same the world over. Bluster, grump or yell, and they bend like a willow in the wind. Push too hard, and they'll knock you down. The Ivon pushed too hard. Now they are convinced they'll knock him down."

One group practiced archery. Some of these women were skilled hunters, strong enough to draw the yew longbows prevalent in the area. They perforated straw-stuffed canvas sacks with skill - skill matched by angry, determined faces.

Another group worked with long-handled axes, scythes, pitchforks, and mauls; tools they were familiar with from hours of working on their farms. Now they learned how to put these mundane and peaceful tools to deadly use.

A third group practiced battlefield bandages, slings, and ferrying each other on stretchers. *Now that,* Patrick thought, *I like seeing. Too many men die from survivable wounds in battle, simply because care either does not exist or is in short supply where needed most.*

"I think," he said, "the Ivon meant to break our spirits. To put us in our places. He wanted to see us come running back to him for help."

"We're running towards him," Noah said, "but with a battle cry on our lips."

"Exactly." Patrick pinched his chin. "I still haven't worked out how we can win this."

The men observed for a while, making notes on each group's progress. They discussed groupings and potential assignments. Cruelly, they analyzed which would be more or less likely to be difference makers. Which were likely to survive. Where they should be placed.

What they did not discuss, a subject never even broached, was whether they should limit the women's activity or place in the fight. The elder females had left no doubt that this was going to happen, and no amount of cajoling or convincing would change their course. They were there to do what the men had not been able to accomplish without them - convince the Ivon that he should leave them alone.

----- -----

"Come on, ladies," Judy encouraged, "If you can hit these, you can hit anything!" The middle-aged mother indicated a range of cast-iron pots and pans hanging from the spreading branches of an old oak. The distaff archers fired blunt, iron-tipped arrows at these, a hit refreshing the swaying movements and providing a satisfactory "DING!" At another of these soundings, she laughed and muttered through a smile.

"If the men had come and asked to treat our best pans this way, I'd have chased them off with a rolling pin."

"Ain't that the truth," said a raspy voice at her elbow. It was Hazel, a full generation ahead of Judy. Too old to even use a bow, Hazel would stay behind with those too old or too young to participate in battle. “Somehow, I don’t mind a dent or two with what’s at stake.”

Forty women, aged fourteen to forty-four, loosed volley after volley, the telltale tinks tolling ever-more-frequent hits.

“They’re getting better, Hazel. I think they can do this.”

“They were ready before today’s exercise. Most of these women practiced with hay bales when they were no more than girls.”

“Exactly my point, Hazel. Those who practiced early need to practice again. The rest are still girls. I won’t take it too far, though.”

As the day went on, Judy removed the largest pans, then the next largest, and so on until the targets were all under a foot in diameter. At that, the group of now-exhausted women were hitting more than missing.

“Now, they are ready.”

----- -----

New grandmother Lori walked from group to group, coaching. Even though they used tools from around the farm exclusively, each had different aspects. She stopped by the axe-wielding women and offered some advice.

“Just like splitting wood, Sarah. Raise the axe behind and above, then guide it down. A straight hit is more important than a powerful one. Trust the tool to hit hard, and guide it to the target. There, yes! Just like that, dear.”

She moved on to the hayforks. Lori had them laid out between crates, spaced just a few inches apart. Smaller women leaned on the crates, facing away from the business end of their polearms. On a curt command, they spun to grab and lift the forks, handle butts couched in notched rocks, tilting up to point outward at chest level for a charging man.

“Up a bit, Lizzie. Jane, make sure the curve of the tips point at the men, not up. Great timing, ladies. Keep practicing.”

Next up were women wielding flails - ostensibly made to crack wheat hulls - fracturing dummies made of fence posts, denting helmets (buckets, in fact) on the same posts.

“Mary, yes! Well done. Again, yes - don’t try to get fancy - OH!” Lori tried to catch Mary, stunned after a stray spin caught herself upside the head. “That’s enough for today. Go see Patti, she’ll fix you up.”

----- -----

Patti, a slightly built empty nester, supervised several different groups. At this moment, she tutored three young women in the cruel art of battlefield triage. They worked with a dozen sheets of paper, each with a paragraph written on them. Patti held six, reading them out to her students.

“Patient one is missing three fingers and has an arrow protruding from his gut. His fingers are not bleeding heavily, nor is the arrow wound. Some very dark blood is seeping from around the arrow, but not much.

“Patient two has a small cut on the inside of his upper leg. When held with pressure, the bleeding is lessened, but it gushes without pressure. The patient is pale.

“Patient three has suffered a crushing blow to his lower leg; a horse fell on him. He is not bleeding.”

“Patient four is unconscious and bleeding from his scalp, or what is left of it. A slice has been removed by a blow that glanced off his skull. His cheeks are red.”

“Patient five has a dislocated hip and is in great pain. He screams incessantly. Superficial wounds otherwise, but he begs to be put out of his misery.”

“Patient six has lost his right foot. He managed to tie his belt around his lower leg above the calf to control the bleeding. Consider these men. I’ll be right back, and you can tell me who gets care first.”

Patti skittered towards women with cauldrons stirring a tarry, viscous goo. It smelled terrible, sticking hopelessly to the rough sticks they stirred with. Agnes, a bent wrinkle of a woman most kindly described as ‘wizened’, beckoned.

“I reckon it’s ready, Patti. The smell is right, and if it gets much right-er, we’ll fall over from the fumes!”

“Let’s test it, shall we?” Patti chose a switch from the willow that shaded this station. Scoring the yellow bark with her knife, she peeled it away - exposing a wet, slippery, floppy stem. This she dipped quickly into the goop, pulling it smartly out. The tar stuck fast to the impossible surface.

“See?” Agnes tried. “That’s as sticky as we can make it.

"All right, that looks good, Agnes," Patti said. "You've got it down, now let's do another and make sure you've practiced. Pour this out into the brick molds, and we'll have some ready-made."

The woman looked over her charges with hesitant approval. They were doing well. Not practiced veterans, of course, but well. Now she must face the young women about the sad results of her triage conundrum. It was never easy to tell someone that a patient was likely to die, no matter what you did to help them. In her scenario, only one had a great prognosis - reset the hip, and with some rest, that man might be all right. For the rest, she would rather not talk about it. But she must.

----- -----

Kelly and his dwarves ate heartily at several taverns in the Greenway, fueling for the inevitable battle. The General himself found a spot with Patrick and Timothy to discuss strategy for the coming attack.

“You’ve trained a good group,” opened the dwarf. “How do you think they’ll fare?

“The archers know their craft better than most. And the hunters know how to dispatch a foe just as they would an elk. Then there are those like Patrick here,” Timothy clapped the larger man on the back, “who have actual military training.”

“Training, maybe. But before Pentref, I never had to test my skills.” Patrick shook his head heavily. “And now we are leading an attack on an impenetrable city. Seems like madness.”

Kelly Siegebreaker laughed out loud. “Impenetrable, you say? Young man, I’ll have you know I have been part of sieges and fortress raids. One here, in fact, hundreds of years ago. It isn’t impenetrable, but you don't need it to be.”

The dwarf leaned in conspiratorially. “You’ll bring them out, and here is how.” Kelly went on to explain his plan, punctuated by nods and pointed questions. After a half hour, Kelly wrapped up. Then Patrick asked the glaring question.

“You and your men aren’t anywhere in this plan. What does that leave for you?”

“First,” Kelly replied, “I don’t have men with me. I have dwarves. And we’ll be under the city in the old tunnels, places we’ve sealed up long ago. My contingent will divide up and seize key points from within the city, and we'll do it quietly. From there, we'll disrupt anything that you and I haven't already discussed."

"And why don't we all use these tunnels to bypass the walls?"

"Because it is better this way."

Timothy slammed a hand on the table, spilling Kelly's drink. "How can that be better?"

"That's why." Kelly picked up the container and salvaged what he could with deliberate patience. "Because men have been known to make rash decisions. This is a dwarven secret, and it will remain so. This way, on the odd occasion we need to come and offer help to our neighbors, we have that 'in.' Literally."

Patrick held Timothy back. "General, we thank you for your help, however it comes. I think your strategy is sound, and we'll make the most of it. May the harvest winds speed you on your way."

"Aye, and may the ground beneath your feet offer a solid footing, and may your stances be sound. I'll see you after, on the inside."

----- -----

The strings of Johnny Brightshirt's instrument lightened their vibrato, fading to silence with his crooning voice. The crowd stayed silent, too. No applause for the song about Billy and Zane, the unwitting martyrs set forward by Johnny as heroes in their own right. Tearful faces, stoic in expression, nodded. The crowd stood, their embraces and back-clapping touches comforting and steeling each other. The crowd dispersed as the bard put his instrument away. Within minutes, Johnny Brightshirt and Patrick Smith were the only two people left in the tavern. Not unusual for an after-lunch break, for certain, and with today's business, entirely appropriate. The large man greeted the young singer with a compliment.

"Your songs have power, Johnny. They always have."

"Thank you. But it isn't the songs themselves that have power, rather the subject matter. *The Ballad of Billy'n'Zane* is filled with meaning and soul."

"The subject matter is weighty, I'll grant you, but your songs move people. They inspire, almost direct." Patrick looked around for listeners, drawing closer to Johnny. He continued, just above a whisper. "Tell me who taught you the songs about Gymdeithas Fasnach."

"No."

"Come now, it's you and me, Johnny. No one else is here. Share the truth with me."

Johnny drew the string of his plush lute case, then grabbed a half-drunk ale from a nearby table and chugged the remnant. "No."

"I think I know who taught them to you." Patrick wagged a finger as he spoke, eyes narrow. "I even think I know who wrote them."

"Patrick, there is no value in this line of conversation. Would you agree to let it go, knowing the knowledge could only serve to weaken the movement?"

"I hardly think it would matter."

"Wouldn't it?"

"How could it possibly make a difference who started this?"

"Reflect on that for a moment. Tell me how you feel, pressed into service as the head of a headless party." Johnny allowed a few moments for Patrick to think, which he did. "Now imagine what the people would do if they had someone to rally behind. What if a single visionary could be credited for the idea, the genesis of Gymdeithas Fasnach? How many people would want to raise such a person as king?"

"Would a King be such a bad idea?"

"Patrick, the whole idea of the movement is to put the power in the hands of the people."

"Huh."

"And that is precisely why I will never reveal who taught me these songs."

"Johnny, I don't know who you really are." Patrick grasped the bard's shoulder. "But make no mistake, I know exactly who you really are."

Chapter 35

The Angels' Flight

Angus secured the bolt and set his bag against the door. He'd asked for the gable room, to ensure no visitors came via the window. That woman had ruined the Greenway for him; he doubted he'd ever get a peaceful night's sleep in this town again.

He was just settling down to bed when he heard a light rapping at the door.

"No! I'm not interested! Leave me alone!"

A male-sounding laugh came from the other side of the plank entry. "Angus, I like you a lot, but not in that way. You don't need to worry. Now open up. We have business!"

Angus sighed and moved his barricade, then opened the door, still in his smallclothes.

Ynghild's smile could not get wider. "But I do!"

"Aah!" Angus jumped back. "How did you do that? I thought it was Johan!"

"I'm here, too, Angus." Johan chuckled. "But not for long. Come, get yourself dressed. It is time to go."

"Go?" Angus queried. "Where to? And can't it wait until morning?"

Ynghild tittered, watching Angus struggle to dress. "No, silly! We three need to penetrate the Angel Gate before it is secured. By tomorrow, Ivonian spies will have carried word of this… gathering, and they'll seal up the entrances to the great city. Even our side entrance. You seem to be having some trouble with your pants; would you like some help?"

"You leave me alone! Hands off!" Angus was shouting now, red-faced. "Find some other dwarf to have your fun with!"

"...ahem. May I be of service?" the innkeeper said from the top stair outside the room. "Whiskey and… what was it? "Discretion"?"

As Angus resisted a deeper tirade, Johan stepped in. “Just discretion this time, sir. It should not be known that we left for a while. If you could keep our departure quiet, we'd appreciate it. We’ll meet you in the stables momentarily for some mounts.”

“Mounts?” roared Angus, after the proprietor left. “You must know I don’t ride.”

“Then it is a good thing you are a quick learner!” Johan started down the stairs.

“Don’t worry, Angus. I’ll teach you.” Ynghild flashed a naughty smile. “I’ll teach you so many things!”

“Try it, and I’ll teach you some manners, girl!” Angus hefted his pack and followed the others to the stables.

Chapter 36

A Rival's Offering

"Start unloading, Captain Sterix. I'll make an introduction." Alene hopped lightly down onto the dry planks of Ivonia's outer docks. "One at a time, as we discussed; we want to be clear that this is a significant offering. We only have one chance to get this right!"

As Sterix barked orders to his men, he concealed his awe and concern. Alene was just a young woman and a slight one at that. She refused all guard and ceremony, speaking to everyone as peers. *That easy way might get her into trouble one day. May this not be the day,* he thought.

Unbothered, Alene strode with confidence down the darkened wharf. This port was set up with many branches, all centering on one trunk, ever-widening until it reached the land nearly a mile away. Two sailors struggled to catch up, each carrying a barrel.

They stopped at the base of the trunk, setting barrels down on the planks. The sailors trotted back, grabbing many more barrels to pile at the base of the dock system.

"Good evening, Ivonia! I come bearing gifts! Who is responsible for the marina at this hour?" She waited for an answer, but most people were asleep. The answer did not come quickly. Looking back over her shoulder, she could still see the lanterns burning brightly on her yacht almost a mile away. Few other lights were maintained here.

Eventually, a night watchman rousted from his sleep and approached. "Miss? What are you doing out this late? The port is closed! Can you return in the morning?"

"Oh, I suppose I could do that. But hold that thought. I might have something that would change your mind." She rustled in her shoulder bag and produced her light, golden crown, and donned it.

The man struggled with obvious confusion. "Are you from one of our noble families? You don't have any blue on at all…"

"Really?" Alene tsked as more barrels were set up behind her. "Does the name 'Alene' ring any bells?"

The night watchman screwed up his lips and furrowed his brow deeply as he racked his night-shift brain for the name. "I'm sorry, miss, but no. Should it?"

Alene had enough. She drew herself up to her maximum height (which wasn't much) and stated in her most regal voice, "I am Alene, Queen of the Veyns. Go and wake whoever should receive me, and DO. IT. NOW!"

Alene watched the still-sleep-fogged watchman struggle with the concept for three seconds before he jerked to attention and then ran off. She watched him race into the three-story building adjacent and heard his frantic footfalls ascending stairs. She turned her attention back to her cargo. Seizing one of the first casks delivered, she set it on another, corked bunghole facing up. She unlaced two delicate Veynsian steins from her belt, then looked up.

Perfectly timed, as always. A dock warden strode up, led by the near-panicking watchman. "What is the meaning of this?" he stated, indicating the pile of goods now effectively blockading the way to the rest of the dockwork.

"A gift," she stated pleasantly, "fine wines and oils for the Ivon, a sign of friendship from Queen Alene!" She pulled the cork and tipped the cask, pouring two servings of the red liquid. "Take your pick, and I'll enjoy the other!"

"Fine wines, you say?" The Dockwarden seemed unconvinced. "I'll be the judge of that!" He grabbed one of the steins and took a swig. Alene followed suit.

"Well?"

"Swill. And no Queen would be out this late or without guards. Take her away!" He indicated that the watchman should take her into custody.

Alene did not resist.

After they had departed, the Dockwarden took another draught, licking his lips happily. "Very good swill." With that, he returned to his building to arrange for men to bring in the cargo.

----- -----

In the uppermost room of the tallest tower in Ivonia, the Ivon paced. Checking preparations, troop movements, and intelligence reports; they were all part of the job and position. This was new, however; defending his home city from an apparent attack.

He sent most of the generals and advisors away for the night, retaining only his personal secretary to take notes. They stepped out onto the balcony to finish up in the midnight air.

From here the Ivon could appraise his beautiful city, white-washed walls and glazed blue tiles lit by oil lanterns below and starlight above. No moon shared light this night, which made the well-lit ship at the outskirts of the port more obvious. He pointed.

"Which ship is that? I do not recognize it."

"I know not, sire, but I can send a runner to learn."

"Do that." The Ivon felt urgent without a reason. "Make it quick."

The secretary jogged off, leaving the Ivon alone - truly alone. He sighed deeply, then stepped back inside to his bookshelf. Tracing spines with a long, delicate finger, he slipped across until he found the volume he sought - Ships of the Cyfandir. He removed the large, illuminated book and stepped back out onto the balcony, standing near a wall sconce with an oil lamp.

Flipping pages, he compared the ship illustrations to the pattern of lights on the well-lit ship in the harbor. When he had eliminated all ships of Ivonian design and registry, he looked up again. *What is my intuition telling me?* He thought. *The Veyns!* He riffled to the section dedicated to his rival, and the first ship was a match - the Queen's yacht!

Just as he made this realization, the ship cast off, moving at a slow pace away from the dock and port. One of the lights stayed with the dock - possibly a lantern forgotten? But in far too short a time, it was evident that this was no mere lantern.

It was a fire.

The fire grew several times, until it began to race along the dry wooden planks of the dock, running ever closer to the shore.

"No."

The fire grew at an incredible pace - as if it had been accelerated - spreading to the branches of the dock system, faster and faster. Men were out of boats, trying madly to douse the fire, but it was simply too big to stop now.

"No!"

The Ivon, the most powerful man on the Cyfandir, stood powerless against a devastating wound to his city. A crowd gathered at the base of the dockwork, right where the wood joined land. There seemed to be a bottleneck of goods, piled right where firefighters needed to be. He saw what would happen next, too late to even call out.

The pile caught fire and exploded, sending flaming strings of hot oil in all directions, growing the fire both on the docks and catching nearby ships and buildings.

"NOOOOOO!" He screamed, sinking to his knees. It could not be worse.

As the moon rose above the horizon, an iridescent sheen reflected off the water. Purples and greens added to typical blues and whites. The well-lit yacht formed up with two larger barques, each coming out of the harbor from different edges. They had not been lit at all. As the ships cleared the sheen that covered most of the harbor, including other ships desperately trying to avoid fire from the docks, arrows tipped with fire arced from the Veynsian interlopers into the man-made cove, where they ignited the very water.

The Ivon leaned over the railing and retched, emptying his dinner onto the cobblestones three hundred feet below. He sat there for a long time, watching his people die and a large part of his navy sink.

Chapter 37

A Train-ing Mission

Bedwyn pounded his finger on a piece of paper aggressively, leaving a greasy stain from his breakfast of eggs and sausage across the schematics. "How does this connect to that?"

"With a Twizzle(R) Tube, of course!" Koksal had no clue why Bedwyn didn't have a clue. "Without that, the aether regulator would overload immediately!"

"Obviously!" It was not obvious to Bedwyn, not at all. "Where is it?"

They went on like this for some time, assembling the new machine. They had stopped several miles outside of town, a small forest separating them and the road. When Bedwyn was satisfied that Koksal was indeed close, he stepped off the train to address his troops.

Seventy stout veterans worked nearby. They helped each other with the fiddly bits of armor and gear, readying for battle. These were the best troops Bedwyn had to offer, dwarves in their prime. Every one of them had served at the battle of Veynsport and were as tuned as warriors could be.

"Thannon, are you ready?" The dwarven king bellowed.

"Yeah!" came the reply from his son.

"Good, 'cause yer goin'! And this time, you'll lead the troops."

Every dwarf stopped their activity, turning to see their only leader in battle for several thousand years passing the torch.

"Aye, sir. It'll be an honor. Where will you be?"

"Riding this infernal contraption with Koksal, making sure it fires at the right time, in the right place, at the right target. There is a farm a quarter-mile from the Eastgate. You'll take that at night and set up as a quick-reaction force."

"What are we reacting to?" asked one of the sergeants.

Bedwyn's eyes twinkled. "Oh, you'll know when it happens. You'll take whatever opportunity presents itself, and Thannon will be the judge in the moment. Say, for example, a gate was breached or a wall happened to fall, opportunities like that."

"I like it," said Thannon. "What is our goal when we get inside?"

"Never a doubt that you'll get in. I knew I promoted you for a reason. Well, General, you'll apply yourself in several ways. If you get a shot at the Ivon, take it. Cutting off the head usually kills the beast. Gymdeithas Fasnach are making their move at the Northgate; you might look to help them from the inside.

"And of course," he continued, "targets of opportunity as you see them. Keep it clean, of course. If you wouldn't do it with me watching, don't do it. Trust me, you'll know."

The old dwarf hugged his son and went down the line with words of wisdom for each and every dwarf present. Bedwyn knew each name, each fighter's family. He'd ask about future plans, and encourage them to hold those plans as a reason to excel and survive.

Bedwyn was a good king.

At dusk, Thannon took his seventy stalwarts cross-country. They scaled the low stone walls that separated fields, skirted houses and barns, and any semblance of habitation. Soon, they could see the torches and lamps that lit the walls of Ivonia proper.

Their pace slowed as they located the gatehouse, and the farm that sat nearby. They waited for the last light in the farmhouse to go out. An hour later, mid-night-ish, they snuck up to the building.

"There's a dog," one of the scouts whispered. "It's lying on the porch."

Thannon rummaged through his pack, producing a greased cloth bundle. "Show me."

A few excruciating moments later, they approached the porch from forty feet away. They were in the vegetable garden, hidden behind bushy tomato plants, when Thannon opened his bundle. Greasy off-cuts from his breakfast brisket.

These he tossed in a dotted line leading the dog away from the house. The canine took the bait, allowing the dwarves quick entry. From there they fell upon the sleeping farmer and his family. Not killing them, but binding and gagging them, set away in the basement with two dwarven guards. The rest headed for the large haybarn that lay closest to the gates; there, they waited.

----- -----

Back at the train, the old dwarf and his goblin friend looked over their handiwork. A long, steel spear - twenty feet long at least - protruded from a cannon-like tube. Barbed points reminiscent of a grappling hook spread out from the head.

Tubes (Twizzle(R) tubes, Bedwyn thought) connected the cannon to the boiler in Koksal's engine, one car up. The car in between held a large steel tank, several whistles protruding. Steam built in the pre-dawn hours, evidenced by a bit escaping aggressively here and there.

"Do you think it'll work?" asked Bedwyn.

"It should. I mean, it won't take a miracle," the engineer answered.

"I should know whether this works. I always know. But I…" The dwarf stammered, "I just don't. And I should. We build pressure as we approach, and use your steam to launch the Gaterender inside the city, reverse, and make a breach for Thannon and company to get inside. It is a simple plan."

"I think it'll work. It is untested for this purpose, but I'm certain we have enough power."

"Is that on this dial here?" Bedwyn indicated a two-foot-round valve with graduated numbers.

"That indicates the power level, yes. We've used as much as ten, but one day I'll be ready to go all the way to fifty. As I'm not sure what that would do to the machine, full power will have to wait. I'm thinking we'll throttle the power to twenty, at least for this purpose. It'll be enough to put that grapnel over the gate or the wall, without penetrating too far."

Goblins making machines of war. I don't like it, Bedwyn thought, *but it is a necessity. If we can't breach quickly, they'll have the advantage. Whatever I can't see, I must angle us towards advantage.*

Chapter 38

Moment of Truth

Zonka checked her work again. Over the last week, she'd used parts of her rag-tied cloak to fashion handholds and footholds on Uvrede's broken-glass-coated scales. Just in case the old girl could still fly. She didn't want to fall off.

And now, as the lights from the great city of Ivonia came into view across the calm, black water, she felt ready. Ready to find and kill all dwarves until - and after - she found the one that haunted her dreams. Uvrede would complete her revenge.

"I've been haunted before, you know." Uvrede's matter-of-fact tone was out of character. Zonka observed a more animated, more interested dragon. "Not like you. I always broke the spell by taking a nap. But the dragons I knew, my subjects, my friends, my family, they haunted me on and off for several thousand years."

"But my haunting is different? A mere orc?"

"'A mere orc' she says, HA!" Uvrede's vibratory giggles were back. "I've known thousands of orcs in my time, served on councils, fought against and with them, and one thing is sure - you, my dear Zonka, are no mere orc."

Zonka laughed with the dragon.

"But that description isn't complete. Even in your haunting, I feel your weight, as if you were still alive. Your very soul has weight, and that impresses me. Ah, we grow close. I'll pull up onto the sand west of the river here and stretch."

Zonka considered this but wasn't afraid of being found out. Her inhaled cocktail of drugs had worked, leaving Uvrede's psyche malleable like clay for a time. No longer susceptible to suggestion, they were in a period during which Uvrede would not even consider questioning Zonka's intentions - or directions.

It was well past midnight when the great dragon Uvrede took her first steps on land in a week. She had expected to be weakened, but a steady diet of fish and consistent exercise swimming here left her energized and ready.

Step by step Uvrede walked onto the beach, where she stretched. Zonka dismounted to watch, as the dragon went through a studied set of moves designed to limber up all parts of her ancient body. She arced, twisted, and rolled this way for a half hour before straightening up and readying herself for flight.

"Ready?" asked the orc who sat on a rock a dozen paces away, munching on a handful of berries she'd picked.

"Don't rush me!" Uvrede growled. "It's been a very long time. At least nothing hurts too badly."

She took a deep breath and spread her wings wide, then raised them, poised for a launch stroke - and paused. She looked over at Zonka, who was tapping a foot on the sand.

"Do you mind?"

"What? Oh, sorry."

Another moment passed.

"I can't do this with you looking at me!"

Zonka sighed audibly and turned away, ostensibly studying the full moon above.

Uvrede swiveled her head in a circle, popping neck joints loudly. She inhaled, and held her breath… Then swept her wings downward as hard as she could.

Zonka rolled to a stop, covered in wet beach sand. When she rose, she found she'd been blown fifty feet directly away from Uvrede - correction, the depression where Uvrede had been a moment before. That space was now occupied by a dragon-sized crater, rapidly filling with the tide.

No dragon to be seen or heard, Zonka studied the sky above. Stars blinked out of existence and back in, a void-like patch heading towards the large lunar shape. Uvrede paused at an apex just in front, her distant shape silhouetted against the lone white backdrop before plunging downward.

Zonka moved out onto the beach proper to see better and was greeted by a rooster-tail in the surf as the great dragon Uvrede skillfully skimmed over moonlit breakers. She ran out of momentum just as her class touched the beach.

She's the most amazing creature I've witnessed in all my years. And I use her power as a mere tool of revenge, thought Zonka. *She is so much more.*

"Now," the dragon beamed, "I'm ready."

Chapter 39

Side-Door Action

"Ow!" Angus yelled. "My armor was not designed for saddles. This HURTS!"

Johan laughed and Ynghild giggled, and not for the first time this night.

Johan pulled rein at the edge of the forest, Ivonia's lights dominating the scene beyond. An abandoned shack showed in the moonlight, a ruined well next to it.

"You are in luck, Angus," Johan said, dismounting. "This is as far as we take the horses."

"And not a moment too soon," the aggrieved dwarf complained. "Many moments too late, I fear. Do you think Dr. Pheuss has anything for chafing and bruising?" Angus slid awkwardly off the horse, his armor leaving telltale scratches in the leather saddle.

"Yes," the man started, "but you won't like them. Besides, Pheuss is very loyal to the Ivon. He won't be helping us soon. At least not a dwarf, especially not one marked by the Ivon."

Ynghild was rummaging through her bag. She came up with some leather wrist restraints. "Will these fit him, you think?" She asked Johan, looking at Angus.

"Now look here, woman, I've had just about enough of your twisted games!"

"Worry not, Angus. I think I know what she has in mind."

Soon they crossed the fallow field in the moonlight. At one point, they paused when they all saw the same group of stars blink out just a little too long; they saw no more. The abandoned hut was little more than a shell, obviously in a state of disrepair approaching collapse. Yet Johan and Ynghild entered with the restrained dwarf in tow. The door closed behind them, Johan lifted a board under the remains of an untouchably corroded mattress.

This exposed a rough set of stairs leading to a presumed basement. Stairs moved and creaked with each step, yet the humans seemed unbothered by their peril as they descended. At the bottom, Johan lit a candle with his firestarter, revealing another room on the verge of collapse. He reached into a broken bookshelf, deftly finding the release that showed it as a secret door.

Behind that door lay a tunnel - more a shoddy mineshaft in Angus' opinion - that led straight towards the city. The entrance concealed again, they navigated the darkened tunnel by candlelight. Five minutes later, the tunnel descended a set of stone stairs, under what Angus suspected was the root of the city wall above. He wasn't impressed.

The way back up led to a steel-clad door with a sighting window. Ynghild called ahead to the door, "Make way for the Ivon's Angels! We have secured the criminal requested by the Ivon!" She took Johan's candle and illuminated first her face, then his for the security personnel on the other side of the door.

The sound of metal screeching on metal turned out to be a seldom-used and ungreased bolt. The door opened, and the middle-aged man inside spoke.

"C'Antrell! It's been an age! Who do you have with you?"

"Nilsson? It has been a while!" Johan hauled Angus along by his still-armored shoulder, roughly. "This is that dwarf who claimed to kill a dragon. The Ivon had me chase him down to answer for lying to the Ivon's face. It took months, but with Ynghild's help here, we got him."

Nilsson laughed as Ynghild closed the door and bolted it again. She smiled and nodded. Then the erstwhile guard spoke again.

"I'm glad one of us is out having fun. I've been in trouble since the incident. I only hear rumors now."

"Anything juicy?" Johan fished.

"Nothing real. The closest to a good rumor was word that last night a woman claiming to be the Queen of the Veyns was locked up for false witness."

"Interesting," said Johan, "I've got to put him somewhere, maybe I'll take him there and get a look myself. Where did they put her?"

"Dockside detention. If you are headed there, I'll just make a note and have you sign for this…" Nilsson regarded Angus, "...thing."

Paperwork done and a hearty hug later, the trio were on their way to the dockside detention center. Ynghild spoke first.

"I hear she's a fraud even in the Veyns. Do we have time for your side quest?"

Angus cut in. "She's no side quest. Alene is a great friend and a worthy foe to the Ivon. She deserves to be there. Plus, if we don't have her, the Ivon has leverage - over both of us." He nodded meaningfully toward Johan, who kept his face stoic and forward.

"Leverage, eh?" Ynghild teased. "Does this Usurper hold a place in my Johan's hard heart?"

The man did not speak, merely led them inexorably toward Alene.

Chapter 40

The Early Birds

Farmers are accustomed to an early rise. This day, these farmers rose particularly early, but not to water animals or milk cattle. They were here to plant. They intended to plant every Ivonian soldier in the ground before the day was through.

And unlike every other battle in recent memory, the men did not come alone. Their wives, their sisters, and their mothers took positions right along with the fathers, brothers, and sons. This was more than a battle for territory. This was a battle for the very soul of Gymdeithas Fasnach and all the souls that had taken the pledge.

Patrick looked at the paper they had voted on and signed it. If this did not work, he was signing his own death warrant for treason against the Ivon, but so be it. He took his stand for the Sliver, for Pentref, and for Billy and Zane.

Timothy read the missive and nodded. Then he rolled it tightly and slid it into the tube attached to a long arrow. This he sealed in wax, then dipped the tip in tar. He walked across the pre-dawn battlefield to stand alone on the road just outside the Northgate. He could see several Ivonian guards standing together, peering into the darkness.

Timothy tapped his candle to the arrow tip, aimed, and drew the bowstring back deeply. Then a bit more, the bow complained about his beyond-capacity draw. His now-flaming arrow rose in a perfect arc, clearly visible for a mile in either direction. As it fell towards the guard tower, two of the three men stepped to the side. But their sergeant stood rooted, mesmerized by such a beautiful shot.

"Amazing," he started, followed by, "Oh!" as the arrow sunk itself deep into his chest. Timothy had taught a whole generation of hunters how to make a killing blow, and this was an excellent example.

The other two guards jumped to the sergeant's side. One tried tending to the man, but he was already dead. The other opened the tube in Timothy's arrow and retrieved the letter. It read:

The People of Gymdeithas Fasnach call.
We call for the return of our sons taken as conscripts to fight for causes they know not.
We call for recognition of our Independence from Ivonia
We call for the return of our stores of grain, stolen by the Ivon's agents
We call for our basic human rights
And today,
We call for the men who killed our children and burned our silos.

We call for justice.

We await your reply on the battlefield, but only for the morning. By mid-day, we will stop calling and act.

The guard took time to read the note. He wasn't a guard because reading was his strong suit. As he understood the importance and urgency, he stopped reading and rolled the note back up. He sprinted to the base of the tower with the missive.

Out in the field, two men on horseback rode from the center of Patrick's line with torches, lighting one to the next to illuminate the faces of the people arrayed against the Ivon. Several thousand strong, with hundreds of bows behind a varied line of fighters.

The alarm went up from the Northgate, raising soldiers from rest. Within thirty minutes, bows stood at the ready across the battlements, with units of foot soldiers mustering inside the gate itself. Thousands. More than a match for the troops arrayed outside.

These men laughed, gave high fives, and whispered jokes in each other's ears, drawing laughter and nods. Morale was high. The message was clear, they would teach these farmers a lesson, and let them know where the real power lay in the region.

----- -----

Several miles east, Thannon observed from the cupola above the hayloft in a barn just outside Ivonia's Eastgate. He could just make out Koksal's land train. Too far to see what Bedwyn was preparing with him. Whatever it was, they'd be successful. Bedwyn always was.

Thannon found himself musing about how much of a privilege he had experienced as the progeny of not only a dwarven King but the greatest strategist in living memory. He hoped that one day he would be able to fill half of Bedwyn's shoes - but also hoped that day would be far, far off.

He looked back at the gate. It was huge. Even seventy dwarves would not be able to ram the gate down. Perhaps Bedwyn could draw out the attack? And the wall, while again not the best work, was tall and thick. This would not be easy.

He studied the land in between the barn and the gate. A hedgerow ran along the southern edge of the road, just high enough to mask dwarves marching single-file. That might be their way.

It bothered him not to know, however. This would be his first action not under the direct command of General Foresight. Thannon was used to knowing how an attack would go. That would not be the case today.

As he thought about it more, he was likewise unsure about why Bedwyn would have separated their group like this. Was it just to give his kid a chance to be a leader? He could not say.

He climbed down to the hayloft and called his troops together for a pre-fight chat.

"Fellow dwarves of the Smaragdine Holt: Hear me! Today we fight an enemy we don't have much contact with. I hope that this will prove to be a much less bloody conflict than the Battle of East Ivonsport, but we won't know until long after it is over.

"Their army isn't showing itself. We have no idea who we will encounter, and even Bedwyn doesn't have a clear picture of the result. Are we worried?"

"No!" Rang out the shouted reply.

"Are we ready for anything?"

"Aye!"

"Will we fight to the last dwarf, no matter what?"

"No matter what!"

"That's right, dwarves!" Thannon wrapped up the call and response. "We are the best ground fighters on the Cyfandir, by a long margin. Our foot soldiers can go toe to hoof with cavalry, even. We may get that chance.

"We are going to win this fight. And I intend to prevail with as few losses as possible. For that, I'll need several things from you:

"First, as we've already established, everyone fights, nobody quits. Just keep going and listen for the changes. There will be changes.

"Second, we fight clean. Once engaged, in each combat anything goes, but we don't attack the unarmed. We don't burn anything that isn't an immediate threat. We don't steal. We don't plunder.

"Basically, if you wouldn't do it with Bedwyn watching, then don't do it at all."

Dwarves young and old nodded assent.

"Finally, I need you to - once the fight starts - be as loud and terrible as possible. Scream the old battlecries. Howl like a direwolf. Cheer each other on.

"That, my fellow Smaragdines, is not how we fight. It is how we WIN!"

The company shook the dust off every surface in the old barn with their resonant cheer. Thannon smiled and returned to the cupola to watch for Bedwyn's signal. They were ready.

Chapter 41

Level Detente

Johan led the trio along twisting back alleys. At one point he stole a blue-and-white-striped cloak and hood from a clothesline and placed it over Angus' shining armor. They kept him bound, with his axe strapped to his back.

"Don't worry," tittered Ynghild, "You look great. Like my aunt Moira."

"So your aunt is a bit of a looker, eh?" Angus chuckled back.

"Not really. She's big in the middle and needs a good shave."

The humans might not be able to see Angus' sneer, but it was there.

A half-hour later they stepped up to the gate at the Ivon's Dockside Detention Center. Johan took the lead, pulling the tin cup that hung from a loose string below the door handle. Pulling until the person on the other side of the door pulled back, he kept tension in the string. "Johan C'Antrell with a prisoner transfer. Open up."

"Never heard of you."

"You must be new."

"Aye, but I still don't know you, sir. Let me check the list."

"Go right ahead."

The string slackened for a moment as the guard looked through several pages of names.

"I'm sorry, sir, but you aren't on the list."

"Look, is Victor in there?"

"On vacation, sir. I'm the only one here."

Johan shook his head and added an increasing amount of tension to the string. "I am Johan C'Antrell. Angel of the highest order, personal confidant of the Ivon. LET. ME. IN!"

"I'm afraid I can't do that, sir. It isn't by the book!"

Johan pulled just a bit more, waiting for the telltale tug on the other end before releasing the tin cup. A satisfying "Thock!" came from the other side of the door, followed by a sound like a dropped sack of potatoes.

"Boring conversation anyway," quipped Johan. "Ynghild, will you do the honors?"

The voluptuous companion stepped forward with a grin, retrieving a small leather tool roll from a sleeve. "I thought you'd never ask." The door was open in a few seconds, and the three proceeded inside.

Johan stepped over the unconscious guard and went straight for the logbook, looking for any sign of Alene's imprisonment. Angus twisted out of his handcuffs - they had never really been connected. The dwarf started down the corridor, hopping up to see who was in each cell.

Four cells in, he spotted Alene and hopped up again to make sure. The small, barred porthole in each door was just about forehead height for him.

"Aren't you a little short for a jail guard?" she joked. Angus grabbed the bars and hauled himself up to look through them.

"It's me, Angus. I'm here with Johan. We're here to rescue you!"

"Johan? Where?" she asked urgently as Angus eased the bolt and opened her door. Alene raced back up the corridor to find Johan. She passed Ynghild first.

"Your Majesty," Ynghild began, "May I present Johan C'Antrell…" She cut off when Alene leapt into Johan's arms and kissed him forcefully. "I see you've met."

The embrace ended as abruptly as it began, and Alene straightened her skirts. "Took you long enough. Where have you been?"

"Everywhere. A lot has happened since we last met. Let me introduce Ynghild, a fellow Gatherer who is likewise disillusioned with the Ivon."

"Charmed, I'm sure," replied Alene, addressing Ynghild. "Can she fight?"

Ynghild crossed her arms, wearing a look between outrage and amusement.

"With the best of them, yes," Johan stated. "She's agreed to help us with the Ivon."

Alene nodded. “Good. When do we dance with the Ivon?”

“As soon as we stop talking and start walking,” said Ynghild. The words dripped out of her mouth, disdain coated with politeness.

----- -----

The Ivon finished reading Patrick’s note and walked to his writing desk. There he held the paper over a candle until it burned, turning the missive this way and that to maximize the fire. He dropped it to the azure floor tiles and walked up the stairs to his northern balcony.

“So they want their conscripts back? What do you think, General?” The Ivon’s calm demeanor belied a furious storm underneath.

“They don’t constitute a threat militarily, Ivon.” The General was matter-of-fact, dispassionate. “Their numbers are even less than it appears, sire. They have women in their ranks. A lot of women.”

“Young women can be as dangerous as young men, with the right weapon.”

“Well, sire, some are young. More are older women, past child-bearing age, I suspect.”

The Ivon considered this for a moment. “That might be even more dangerous. Well, let us not keep them waiting. Send them their conscripts.”

“Sire?”

“You heard me. Send them back. In fact, let me be even more generous. Mix them into non-conscript units. Send them all together in a charge. We will see what happens when grandmother meets grandson in battle, eh?”

“It… shall be so.” The General turned to leave.

“Set our heavy infantry as a relief force, but let the conscripts give all they can first. Then mop up.”

The General nodded and turned away again.

“No survivors, General,” the Ivon said. “Be sure of it.”

----- -----

A few back alleys later, Johan and company entered a small shed that concealed an entrance to the cellars and tunnels that ran under the Ivon’s palace. Carved into sandstone, much of the way was plastered - thick white stuff. Angus was not impressed; this was novice-level tunneling at best.

Eventually, a blue door with an Angel's sigil blocked the way. Johan produced a key and opened the door silently; they all slipped in. Ynghild and Johan then moved to block the entrance with barrels and furniture, making it difficult to follow them.

"There will only be a few guards between here and there. We don't want somebody like Brennan to pop up behind us," Ynghild explained. "Angus, I'm sorry, you won't like this next part." She indicated a small gap in the wall, hidden in the shadows. "Follow me. And be as quiet as possible."

It was a very dark and very tight set of spiral stairs, Angus discovered. His armor brushed against plastered walls on either side. After a few moments of walking in the near-dark, they reached a platform.

Johan whispered, "Yng, you set up Angus on a rope to keep us from getting separated. I'll rig Alene."

Ynghild replied with a like-whispered, "It'll be my pleasure!" With that, she recovered a bundle of rope hung amongst a dozen similar kits, and snaked the loop around each leg, his waist, and a loop pulling each shoulder back into a proper posture. "Now stand up straight, this might pinch," she said, as she tightened the harness around him.

Angus, extremely uncomfortable with the fact that this woman was tying him up again, looked up. Even with his dark-adept vision, he could not see the ceiling in this smallish room. He turned obediently when Ynghild pressed his shoulders, and she connected another line to his harness. He tried to splutter when she pressed a balled gag into his mouth and secured it from behind. Then she pulled the pin that held another line on the other side of the wall, saying sweetly, "Shush now, or he'll hear!"

Angus wanted to object, but he found himself pulled off his feet by the harness, wind whistling in his ears as he ascended hundreds of feet in seconds. When he could no longer see his party, he felt the rising decelerate to a stop. Something whooshed up from below, and Johan dangled beside Angus in mere seconds.

Johan helped them to the platform and unharnessed the two. Alene and Ynghild followed, nearly silently. Fits of laughter and giggles had to be stifled; Angus was not amused. His face after

Alene removed his gag said it all - there would be a reckoning after this, for both Angels.

----- -----

Sammel raced to don his chainmail and grab his spear, speeding past the sergeant on the way out of the barracks. The morning had come too quickly. Was this another of their endless drills? Would he end up digging another latrine at the training grounds? It was always impossible to tell.

In the early morning light, he was astounded at how many recruits and conscripts mustered. They formed up quickly, marching toward the Northgate. A soldier Sammel knew from his early days at the Greenway walked up to his sergeant, handing him a green bundle and sharing a couple of words before moving on to chat with the next group of conscripts.

"It appears the Lieutenant wants us to honor where we come from today. Green sashes to indicate where in Ivonia we come from. Stay true to your training, stay true to your homeland! And whatever happens, stick together, green with green!" The sergeant was sharp but muted this morning.

Lines of conscripts formed up with white-clad Ivonian soldiers, each wearing a simple blue sash that indicated a birth here in the city proper. Also, the lighter, more maneuverable troops in light armor lined up, carrying polearms for the most part.

As they approached the Northgate, it swung open, and the column proceeded through without breaking pace. Once past the wall, moat, and new fortifications, they split left and right to make a line of soldiers a thousand men wide and three deep. Conscripted and native-born units alternated places.

While Sammel noticed this, it was the other end of the field that concerned him. Several thousand farmers, hunters, and craftsmen faced them. Dressed as a working person might from the Greenway to the Sliver, these people looked familiar.

"Are those women in their ranks?" he asked the young man next to him.

"Aye, it appears so."

"Those look like our people," Sammel whispered.

"Aye, it appears so," whispered his sergeant, walking the line to check his men's readiness. "Remember what I said. Stay together for your homeland, no matter what." The Pentref native winked.

----- -----

Timothy sidled up to Patrick. “Are you seeing this?”

“Aye,” Patrick replied grimly. “We’re outnumbered.”

“True,” replied Timothy, “but by who?”

“Skirmishers. Thousands of skirmishers. Why no heavy infantry? Why no cavalry?”

Timothy laughed. “There might be a reason I’m the hunter and you are the blacksmith after all. Look more closely.”

“Half of them wear the Green,” Patrick marveled. “Do they not know?”

“I guess we’ll find out soon enough. I’ll have the archers aim for the blue first.”

“Good call.”

Chapter 42

Major Strokes

Once the last line of Angus' harness had been removed from its uncomfortable placement, Johan led the four up another sideways staircase. This one curved as it rose. At the top, Johan and Ynghild emerged first, sliding from a hidden niche in the angled rafters. They silently navigated the perfectly smooth timbers until they were each right above one of the Ivon's guards.

Knives drawn, they dropped onto the unsuspecting elites and worked quickly to muffle voices and slit throats. They signaled for Angus and Alene to come down.

Alene launched herself from the niche to a bar on the fixed ceiling lamp. Swinging past, she tucked her feet and landed after a double backflip to end between Johan and Ynghild. "Nice work," she whispered. "Now what?"

Johan replied by hurtling over to the place where Angus dangled from his fingertips, six inches too short to land on the desk. "I'll have to find another way out, I think, when this is done," he said in Johan's ear. "Dwarves never come up lacking, but sometimes we might be a bit short." Johan chuckled softly.

Alene was next to speak. "Where is the Ivon?"

Johan pointed to a northern passageway with a short stair and a door. "Up there, probably with advisors to watch the action at the Northgate. How should we take them?"

Ynghild smiled in her sultry way. "By surprise, of course. But first, I think we have two more guards outside the entry, no?"

They formulated a plan and took their places. Johan sat just inside the doorframe, and Angus behind the door. Alene and Ynghild opened it, looking every bit the helpless waifs they weren't.

"Could you please come help us? We're having trouble getting dressed for the Ivon."

The guards weren't surprised that there were unaccounted-for women in the Ivon's chambers and stepped in. Johan stabbed the first in the neck, then Angus stomped the door into the second, knocking him down. Two strides later, the killing blow came from Angus' axe, no sound allowed.

They shoved the corpses under the Ivon's prodigious bed and took positions for their next task - killing the Ivon.

----- -----

Dawn broke as the great city of Ivonia looked to its north and east gates for the coming battle. Light shattered the darkness with inexorable force, illuminating a populace and the challenges they'd face before dark.

Sailors worked steadily to put out smoldering remnants of the fires set by Alene. They could not field a functional navy until considerable repairs were effected; that would take some time. They were armed and angry, however, and ready to repel any attacks from the sea.

Their watchmen scoured the horizon, aware of a small contingent of Veynsian Navy and tracking more. Every eye strained to ensure no further sneak attacks. What they did not see was the shape that rose from the beaches to the west, clearing the impenetrable cliffs on that side of the city with ease.

Uvrede gloried in the power she still had. Leaving another crater on the beach where her launching wingbeats moved barnfuls of air in seconds, she gained altitude with the sun's rise. The sunshine felt wonderful. Once a thousand or so feet up, she looked over her shoulder to see if the ghost of Zonka still haunted her.

"I'm still here," the crone replied to the question unasked. "If I were still alive, I might be afraid. I never got the chance to fly."

Uvrede smiled, a great toothy chasm framed by gold-rimmed lips. "Fun, isn't it? Don't lose me now, this is what we came here for."

"That it is. What shall we do first? Take a look around?"

"Yessss. Let's do that." Uvrede's old Drakhonic accent drawled heavily this morning. She seemed transported to an earlier time when her power was greatest. The broken glass in her scales positively jingled.

Within a few minutes, they circled high above. The city looked much like the maps Zonka had studied and she got her bearings from certain landmarks. Two roads led in and out of the place, one to the north and one to the east. These intersections were named Northgate and Eastgate. *Humans are so creative,* she thought dryly, *I wonder what they call that tall tower? Likely the tall tower.*[11]

"Let's fly over the southern edge, if you will."

"Of course."

They sped downwards, tears blinding Zonka. She closed her eyes against the wind as they approached, opening them briefly here and there to keep oriented. As they got within a few dozen feet of the city's peaks and balconies, Uvrede spoke again.

"It has been so long since I've done this. Would you mind terribly if I were to use some of these rooftops for target practice?"

"Oh, do!" Zonka tittered. "Please do!"

Uvrede slowed here at a lower altitude for accuracy, targeting the taller towers on the southern border. Blue tiles exploded again and again as fires lit up the wooden trusses underneath the rooftops. It was quite a spectacle.

They continued this way for a minute or so until the Eastgate emerged into sight. Zonka saw the sparkle of plate armor and tapped the dragon on the shoulder. Uvrede, still not questioning how she could feel a ghost, looked back, then followed Zonka's pointed finger.

Giggling that vibratory dragon laugh again, Uvrede gleefully squeezed into the road that led to the armored cavalry Zonka had spotted. Wings held high and back, she breathed flame over a large portion of the horsemen, who opened the gate. Uvrede skidded to a landing, cobbles flying like shrapnel as she slid her tail around in an open plaza, breathing fire and igniting a four-story conflagration all around her.

Surrounded by flames on three sides, she grinned as the unit before her made individual choices. Most writhed in flames, dying horrible deaths; the remainder raced out of the gate they had just opened. As the last horse escaped through the wall, the dragon heard an other-worldly whistle from the gate's far side.

She rose again to investigate, propelling loose cobblestones and debris away into the surrounding buildings and fanning the flames.

---

[11] She wasn't wrong; or at least not far-wrong. The Ivon had to have the tallest tower, so he named it thus. He even signed a law stating that no tower could ever be more than half as tall as his tallest tower, to preserve his view.

----- -----

"They've opened the gate!" Bedwyn was excited and concerned. He hadn't expected this, not at all. "Full steam, Koksal, let's make sure they can't close it again!"

As Koksal increased speed westward on the East Road, he pulled the whistle loudly.

"What're you doing?" shouted Bedwyn. "You'll give us away!"

"I wouldn't want to run over anyone accidentally," replied the goblin engineer. "I'm still traumatized after the battle at East Ivonsport. Do you know how long I worked to clear the ways of pieces of people?"

"Well, what's done is done. They know we are here now. At least it looks like heavy cavalry, and a small unit at that. We'll be fine."

The dwarf saw Koksal's expression freeze slack-jawed. Following his gaze back towards Ivonia's Eastgate, he watched as a gigantic dragon ascended above the wall. A lone orc rode the dragon's back.

"That's new. A real dragon, and a big one at that! Koksal, turn that steam up. Our wallrender grapple just got repurposed into a dragonspear. Give me everything you have, or we might not make it through."

Chief Engineer Koksal turned the knob below the power dial until it was wide open. The overtaxed boiler groaned and shook and tortured valves rattled. "She can't take much more of this, General!"

"She'll hold together. Either this works or we won't be here tomorrow."

"Even if it does work, we might not survive the blast!" Koksal shot back, fretting over the controls.

The dwarf frantically worked on the elevation and angle, desperately hoping for a fatal hit on the only shot he'd get. He paused to watch the dragon incinerate the last of the cavalry and saw the barn next to the road explode with dwarves running to attack a dragon.

"Blow that whistle, Koksal!"

The goblin leaned on the whistle with all his might, and it worked. The dragon once again looked with curiosity towards the land train, making a beeline for the unlikely pair of dwarf and goblin.

"Almost there... Almost there..." Bedwyn repeated, until he was sure of his shot.

ShhhhFOOOMP! The bolt sailed away, faster than any projectile Bedwyn had ever seen. Hoses burst, tanks ruptured, and the center of the train suffered catastrophic failure from the impact, sliding sideways to a stop.

Bedwyn Foresight watched as the giant projectile sailed at the dragon in slow motion, heading straight for its heart. He watched as she started to roll away. The point shattered the remnants of glassy armor on her chest, sliding down to her belly, trying to find a purchase but never succeeding.

The furious but only lightly wounded dragon headed straight for the train, exuding flame as she came into range.

"I should have seen this coming. Go on, Thannon, you'll be gre-"

----- -----

Company captains raced back and forth along the Ivonian lines, shouting instructions and encouragement for the imminent charge. "Don't break formation!" and "Keep fighting as long as you draw breath!" and "Never give up, never surrender!" Every quote closed with a variation of "for the Ivon!"

Sammel felt the cold sweat come, body shaking from the adrenaline rush. He'd never seen combat before, despite training for two years straight. His physique rippled with muscle now, and he knew - theoretically - the fast ways to kill a man.

After five minutes of these short speeches, horns blew. Several thousand men took the first step in a charge that would see hundreds, if not thousands, of people dead. The second step came faster, and within three seconds, they charged screaming at a full run.

The Battle of the North Green had begun.

Chapter 43

Cunning Riposte

Booms of explosions washed over the tower, with no source in sight. The Ivon tsked in annoyance, unwilling to give up his prime seat as his revenge unfolded.

"Go see what that is, will you? I want to watch these traitors kill each other."

"Yes, m'Lord."

Two captains left smartly, leaving the Ivon alone with a general and a colonel to watch the main battle unfold.

"Nothing else matters. These adherents of Gymdeithas Fasnach started our conflict, and we'll let them end it, too. Send in our heavy infantry behind."

The Colonel waved two colored flags in a pattern, stopping for a beat at each pose. A keen-eyed observer might recognize a matching semaphore operator on top of the Northgate, replying and translating orders to the sergeants on the ground.

Horns sounded and the line of light infantry containing the conscripted troops began their charge: first a few walking steps, then a jog, then a fast run.

"Yes, minions. Destroy each other and ensure that no town or village will dare dispute my rule ever again!" The Ivon laughed villainously, a "Muahahaha!" that left no doubt as to who the bad guy might be.

The Ivon no longer cared if he was viewed as the bad guy. He desired only to be feared and obeyed, not loved and respected. He had designed this battle to fulfill the fear part.

----- -----

The captains stepped through the door into the Ivon's chambers. Initially headed to the large, south-facing balcony, they paused when beckoned to the Ivon's bed.

"You aren't the Ivon," a shapely woman stated from her reclined position on the deep blue duvet. She wasn't wearing much. "But I suppose you can distract me while I wait."

The captains appeared confused, forgetting for a moment their task. They both stood riveted to the spot, staring.

"Who are you?"

"Me? You can call me Allus. I'm the last woman you'll ever see." She smiled wickedly.

"I don't-" started one man, cut off as Johan's knife cut his throat. The second turned just in time to see Angus' pick enter his ribcage and stop his heart.

"Impressive. Did you two practice that?" Ynghild asked.

"These two have saved my life before," said Alene, stepping from behind a curtain. "Together they slew sixty archers that threatened me and my men at Veynsport."

"Really!" replied Ynghild. "Sixty is a rather unbelievable number. Johan is good, but not sixty-men good."

Johan and Angus busied themselves with tossing the dead captains and the blood-soaked rug they had occupied over the railing.

"Sixty was the number. They were both sorely wounded and near death." Alene insisted. "If it weren't for Indaria, they…"

"Indaria?" Inquired Ynghild.

"Yes, the elven mage Indaria."

"Ah, that makes the story so much more believable," chuckled Ynghild.

Alene stopped talking and turned red as Johan and Angus returned to their hiding spots for the next foray. She shot Ynghild a venomous look before stepping behind her curtain again.

----- -----

Over the wall, Uvrede spotted the retreating cavalry racing away unformed. She spat flame and ended each one without changing her now-lazy flight. A large barn just off the road grabbed her attention, and she flapped once toward it before another eerie whistle sounded farther down the road. Ignoring the mundane barn for a moment, she flew on towards the whistle.

"Dwarves!" screamed Zonka. "That machine has dwarves aboard, I can see them from here! Destroy them! Kill them all!"

"I thought you said this would be hard," laughed Uvrede. She turned her head back forward in time to see a projectile coming right for her. She rolled midair, a maneuver taught to her by her mother so many thousands of years ago. Sacrificial glass armor shattered on the impact.

The move, together with her armor, saved her from what might have been a fatal blow.

"That is as close as I've ever been to death," the dragon stated calmly. "Time to end this one."

Two wingbeats brought her within breath range, and she reduced the train to a sputtering pile of slag, secondary explosions continuing for seconds. She wheeled and rose high again, re-assessing the situation.

Zonka stopped her maniacal cackling long enough to congratulate the dragon on her victory. "You keep up this pace, and I'll stop haunting you very soon. We kill dwarves until we get to the right one - the dwarf that haunts my dreams, then we can part ways."

"My dear Zonka, I'm not excited about parting ways. You have become something I haven't known in many millennia." The dragon choked back a sob. "You have become a friend."

"I feel the same." Zonka was being honest for once. "Two old birds like us have a different perspective than most. It has been a true pleasure getting to kno- DWARVES! Off to the north, see the shining armor?"

Uvrede left the Eastgate as suddenly as she had arrived, heading towards several lines of infantry a mile or so to the northwest. So many dwarves to kill. The feeling was delectable.

----- -----

As they ran, Sammel experienced a wide range of emotions. Euphoria that he was about to find out how well his training had prepared him. Fear that he might be among the dead at the end of the battle. Concern over likely wounds and the pain they might bring. Terror at the thought of being forever changed physically and emotionally.

His feet hit the ground in rhythm with his companions. Would they hesitate when they had to fight their own? Would he? Could he kill another from the Greenway? For that matter, he wasn't sure he could kill any Ivonian. But here he was, moments away from finding out.

Then he heard his sergeant's voice yell out, "Men of the Green, hold up!" That call echoed throughout the line and his platoon slowed to a walk. Sammel looked to the right and left and saw all of the men with green sashes now held mid-field, as the rest continued their charge.

Arrows arced high above the battlefield, raining heavily on the ranks of city-born Ivonian skirmishers. Men fell out of the ranks and died, or writhed wounded on the reddening green grass. By the time the troops clashed with Gymdeithas Fasnach in close combat, their numbers had dwindled to the hundreds.

"For the Greenway! For the Sliver! For Pentref! No Prisoners!" Tears streamed down the sergeant's face as he directed his platoon to dive into the rear of the Ivonian ranks, finishing the blue-sashed natives off. Sammel moved on with the group, mind full of questions and relief at not having to fight family and friends.

Sammel's first kill was dispatching an arrow-wounded Ivonian as they passed. 'No prisoners' was a very specific directive, but one he understood. Prisoners would take a portion of Gymdeithas Fasnach's troops to maintain, and their already thin numbers would be a concern.

As the lines met, handshakes, greetings, and embraces ensued. The celebration was brief, as a new line formed up on the opposite side of the field - the Ivon's elite troops. Heavy plate armor shone in the morning sun, naked swords and shields glinting as they were readied for action.

----- -----

"Open the gate!" screamed the violently promoted new Captain of the Ivon's First Heavy Cavalry. A great, roaring, shimmering bronze shape had just incinerated roughly seventy percent of his unit, leaving burning corpses blocking him and the vanguard in the eastern gatehouse.

"What the hell was that?" shouted his second, terror showing in wide eyes. "I've never seen anything like it!"

"Does it matter?" replied the Captain. "I think we might outrun it, but I have no idea how to face power like that."

"It's a dragon, I saw it plain as day." That comment came from an indigent old man slumped against the wall. "Never really believed the stories."

As the drawbridge before them lowered over the moat, a new wonder sounded - a high-pitched whistling, like a boiling kettle. But this whistling was scaled up like the massive, fiery attack they had just survived.

"Away! Make for that barn!" commanded the Captain, remembering his training. "Fast as you can! We'll regroup in there where that… thing can't see us!" He kicked his steed into a gallop, launching towards the agricultural building.

He raced along the road, shod hooves clattering on cobbles. This was bad for his horse, so he swerved to the grassy shoulder as soon as he could. His mount found an extra gear in the softer footing, and the Captain wondered if they might make cover in time.

A stolen glance over his shoulder confirmed the old man's guess. The Captain had heard of dragons in fairy tales but never expected to see one. Dragons were supposed to be great, powerful creatures that could burn a knight to ash with a breath.

This Dragon shimmered in the morning light, rays of reflected dawn shooting off in all directions. And it was a great beast, the size of a several-story home! And something rode it, too. A hulking humanoid shape trailing crazed, rough ribbons in grays and greens and browns.

The dragon watched initially over the woods to the east, in the direction of that amped-up whistling. But just as the Captain thought they might have escaped, the leviathan swiveled her head in their direction. Flame gouted from its mouth, catching first the horsemen at the rear, then continuing to the front of the column.

The Captain had remembered his training, but it wasn't enough to save his men, or himself. He screamed in agony as the flames took him.

Chapter 44

Coup Count

The Ivon watched the first lines converge, a wicked, toothy smile bisecting his visage. His skirmishers contained most of the non-naturalized conscripts, but as the lines closed the gap, a new one opened. A portion of the skirmishers paused their charge, making a second line behind the main charge.

"Is this a new strategy of yours?" He asked the general nearest. "I'm not familiar with the maneuver."

"Neither am I," said the first, turning to the second. "Is this yours?"

"Unfortunately, no." The man signaled with flags to the relay at the gate. "But I do see what is going on. And you won't like it."

The trio turned back to observe the clash unfold. The forward part of the skirmisher line crashed into Gymdeithas Fasnach's but with much less impact due to their diminished numbers. The second line crashed in soon after, attacking the Ivon's men.

"Explain." The Ivon's demeanor was stoic, but both generals knew that it was a waterbird expression - calm on top, but frenetic under the surface.

"You've been betrayed, sir."

"Betrayed?"

"Yes, sir." He offered his spyglass. "Note the green sashes. The conscripts must have organized, and they held back in order to attack our native skirmishers from behind. Dreadfully dishonorable."

The Ivon watched as his native-born skirmishers diminished, until the conscripts stood amongst the antagonizing force, exchanging embraces.

"This I cannot accept. Destroy them."

"Consider it done, M'Lord. See now, your elite heavy infantry lines up across from them. The villains may be reunited, but they will shortly be united in death."

On cue, the Ivon's best troops formed up where the skirmishers had stood moments earlier. They doubled the numbers Gymdeithas Fasnach fielded. The result was still guaranteed.

"They haven't returned," tsked the Ivon, looking over his shoulder with annoyance. "I should like to learn what those booming noises were."

"The Norfield is set, Ivon. We can adjourn for a time to observe the happenings to the south."

The three started towards the door that led into the Ivon's chambers. The Ivon himself paused for one last look to the north, aware of a rising smell of fires and burning.

----- -----

Angus stood behind the inward-opening door, pressing his back to the stones. He watched as a tall man, entirely clad in blue, stepped in with confidence. He tried not to look at Ynghild, who had draped herself across the Ivon's four-posted bed in a particularly alluring position. The general was not likewise inclined to dismiss her.

She spoke up.

"Why hello, boys. You aren't who I expected, but I can work with this."

"Who are you?" The man spoke with a commanding voice. "Why are you here?"

"I'm surprised you don't know," She giggled playfully, "Perhaps I should leave you two alone?"

On the word "two" her eyes met Angus', and he shouldered the door shut behind the second blue-clad man, raising his axe overhead for a strike. The man turned, gasping, just in time to experience being of two minds. Angus' axe stuck deep, and he released it as his victim fell forward to block the door with his draining corpse.

The remaining general whirled to face Angus, bejeweled saber in hand. He took two steps to the left, snatching a thick robe from a hook. This he flipped over his arm several times, forming a rudimentary shield.

The dwarf reached towards his belt knife, certainly a deadly tool. He smiled as he moved his hands out in front of him, clapping metal gauntlets and affecting a smile. The two squared off and prowled in a circle, eyes never leaving the other.

After a few steps, the general tried a thrust - and missed. His foot had slipped on the waxed, bare stone floor where a rug usually resided. He looked at the floor and saw the remains of bloody drag marks leading to the southern balcony.

He made to shout for the guards but found himself unable to scream. Blood bubbled from his throat where the now-standing Ynghild had slashed it, sneaking up when his back was to her. The light left his eyes as he crumpled to the floor.

Angus dragged the corpse to the balcony and tossed it over, then went back to retrieve his axe. He leaned the red-gleaming blade in his hiding place as Ynghild threw the lock. Angus repeated the disposal as a thud sounded on the other side of the door.

"Did you lock me out of my chambers?" The Ivon was furious. "Open this door immediately!"

Angus ducked around the edge of the southern balcony, eyeing hiding spots in the rafters he knew held Alene and Johan. He wished for his axe.

"I don't know how that happened," babbled a worried Ynghild as she opened the door and stepped back. "One of your men must have-"

"Where are my men?" He shouted. "What have you done?"

Ynghild backed up until she was against the bed and leaned over conspiratorially. "They said you were stressed. I thought I might help with that."

The Ivon strode over towards her, hand raised high for a disciplinary slap. "Where are my men?" he shouted again but was cut off by a weight on his shoulders.

Alene landed her feet expertly upon the Ivon's shoulders on her way down from the rafters. The two landed in a heap, Alene executing a perfect shoulder roll, coming up to her feet facing the prone Ivon. "Your men are the least of your worries. Do you not see the smoke rising? Your city burns!" She finished looking over the balcony, gesturing to the evidence.

The Ivon rose to his hands and knees, only to fall forward again, one hand shooting beneath his bed as he landed. He retrieved his hidden crossbow, pointed at Alene, and fired. The shot hit her in the leg, the impact knocking it out from under her.

Standing, the Ivon strode to loom over Alene, who writhed on the ground.

"Who," he asked Ynghild, who stood next to him, "is this impudent waif?"

"I have no idea. Perhaps your men sent her up to play with us?"

The Ivon's hand shot towards Ynghild, redirecting her knife. He dropped the crossbow and grabbed her hand just above the wrist. With a quick step behind and a strategic twist, she was bent over with her own knife at her back.

"Oh, niece, what have you done? I taught you everything you know!" He slapped the pommel, effecting a backstab on the intended backstabber. He pushed her away, she slid to a stop next to a rising Alene.

Ynghild coughed, sputtered, and gasped, spitting blood onto the stone floor. She looked up at Alene, who met her gaze, then faced the Ivon.

"You still don't know who I am?" asked the Queen. "I am Alene, the rightful ruler of the Veyns, conqueror of East Ivonsport, and last night I burned your fleet. Now I am here to finish the job." As she spoke, she raised her Veynsian shortsword behind her and up, ready to strike.

"How very quaint, a Queen coming to do her own dirty work!" The Ivon laughed in disdain. "You are already beaten, child. Why not join me instead? There are many benefits to allying yourself to me, and to Ivonia. I'd rather not kill you."

"You," she spat, "disgust me. You have sent armies, navies, and even spies to attack and undermine my country and my rule. Now you will answer for your crimes. You will answer to me!"

"Ha!" the Ivon retorted. "I'll enjoy this then." A thud of men breaking into the room from the stairway beyond resounded, then again. "Let's do this. I've never killed a queen before!"

He stepped to a wall holding a myriad of sword choices and selected a rapier. He swished it through a quick pattern, then took a guard position opposite Alene.

"I don't know what you were thinking, coming here. I have yet to meet a female that can compete with me.

----- -----

Uvrede flew through the rising ball of flame and steam leftover from Koksal's train - there would certainly be no survivors. She wheeled to the south then west, remembering that barn just outside the gate.

"Climb. I think I see something," Zonka yelled. She had to shout, as the wind whooshing over her ears overpowered them.

Uvrede flapped, flapped, flapped the air downward, rising aggressively above the field, barn forgotten.

"Head north, please." Zonka was right onto the next target, not satisfied with one dwarf. As they reached several hundred feet above ground, a sparkling glint caught Zonka's eye. Soldiers in glistening plate armor, not unlike what the lone dwarf that haunted her dreams wore. "There!"

"A battle." Uvrede was not impressed. "Not a great battle, as those in the armor hold an advantage over their foes. See their numbers."

"The shiny ones - I think they're dwarves!"

"I don't think they are dwarves."

"They are!" Zonka screamed. "Burn them! Burn them all!"

Uvrede shrugged and started in that direction. It wouldn't be long before they knew for sure.

----- -----

Alene sneered and shouted a wordless warcry as she sliced downward strike after downward strike, tight circles alternating sides. Her footwork showed extensive training marred by the obvious crossbow bolt still protruding from her leg.

The Ivon took a one-half step back for each attack, parrying expertly. Just before he reached the far wall, he added a little sideways slap of his saber to a parry, effectively twisting the shaft in her leg. She screamed in pain and sank to her knees.

Across the room, Ynghild dragged herself to lean on a chest. Clearly out of the fight and losing blood fast. She wisely left the knife in place, knowing that she would bleed out faster if she removed it.

The door shuddered again, muffled shouts of men behind. The Ivon pointed his saber at Alene, prowling around her in a sinister orbit; his blade pointed at her throat.

"You've lost." He emitted a low laugh. "You did not bring enough men, while more of mine are just outside. I'll enjoy devising my revenges for your attacks. Choices have consequences." Without taking his eyes off of her, he backed towards the beaten door.

As he neared it, the Ivon felt another presence to his side and glanced. He saw Johan, face splattered with blood, just in time to feel Johan's foot stomp his hip. The Ivon folded as he was launched away, sliding on his bottom to land before his throne.

"Et tu, Johan?" The Ivon coughed. "It seems that everyone I hold dear is showing their true colors today. Small matter," he continued as he stood, "you won't be able to match my guards in your states. Give up now, while you still can. I might grant you a swift death, Johan."

"Excuse me," said Angus, striding across the room to retrieve his axe, "I'll need this to hold the door. Don't mind me, Johan, I'll give you the time you need."

"Angus, my dear friend," said Johan over his shoulder, "you always seem to be in the right place at the right time. I'm glad you are here, now." The man turned back to the monarch.

"You think we've betrayed you? You've betrayed us. Not just the abuse Ynghild and I have endured at your hand personally. No, you betray your people daily."

Johan moved closer to the Ivon, who now stood in front of his throne. The Ivon set his saber down gently - where he might be able to reach it should his Angel attack. Then he exclaimed with feigned piety:

"You speak as if you didn't learn your craft from me; as if you yourself had not participated. Your whole professional life has been in my service. You've stolen for me, you've murdered for me, and worse. You know my secrets because you are entirely complicit!"

"No longer! I choose who I serve, and it is not you!" Johan's eyes swept across the room, tarrying a moment on Alene's before looking over the southern balcony. "I choose to serve them, the people. Not just Ivonians, but all of the people."

The Ivon grimaced and his voice broke out angrily. "You owe your loyalty to me! I made you what you are today. I trained you, mentored you. And even now you carry the Angel's knife at your waist - I see it there! If you can't let go of the symbols that bind you to me, how can you ever be free? You are mine!"

Johan, facing away from the Ivon, felt the scrimshaw hilt of the stiletto blade the Ivon had given him on his graduation. It did indeed bind them, more than symbolically. Some of the more dastardly deeds Johan had done in the Ivon's name involved that very blade. His thumb loosened the knife in its sheath.

The door burst off its hinges, and three of the Ivon's royal guard followed it into the room. They paused when they saw Angus and took in the scene of Johan and the Ivon, and two wounded young women at opposite ends of the room. The Ivon was the only one unhurt - or at least unbloodied.

Johan moved with a blinding speed, drawing the knife and spinning to face the Ivon. "This knife? You can have it back, and everything that binds us!" With that he finished his spin, putting all of his motion and emotion into the blade.

The knife came too fast for the Ivon to dodge, and it lodged deep into his throat. The Ivon could only splutter and hack - he sat back onto his throne, dying. Johan approached speaking; the rest of the room was transfixed, watching the scene unfold.

"In exchange, I take your life as payment for the evil you did. I take your life for the evil you made me and Ynghild and Brennan and so many more do." Johan's face hovered in front of the Ivon's dimming eyes. He whispered the last. "I take your life for what you made me into."

From the corner, Ynghild wheezed, "That's not all you take. You take his crown." She pointed to the tapestry bearing the long-held motto 'Potentia per Sanguinem'. Johan looked and read it aloud, realizing its meaning for the first time in his life.

"Potentia per sanguinem,"[12] he said to the Ivon, retrieving his knife. He held it aloft, showing it to the royal guard. Each man knelt, fist to breast, saying in turn, "Ivon Nova."

Ivon Nova. The New Ivon.

---

[12] Potentia per sanguinem, or advancement through bloodletting, wasn't an official method in most places, but a past Ivon had made it so - largely to retroactively justify his violent rise to power.

Chapter 45

A Shining Example

"Those are not dwarves, Zonka." As the eternal orc and her eternal dragon approached, they discussed their next target. "Are you sure you want them dead? That is a large enough force to be useful."

"They look like dwarves to me!" Zonka panted. Images of a recumbent dwarf in shining armor ambushing her in her own home taunted her psyche. "Kill them! Burn them all!"

"I'd say it was your funeral, but we've already done that. This is your haunting. Their funeral." The dragon queen chuckled as she exhaled, then inhaled for her next burn.

----- -----

As the men lined up against their challengers, they joked and laughed with each other. This would be a day at the park. Very few of the men and women arrayed against them had any amount of armor, and many bore informal weapons.

"READY!" Shouted the commander from the center rank. The command was echoed by each unit leader along the line.

"STEADY!" The command riffled likewise.

"CHAAARRRRRRAAAAAAGH!" This command did not resonate and repeat, as a great whooshing noise washed over them, followed by heat and flames and agony.

----- -----

Johan was fast to press his advantage. "Strike his emblem. This marks the beginning of House C'Antrell! Send for my personal retainers, tell them to bring my coat of arms."

As one of the men scrambled down the stairs, the Ivon Nova continued. "Bring my father; he will command my forces through the rest of this…mess. Send doctors for these women, and put out those fires! I have other business to attend."

"Angus, I have need for a Protector like Alene. Are you interested in the job?"

"Hey! He's mine!" protested the queen from her seat.

"Not in the long run, Johan - er - Ivon, but I am here today."

"That you are. Watch my back."

"Aye." Angus eyed Ynghild, whom he still didn't trust. Though he thought the woman may have a different attack in mind.

Johan looked over the city to the south, noting that all of the fires were in a line, regardless of location on the street. *That indicates either dramatic planning or an attack from…* he raced to the northern balcony just in time to see the Ivon's best troops - *his* best troops - reduced to a long pile of writhing slag.

Grabbing the semaphore flags, he got the attention of the relay at the gate. This took a moment, as the relayman's first instinct was to hide from the great dragon now wheeling far into the western sky. Once contact was established, he sent the following message:

CEASE ATTACK
PARLAY
SHELTER
DRAGON
IVON NOVA

As the last was received, Johan himself cut the Ivon's flag from the north balcony. He waited to see a small parlay party sent north to invite Gymdeithas Fasnach into the walls. Angus, seeing a moment of transition, interjected.

"Well, Ivon, it seems you have a whole host of new problems. But one stands out. How do we deal with that?"

As the dragon continued her circle from west to south, the Ivon Nova went to the larger balcony. The dwarf followed, and they were joined by Alene and Ynghild, propping each other up to see this once-in-a-lifetime sight.

Johan started. "I have no idea. Perhaps we find a Dragonslayer? Do you know any?"

"I'll ask around," replied Angus, mirthlessly. *I am Angus Dragonbane. Last time was an accident, and now I'm asked by a head of state to repeat. And this dragon makes Szycthyis look like a toddler! I've no idea how this might work.* "I wish I had my spear. This axe will be useless against a beast that large." He pointed at Uvrede, who seemed to take personal offense, roaring as she turned to face the tower.

"Don't you know it is rude to point?" laughed Ynghild. "But seriously, hurry it up. It looks angry."

Johan jogged to the back side of the Ivon's chambers - *his* chambers - and pulled a large wall-hanging tapestry aside on a hidden-hinged mount. Angus followed, and tears formed at the corners of his eyes.

"May the Powers Deep bless you, youngster. If you weren't royalty, I'd hug you!"

----- -----

Rising after destroying another large part of Ivonia's small army, Uvrede raced out of bowshot before spiraling higher.

"These were not dwarves."

"I don't care anymore." Zonka scanned the horizon. "I know he is here, I can feel it. He is always where the action is. He probably causes it."

"There are thousands of buildings below us. None look dwarvish. If you want me to burn it all, we'll be flying for days." Uvrede felt a pang in a wing. "And I should let you know, I'm tiring. It has been thousands of years, after all. Perhaps we come back and finish tomorrow."

"Possibly, but I feel his presence. Look there, on that tower. Is that a glimmer? Gormoital perhaps?"

"Mmmm. I see that. Let's look, then I think I should rest."

"That is him! The one we came for! FLY!"

Uvrede flew. Roaring, she changed direction, flying along the wide avenue that led from the docks to the tower. Then, abruptly, her right wing cramped up. She corkscrewed once before recovering, just before hitting the cobblestones.

Rearing up, she braked with her wings while her claws ripped thousands of cobblestones up from the road, sending rocky shrapnel through windows and down alleyways. Stopping, she folded her wings and stretched her neck.

"What are you doing?" shouted Zonka. "We were so close!"

"Zonka, I'm old. My wings failed me. But I still have legs. I'll climb that tower If I have to." With that, she stood on four legs and walked the rest of the way, eyeing the tower for likely claw holds.

----- -----

Patrick and his army looked more like a hoe-down gone violent than a mass of soldiers. They hollered and yelled about winning the battle, how to defeat a dragon, and whether it was time to retire to their fields.

The chaos frustrated the leader, especially with the same chaotic ideas running around his own head. Then he spotted a semaphore signal from the gatehouse, beyond the burning line of troops and grass. It stated:

IVON DEAD
BATTLE OVER
DRAGON
ENTER
SHELTER

New possibilities swirled in Patrick's mind. He glanced up to note the state of the Ivon's banners; being struck and cut down from every standard and flagpole; some without ceremony at all.

It took little time for him to reason that his people would fare better against a dragon in the city than out in the open field - the remains of the heavy troops before him spoke to that fact. He moved quickly.

"To me! Relay my words - The Ivon is dead, the Dragon is here, the battle is over and we shelter in the city! Run!" He showed the way by running around the nearest end of the dragonfired stripe.

As they always had, Patrick's people followed him, one and all. They formed two lines, skirting both ends of the conflagration, coming together again unformed when they approached the drawbridge. There they slowed to a stop.

Through the darkened tunnel, they saw thousands of glints of reflected light dance on the stones above. A new armored host, nearly a hundred strong, trotted out. Timothy was at Patrick's shoulder in an instant.

"I thought they were done. I thought this was the best they had! We can't take on heavy infantry massed up like this. Besides," he finished, "these guys are huge! Look how wide they are! We'll be slaughtered!"

Patrick smiled and started jogging in. "Look again!" He called over his shoulder.

As Patrick got on level ground with the oncoming host, it was clear that these were not ordinary men. They weren't men at all. These were dwarves!

----- -----

The collection of antique and storied weapons hidden behind the Ivon's tapestry[13] spanned the gamut from swords to axes, flails to spears. But at the center of the display stood a fifteen-foot-long spear. Angus admired it for a moment, taking in the details.

The spearhead was formed from what looked like pattern-welded layers of steel and gormoital; known locally as mithril. The pattern was incredibly regular, all layers coming to a common point at the very tip. It sported a broadleaf shape, with a round, bejeweled ring where the tip met the long, wooden haft.

Runes (elvish, perhaps?[14]) ran the length of the wood but appeared to be wrought into the very fibers instead of carved as if the wood had grown that way. Lines of the ancient text spiraled and wove themselves through each other, following a pattern like one might see from a vine-wrapped tree trunk.

Another bejeweled ring joined a second broad-leaf spearhead at the bottom, just as spectacular, but not identical. Each one appeared to be the masterwork of a master of multiple disciplines. The dwarf pointed at it.

"That's the one," he said, "if you want a dwarf to kill a dragon, that's the kind of tool that might make it happen. I used to have a spear once, and I was somewhat good with it."

Johan dislodged the spear from its securement, frowning with concern as he struggled against its wobbling nature. The haft was

---

[13] This tapestry was an art work entitled peaceful farmers; depicting a group of men using tools like scythes and flails and pitchforks to gather and process wheat. The ex-Ivon had appreciated irony and juxtapositions.

[14] It was, in fact, elvish. A fact that Angus would soon learn, at great cost.

long and slender and was considerably more flexible than Ivonian spears the new Ivon had encountered.

"The Ivon called this his 'Sleagh Mhor'. Said it had killed monstrous creatures, including dragons. This seems a little rickety, Angus, but you're welcome to try it!" Johan tossed the spear vertically to the dwarf. Angus received the spear, bringing it to a horizontal position. Then he started to convulse…

----- -----

Geirdriful said the ceremonial words from memory, even though they were inscribed on the spear in front of her. Her lithe hands held an easy, powerful grace as they cradled and caressed the long weapon, each rune glowing as it was intoned and leaving a sparkling blue trail as the words faded into echoing memory.

She raised the polearm above her head, slowly twirling the double heads as the glow on the haft approached each end. When the glow reached the rings collaring the spearhead, they, too glowed; but in a rainbow of coloration that matched the many small gems and jewels. Fully in the dancing trance now, the svelte elf tipped one spearhead toward the stone floor, sliding it along the surface, sparks rising.

----- -----

The humans watched in alternating wonder and horror as Angus, the portly dwarf in heavy armor known more for his gluttony than his grace, danced. No normal dance this, each step was foreign in form and fully counter to the dwarf's normally reserved, efficient movements.

His legs crossed over each other, pirouetting en-pointe in his heavy leather-and-metal footwear. He spun in the opposite direction of the staff, lending more speed to an ever-accelerating movement. The spear whooshed through the air at first, then glowed from the center; armored hands danced from place to place, guiding the spin.

Angus spoke words in a drone at first, alien phrases in a foreign tongue. The dwarf's voice rose into a sonorous song, dual-pitched with high and low notes at once. His beard vibrated in pulses as the sounds harmonized and excited the red hairs. The glowing words grew like vines to reach the ends of the spear, activating brilliant multi-colored lights emanating from the rings.

When Angus dipped one spearhead to touch the floor, it rang out like swords sliding across each other. Sparks flew in all directions, leaving a large gouge in the stone floor. The point that had contacted now looked larger and had a thrumming buzz of its own.

Johan watched in amazement as Angus released the spinning spear and flipped over it, catching it before it hit the ground. As the dwarf started moving towards the balcony, still dancing for all he was worth[15], he let the still-mundane spearhead out several feet, contacting the Ivon's throne just above his head. The ironwood throne shattered as the second spearhead awakened, emitting a similar, pulsing with a green glow that danced with the blue of the first.

Then things got interesting.

---

[15] …and a good bit more than he was worth, as far as Johan could tell. He'd have to find out where Angus learned to dance, and go learn from that teacher, just to advance his bardic skills…

Chapter 46

Let's Do Lunch

Uvrede stood at the base of the tower, wrinkling her nose. "Humans are so crass. They leave corpses everywhere without properly disposing of them. It is disrespectful, and it stinks!" She burned the corpses at the base of the tower and the banners that had fallen to a crisp then looked up again.

"Are you sure you can climb that?" Zonka asked. "I'd rather see you fly…"

"I'm saving the last of my strength for the flight out," the dragon answered. "Even great dragons like myself are mortal. We'll need to leave soon before they can muster the whole city against us. But we can make a morsel out of your favorite dwarf first. I'm a bit peckish…"

With that, she rose up on her hind legs and grasped the stone wall with her front. Foot-long claws drove right into the stone as if it were dirt, and she started her three-hundred-foot climb with confidence.

----- -----

Geirdriful[16], now wielding a fully activated sleagh mhòr, danced and rolled and flipped and cartwheeled her way to the ready spot - an ancient stone where the ceremony would be complete, her forms run, and her test fulfilled. After this, she would be prepared to fight every foe, no matter how monstrous. She would be ready to slay dragons.

She stopped the spear and ran to the stone, lifting herself up on the tip of the spear to stand, propped ten feet off the ground. One

[16] Geirdriful was the long-passed elf responsible for animating Angus' dance. At this point in time, she only existed in Angus' head, a memory of a shared dream awakened and re-enacted after holding her storied weapon.

hand held the bending spear just under the spinning collar, the other raised in a ceremonial salute to her imaginary foe.

She balanced there, ready. She looked at the crowd of supportive elves all around her and smiled as she basked in the applause - still perched on the spear.

----- -----

Snapped back into reality by the stiff, cool breeze filtering up through his armor joints, Angus looked down to see the source. He was no longer in the lithe body of an athletic elf, but back in his chunky, armor-laden corporeal form. More importantly, his whole form was leaned over the edge of the tower, standing sideways on a spear, three hundred feet above the cobblestones!

...and somehow, that wasn't the worst part. Those cobblestones were obscured by a dragon - a gigantic dragon, much bigger than the one he slew - climbing the tower. Looking at him! *Did that thing just lick its lips?*

Angus looked at the tip of the spear and saw the lower spearhead spinning like a top in a small divot in the stone. Everything he was, plus the spear, balanced on that single whirling point. He tried a small movement and wobbled. The wobble became a cycle of circular swaying, timed with the spinning of the speartip.

"Stones, but this is high!" Angus shouted. "I need a hand, grab the-"

It was too late. The speartip slipped, sending a small chunk of sandstone whizzing by Alene's ear. As the spear straightened, the dwarf hung in midair for a heartbeat before falling, eyes wide.

Angus adjusted his grip to a two-handed one and tried to jam the spear into the tower. The tip merely spun faster and left a deep vertical scar as he descended toward the dragon. She opened her mouth wide in anticipation.

That toothy maw seemed to grow second by second, and Angus managed to orient his spear in such a way that he might wedge the spear to hold the massive jaws open. But as the tips intersected the teeth, the spear flexed and bowed, slipping right past the jagged opening, continuing downward.

One tip cut deep into the creature's tongue while the other cut a groove in the upper palate. He lodged there, hanging above a teasing uvula by a bending spearhaft. The entire head shifted and swayed violently, and gravity seemed to increase to a point where the dwarf lost his grip on the weapon and slid the rest of the way into the Dragon's dark gullet.

That is how Angus Dragonbane was eaten by another dragon, and dragonkind achieved its collective revenge.

----- -----

Black Zonka cackled with glee as the helpless dwarf fell to his doom in Uvrede's maw. The sunlight glittering off of his armor reflected the blue metal she knew he wore. This was the dwarf - THE dwarf - that haunted her dreams every night. As he disappeared with his sideways spear, she shouted her thanks.

"Uvrede, my revenge incarnate! You have made my sacrifice worthwhile! Now I-"

She broke off as she clambered for handholds, the great dragon's wingbeats launching them again into the air. They climbed straight up, past the top of the tower. Uvrede made a different noise, like a gagging. Like something was caught in her throat. No words came from the dragon.

"Where are you going?" Zonka yelled as they flew towards the Eastgate. They were several hundred feet off the ground still, dropping slowly as the great dragon's wingbeats faltered. "How can I help?"

Then she noticed a glow and a growing heat beneath her perch - shining through the scales and skin below her. She had a moment for a final two words:

"Oh, no."

----- -----

Thannon saw the Dragon disappear from sight as it closed on the tower. "It's gone to ground, we might have a chance! Look for anything that will serve as a long spear - that's as big of a dragon as I've ever seen!"

They got a couple blocks before they saw the dragon launch again, straight up the side of the building, then over to the Eastgate, where it lowered again.

"Change of course, boys. Let's pursue!" And pursue they did, as fast as their little legs would propel them.

----- -----

Patrick watched the same story unfolding and chose a different tack. He called his bowmaster, Timothy, over.

"Take every longbow you can muster to the green, and head to the Eastgate. You know how to take down an animal in the hunt; this can't be that different. The rest of us will travel by foot inside the walls to get there. Meet at the gate, and we'll go from there!

----- -----

"ANGUS!" Shouted all three humans as the dwarf fell out of sight, taking the spear with him. They raced to the balcony and looked over just in time to see him disappear into the mouth of the largest creature any of them had ever seen. She devoured the spear with him, and still easily closed her maw.

They stepped back a breath later, as the dragon shot straight up, past the balcony. It crested and started east, losing altitude as it left the city. The trio watched wordlessly as it passed over the wall, where two thick beams of multicolored light burst from its neck, one up and one downwards. Large portions of flesh and muscle disappeared into red mist surrounding the light, and the beast tumbled from the sky.

They watched as chunks rained down on the farm just past the gate, one big hunk breaking a new skylight into the big hay barn. The bulk of the dragon landed and started rolling and cartwheeling, leaving a trench in the right lawn; small fires started here and there.

"Let's go, he might still be alive!" shouted Alene. Johan and Ynghild exchanged looks that suggested there was no hope but slid down the descent ropes anyway. At the bottom, they clambered into the royal coach the Ivon kept ready at all times, urging the driver to make the best possible speed for the Eastgate.

Chapter 47

First on the Scene

Twenty minutes later, all three groups along with thousands of Ivonian survivors, flowed out of the Eastgate and gathered a safe distance from the mangled dragon. The dwarves trotted straight through at a heavy-breathed jog, clattering in time.

The wagon was first to pull up alongside the dragon. The humans jumped out, searching for signs of hope that Angus might have survived. Johan reached the head first, followed only a few steps behind by Alene. What they saw took some telling.

The dragon had slid for several hundred yards, tilling the earth and leaving deep grooves and trenches with each part. The debris field was a hundred or more feet across. It had come to rest against and on top of a long rocky structure that Johan didn't recall; the structure had the look of melted wax but was as solid as iron.

Alene understood what they were looking at first, and she said so just as the dwarves arrived with Thannon.

"This looks like Koksal's train. He was key to our victory at Canolbwynt. I fear we've lost two heroes here."

"Three." Thannon choked up as he said it. "King Bedwyn, my father, was with him."

Johan looked at the width and fury of the burn scar that ran crossways to the trenches. "Nothing could have survived that fire. I'm sorry, Thannon." He offered an embrace.

Ynghild stepped up onto a pile of fresh-mounded earth to get a better view.

"This is an important day. A day of transitions." She spoke loudly and clearly, a voice designed to address the thousands surrounding her.

"People of Ivonia, I bear news! The Ivon is dead, slain in a fair fight by none other than Johan C'Antrell! House C'Antrell is a royal house, and by the old laws, Johan shall be the new Ivon! The Ivon is dead, long live the Ivon Nova!"

Ivonians all around took up the chant, which Ynghild let run until a grim-faced Johan sent a grimacing nod. She continued.

"And with the heroic passing of King Bedwyn, I suspect the authority of the Smaragdine Holt passes to Thannon?"

A nearby dwarf shouted, "Pending a confirming vote of the dwarves of the Smaragdine Holt, yes. Thannon is our new King."

Thannon knelt facing the hulk of Koksal's train and did not turn as his contingent, along with thousands of humans, cheered for him and his father.

"For Thannon! For Bedwyn!"

Patrick shouted from the crowd to Johan, "Where is the Dragonbane? Where is Angus?"

"In there. The last thing she did was swallow him whole! She flew away right after and crashed here, after an explosion in her neck!"

"Angus Dragonbane is in the belly of that?" King Thannon drew his sword and started hacking at the ruined neck of the dragon, hoping to make access to find Angus. Every dwarf and many of the men ran to help. Within a few minutes, they found an unconscious Angus in the uppermost crop, surrounded by ground-up fish, rocks, and sand.

After they dragged him to the grass and cleared his windpipe of fluids, Ynghild rushed in and offered him the 'kiss of life', a method where she shared her breath with his to start him breathing again. After just a couple of breaths, Angus coughed and spluttered, sitting up and wiping his lips.

Ynghild giggled, playing with the bile in his beard.

"I wasn't done with you yet!"

"Madam, have you no shame?" Angus shouted. "I said no, and no means no!"

"Angus, Angus," Johan interjected, "she just saved you, got you breathing again. *Then* she flirted. Give her a break!"

Thannon stepped in. "I want to hear how you did it! How did you defeat the dragon from within?"

"Over here!" One of the dwarves pulled a long, double-ended spear from the holes in the dragon's neck. Johan, the compulsive storyteller, was already starting.

"Yes, that's it. I loaned that spear to Angus from the royal collection, and he launched himself into the dragon's mouth, just to get at its weak spots. A masterful and intentional act, I'd say."

"Well," Angus stammered, "I don't really…"

"I saw it myself!" Johan insisted.

"So did I," affirmed Alene.

"All true," agreed Ynghild. "He took hold of that long shaft and-"

"That's enough out of you!" Angus' reddening face neared purple, and he stormed off towards the nearby barn to wash himself in the horse's trough.

----- -----

Kelly martialed the first fifty dwarves he found in the city. Every operation had succeeded with minimal damage and casualties; "unprepared" was a phrase offered repeatedly.

This Dragon was another matter. She had flown east, and the band of dwarves approached the Eastgate now. It was charred, gate open, and a terrible slag of soldier's and equine remains had to be navigated before they came out to see the finality of the dragon's plight.

Dozens of dwarves and hundreds of humans milled about, surveying the wreckage and chaos of the scene. Kelly led his men to the nearest group of dwarves, where a red-bearded dwarf was… bathing in a horse trough? Kelly noted the green in Angus' beard as he came up for air.

"Angus, is that you?"

"Aye, who's asking?" The younger dwarf cleared his eyes, then rapidly stood at attention right on the slimy boards of the trough. "General, Sir!" He added with a sharp salute. The jerky motion conspired with the lack of traction to drop Angus back into the water, the impact splashing all near.

Angus' still-armored foot busted through the end of the trough, drenching the General in fish-and-bile-laden horse water. Kelly was not amused. He tried to flick water from his arms and picked a half-digested squid from his visor.

"You never cease to amaze me, Redbeard!" Kelly was furious. "Are these antics how you intend to make things right?"

Thannon stepped up, laughing. "What is the plural of "Dragonbane, anyway?"

“Well,” Kelly started, “I don’t think there is one. I’ve never heard of anyone, dwarf or otherwise, who killed two dragons.”

Thannon smiled broadly and gestured to Angus.

“You have now.”

“No.” Kelly sobered from his anger-drunk state instantly. “He didn’t. You didn’t. How?!?”

A new voice, a familiar human voice, called out. It was Johan, carrying the mundane-looking, double-headed spear with reverence.

“With this.” Johan enjoyed the flustered Kelly, too. “I don’t know how much you made him practice with spears, but it paid off. I’ve never seen a dwarf move like that. Or anyone, for that matter. I don’t think I could have done it. But he did. I watched it with my own eyes.”

Kelly looked at the spear, then at Angus, who was only a third of its length.

“We don’t train with anything this long, nor this floppy. Where did you get it, Angus? How long have you been working against Artemus’ orders?”

“I haven’t. Johan tossed it to me in the moment of need, and I figured out how to activate it. Still puzzling that out. But it wasn’t a training thing.”

Johan stepped up to Angus, offering the spear again.

“I think this needs to be yours, Angus. You definitely know how to use it.”

“Shist no!” Angus shied away from the offering. *I don’t know what it was, but that Dream was nearly the death of me!* “I’m off spears for the moment, and this one is clearly too big for me.”

“It might come in handy.”

“No, thank you. Keep it for me; put it in a museum or something.”

----- -----

Johan walked back to the tower with Angus. His guard stayed back a hundred paces in the waning afternoon to give them privacy.

“I saw you use this spear.”

“Aye.”

“But it was something special. Like a dance.”

“Aye.”

"I was surprised - no, amazed - at how you moved. You were one with this weapon. I couldn't train that in a lifetime."

"I was surprised, too."

"I think I know how you did it."

"How did I do it?" Angus asked, eyebrows raised.

"You didn't."

"The aches and pains from overstretched joints beg to differ."

"It wasn't you, though. Who was it?"

Angus executed a full walking rotation, making sure they were truly having a private conversation.

"You won't believe it if I tell you."

"Try me."

"Well, ever since our time in that blasted vine, I've had… episodes."

"Tell me about them."

"It is odd, like somebody else is in my head. I know things I can't know. And sometimes, like you saw, I do things I can't do."

"How does that happen?"

"I'm still figuring it out. You tossed me that sleagh mhòr - how do I even know the name? - and I wasn't Angus anymore. I was a powerful young elf, one who had trained for thousands of years to be able to activate the weapon and slay monstrous beasts."

"Like dragons?"

"Like dragons."

They walked silently for a dozen steps.

"It changed me, too. The Dreaming - that's what it's called - leaves its mark. And not just this." He tugged at the green braid in Angus' beard and doffed his cap to show that some of his hair had likewise turned. "I'll be in the middle of a set, and I'll move on to a new song. And the crowd will stop singing along." He breathed a bit before continuing.

"Then I realize that I'm speaking a language I don't know, singing a song I never learned, about things I've never seen. I have other people's stories."

"There are worse things for a bard to have."

"Sure, but I don't get to be a bard anymore. As the Ivon, I'll have duties, schedules, and …responsibilities. Ugh."

----- -----

Zonka opened her eyes and felt the pain wash over her. She took a moment to assess her wounded state. A badly broken leg and something in her ribcage hurt. Her breath gurgled. This was bad.

There was a Zonka-shaped hole in the shingled roof above her - her landing spot after the explosion from the dragon. She'd landed in a pile of hay on the loft of that big barn, the softer hay preventing further injury.

She felt a pang of remorse over Uvrede's death; the dragon was an ancient queen with irreplaceable knowledge. But none of that mattered unless Zonka could figure out how to survive her wounds. She looked around and found that the stables below had several draft horses. She took some time to study their nuances before picking one.

She waited until dark to work her way down the chute, and hop-hobble to steal a bag of carrots hanging on the door. These she used to get the horse ready for a simple blanket. She left the barn in full darkness, heading east along the road.

Riding nearly bareback, the world's oldest orc tried very hard to get to help - so she could keep growing older.

Chapter 48

Dinner and a Show

Johan stood in his finest dress blues, along with his father, Joseif C'Antrell, behind the heavy, deep azure curtains. The elder spoke first.

"I'm proud of you, Johan. I'm sure your mother is, too. You've become everything we ever hoped you would, and more."

"Thanks, but this wasn't in my plans. I never wanted to run a nation."

"It's a little late to be concerned about that now," Joseif laughed. "Your de facto rule is about to become fact."

"He was an evil man."

"True. But he wasn't always. When we were children, he was good." Johan's father reconsidered. "As good as a very rich child can reasonably be. It was his unchecked power that changed him."

"I don't want to become evil."

"Then don't become evil." Joseif laughed again. "Best way to do that is to embrace checks and balances. Listen to your advisors. Encourage dissent. Remember that you'll be wrong sometimes. Welcome critical review."

They hugged for a moment before Josief continued.

"Enough of that, it is time. Let's make you the most powerful man in a thousand miles."

They stepped through the curtain and into the grand auditorium, where blue-clad nobles and business owners were arrayed at his feet. Three tiers of benches surrounded the spacious banqueters, each level bearing more white and less blue, a quite literal show of Ivonia's deeply stratified social structure.

Johan raised his hands, saluting his people as his people for the first time. *I'm already unhappy with this,* he thought, *it looks like people with money are worthier than those without. It just isn't true! But how to fix it without destroying our economy? I don't know.*

Joseif took the ceremonial crown of sapphires set into silver and approached Johan. His face beamed with pride.

"Johan Percival C'Antrell!" Joseif grinned as Johan grimaced at the use of his middle name. "You have deposed the Ivon, leaving the country un-managed and undefended. You now face the Choices - will you take his mantle upon yourself, to manage Ivonia for the good of all?"

Johan replied simply, "I will."

Joseif nodded and went on. "Will you defend us from threats within and without?"

"I will."

"Will you endeavor to educate us, young and old, to ensure progress?"

"I will."

"And will you bring the best of art and culture to enrich our lives?"

"I will." Johan's mind switched on. *Those last two are my out! But how can I be a bard and a leader?*

"Then it is my pleasure, as head of the Council of the Great Houses of Ivonia, to crown you as our new Ivon. We offer our trust and backing, as long as you are willing to keep true to your choices."

Applause, cheers, and adulation went on loudly for twenty minutes; far longer than any ovation Johan as the bard Johnny Brightshirt had received. His mind swam with meanings and possibilities, but for now, he soaked in the praise.

----- -----

As Indaria gently lifted the cedar bough, small splashes from the gentle rain reached her face. A leatherleaf fern blocked her view into the meadow, and she used her other hand to slide it to the side. Within the meadow, she watched a young male deer and a rabbit friend nibble the nutritious green tips.

She thought of flowers, and those same flowers came into view. She listened to the sounds of nature, hearing how close to music it was, and then it was music. Raindrops tapped in time, just enough variation to keep it from being a perfect beat. The deer tapped a foot on a mossy, hollow log, creating a bass thump. The rabbit hopped through the rushy margins of the creek, rustling sounds punctuated by splashes of shallow water. Every few beats, a rock would be displaced and make a perfectly counterpointed clatter.

She spotted a trace of elven male footprints, just slightly larger than her own, then lost them just as quickly. The cadence of the musical forest increased, taking on an excited, inquisitive tone. She stepped out into the meadow just in time to see a lithe, shadowy figure disappear into a shady part of the woods on the other side of this perfect clearing.

Indaria ran towards the figure in pursuit. It must be an elf, no other humanoid exhibited nearly as much grace and fluidity of movement. She thought it must be a male. But why was he running?

She pursued him for hours, days, and weeks. Strangely, Indaria felt no hunger, no need for sleep; though she did sleep from time to time. Once she woke with a start, feeling something near her. Her mossy bed was still warm next to her as if there had been another warm person near.

Never any conversation, nothing more than fleeting moments of a feeling of closeness, then a desire for nothing more than to pursue this other person. She needed to understand him. And a need to understand this newer presence - one she felt only as a gut feeling. No outward evidence, just an awareness of a new presence developing.

Then a bright light broke her Dream. Air rushed into her pod-like cocoon, large, soft hands pulling her recumbent form from the slimy, green goo that covered her. Indaria fell from her perch high in the tree, perhaps thirty or forty feet. She couldn't see clearly, but the old tree heard her yelp and lowered her, branch by branch to lie safely on the ground.

There she lay, fading in and out of consciousness, for a very long time.

----- -----

Two nights of travel on horseback in the dark was a lot for an old orc like Zonka, but her broken leg made it so much harder. The swelling in her side indicated something, her liver perhaps, was badly damaged and probably bleeding. But through sheer determination, she found the tree she sought in the forest north of Veynsport.

Climbing with one good arm and one good leg was even more difficult. The old crone used every trick in the book, including her extensive knowledge of knots and rope pulleys, to reach her target far above the ground.

Knowing how short her remaining time was, she took no time at all to cut a slit big enough for her to slide into the peaceful pod before her. A small person was captive inside, probably already dead. She mustered enough strength to toss that corpse out and climbed in, pinching the open sides of the pod together with all the grip she had.

She wrestled against being ejected for some unknown time before pain and sleep overtook her powerful will. And after she was asleep, the dreams began, if dreams you could call them. Some might use the term “nightmares.”

Chapter 49

A Decent Proposal

Johan the Ivon walked down the charred and hastily repaired docks alongside Alene, the Queen of the Veyns. At first, one might think they were alone; but a schooled eye would see the Ivon's security taking up strategic positions to protect the Ivon should a threat arise.

Alene's eye was schooled, and she commented with a giggle. "You'd think they were worried about you. What harm could a small woman like myself do to you?"

"That's not something I care to explore, Alene," Johan replied. "I've seen you in action enough to understand your power. And just look around!" He gestured to the half-burned navy and the scorched commercial fleet. "This was your doing, was it not?"

"I'm sure I don't know what you mean!" She giggled again, hiding her smile in her shawl against the cool, fall morning. "That fire was well-timed, however. It ensured that the Ivon Prior couldn't move troops or attack the Veyns had things gone his way. Yes, I'd call it a well-timed accident. Fortuitous."

They walked another dozen steps, and his hand found hers; they intertwined fingers. Then Johan broke the silence.

"I know you said we couldn't be together publicly, as I was a former spy and you were a head of state."

"I'm not sure you ever stopped being a spy," she answered. "I'm pretty sure you still are."

"That's fair. But publicly now, I am a head of state as well. We are peers, are we not? Surely you would allow me to make our relationship official."

Alene stopped as Johan walked two paces while turning. She tilted her head.

"Johan, no. It can't be. We can't be. Our men just warred with each other in two cities. Even in the aftermath, Ivonia has significantly more power than the Veyns. Such a mismatch might be seen as a mismatch, right? As if the Veyns had capitulated? I'm sorry, Johan, but it isn't the right time. And I have to face the possibility that it may never be the right time."

She stepped up to him and grabbed his face, pulled him in for a kiss.

"No matter how much I love you." She let him go and walked the rest of the way to her yacht alone. Johan stood and watched, without moving.

An hour after she sailed, as her yacht disappeared over the horizon with Johan watching at the end of the docks. Ynghild slipped an arm over his shoulder. He inhaled deeply, weakly defending against her alluring perfume.

"You'll need a second," she stated. "I'll take the job."

"Yes, you will."

"She's gone. Put her out of your mind."

Johan sighed deeply, eyes still on the darkening water. "That's easier said than done."

"I'm sure we can find ways to keep you occupied." Ynghild slipped her hand down his arm as she turned to walk back to the city. "You have a city to rebuild, alliances to forge, and power to consolidate. Whenever you are ready, Ivon."

While the Ivon needed to attend to matters of state, Johan remained preoccupied; watching the empty horizon until there was only darkness. Only then, covered by the night, did he allow himself to feel his loss. He walked back slowly so his tears would dry before his next meeting - with Patrick, Timothy, and the other representatives of Gymdeithas Fasnach.

----- -----

That meeting took place on a large, flat roof of a four-story administrative building. It was on the northwestern side of the city, high and with a sweeping view of the Greenway. On a clear day, one could see the Sliver in the mountains to the north. This evening, bonfires marked the towns between here and there, with faint hints of light from the place Johan knew the Sliver to be.

Johan strode up the stairs where he knew the rest of the party was waiting for him. Ynghild was resplendent in a shimmering blue dress, entertaining the dozen guests with small, idle talk. *She's good at this. I wonder if anyone will recognize her? She's worked in each of their towns at one time or another, gathering information and recruiting unwitting informants. But she never looked like this...*

He walked in calmly, using his bardic skills to press his presence further than his person. He stood for a moment behind his seat at the head of the table. Skating his eyes across each set facing him, he expressed a slight smile, trying for confident, not smug.

"My dear friends, I am grateful to have all of you here today. The reasons for our meeting are terrible. Many of you have legitimate grievances that we will never be able to address fully. And yet we are here.

"We see before us," he gestured broadly north, towards these peoples' homes, "a land of plenty. I hope you'll agree that there is more than enough to go around, yes? And I hope we can leave this table with all satisfied, ready to move forward and rebuild."

He sat down, sliding in his own chair pointedly. "Let us hear what you have to say, and come to agreements."

A stout, middle-aged man stood first. "I am Ernst, and I farm between the Greenway and the river. We labored all year to bring in a record harvest, and now it is gone. We face a winter without even enough to eat, because of the former Ivon's spite and greed. How will you make that right?"

Johan nodded sternly. "He was wrong to take your grain. We will return what is yours. Will you work with my stewards in the morning to make your claims, and we will endeavor to return all that was stolen? And for any that cannot be returned, I offer double the market price in compensation."

Another stood as Ernst sat, nodding. "I am Able. Your men burned many of our silos and barns."

"I will send crews to rebuild, including skilled planners. We will defray any excessive costs; I only ask that we use timber from the nearby forests. Is that fair?"

This negotiation continued for an hour, with Johan offering far more than the citizens of Gymdeithas Fasnach expected. Except Patrick. He knew a secret. When Patrick was the last guest who had not spoken, Johan the Ivon made eye contact with him directly.

"Patrick, have you no demands?" Johan used his most proper, enunciated style for his new persona, the leader of a great city-state.

"Personally? No. We at the Sliver have no real needs, as long as our agreements with Gymdeithas Fasnach hold."

"And you are the leader of Gymdeithas Fasnach, are you not?" Johan said with a wry smile.

"Not at all. That's not how we work. I'm not sure how the idea was originally intended, but we have all chosen a distinct lack of leadership in favor of an anarchic democracy."

"Interesting. How is it working for you so far?"

"It serves. We may have different choices in the future."

"You are wise to see that. The same might be said for Ivonia. But whatever choices we make, let us try for peaceful relations in the future."

Patrick raised a glass in salute. "To peaceful relations!" The whole table responded in reply.

While most cheered, Johan and Patrick shared a knowing wink.

Gymdeithas Fasnach served.

----- -----

Playful dolphins splashed along the bow in the moonlight as Alene, Beatrice, and Angus lounged on the low forecastle of the Queen's yacht. They reflected on the day's events, and how the Cyfandir would be with its new arrangements. After a while, Beatrice broke her news.

"I think it is time for me to retire."

"You can't!" Alene objected.

"I can, and I will. I deserve a rest, after raising you."

Alene sagged against the railing. "But I still need you. I can't make it without your help."

Angus butted in with, "I think you've shown that you can. You aren't just a grown woman, you are a queen. And a good one at that!"

Beatrice smiled. "That she is. And I deserve a break. I'm ready for warmer climes."

Alene effected a full pout. "But where will you go? Winter is coming on quickly."

"I miss the island life. The atoll, I think, is the place."

"There's nothing there but fish and trolls. You'll be bored to death." Alene pleaded. "What about your inn, the Hoot Owl? They need you, too."

"I've found a buyer. A nice widow, capable and interested. And I have an idea on the island. It seems that Angus and his friends have nowhere to call home while they work there. I might make a small tavern with a few rooms. Keep just enough hustle and bustle to enjoy, but none of the stress. I might trade a little too, with our friends the Nyanjan."

"A nice idea. But who will pay for it?"

"I think you will. I've footed the bill for you for almost two decades. Give me a land patent - Johan won't argue - and send a crew to build for me. I'll take care of the rest."

Angus raised a hand, concerned. "This won't change my claim on the marble there, will it?"

Alene looked at them for a few moments before speaking. "All right, you two get together and draw a map you can agree on, and I'll back it. Angus, you keep the marble flowing, and Bea, keep me in my favorite tropical fruits. You know what I like."

----- -----

Indaria wasn't sure how long it took her to regain control of her mind and body after being ripped from her Dreampod. Hours, probably. Her reality had merged with the Dreamvine, and she was aware of a deeply powerful presence within the vine. She had sparred and hunted for it unsuccessfully, but she knew it wanted to be near her, to be with her.

To be with her. She placed a hand on her stomach as she started to feel a bit ill. She looked up - high up - to see her pod, stuffed near to bursting with a larger being. She stood, stretching limbs that had been too still for too long. She was covered in drying, phlegm-like goo, which hampered movement, but she was at least unbroken.

She closed her eyes and touched the tree, a mighty, spreading valley oak. As if bidden, a single long branch twisted around the trunk and down, coming to rest at her feet. She stepped up and the branch wound its way upwards to the wounded and dripping dreampod.

The pod thrashed. Rather, the being inside the pod thrashed. Indaria could see that whatever was inside was not experiencing a peaceful Dreaming. The wound in the upper side of the pod seemed to be stitched together from the inside. The elf placed a hand on the pod and felt.

It isn't human. Too big, too powerful. And in so much pain! She placed a second hand on the vine itself, reaching out to the entity trapped forever within. *What is happening?*

The response came in feelings, intentions, and faded images. First, a clear image of an orc, large, old, and female. Wounded. A badly broken leg, with viney tendrils pulling and twisting against the damage, causing more pain. A swollen side was being squeezed and poked. The Dreamvine was angry.

Why are you angry with this orc? She needs your help! More images flashed, including the orc's face and hands, ripping open the pod and tearing Indaria from her resting spot. Then an elven agreement, one traditionally grown into the wood of a tree, was ripped apart and burned in a fire.

A broken agreement? Indaria realized that the entity within used elven references, practices that had fallen into disuse millennia ago. *Are you - were you - an elf?* The struggling in the pod ceased. Indaria felt the struggle end but knew the orc was still alive. She received images rapidly of a brilliant dawn, of a blurry face that suddenly became clear - hers, but with green eyes and brilliant green hair, of a male elf, dark-skinned with similar green hair and eyes, staring at her.

I understand - at least enough. Please, keep her alive. I know she has angered you, but she is important. I know how much you miss elves now. I'm going to bring you home - to my home. We'll work together for a time.

She felt the grudging consent and saw images of the unconscious orc receiving healing care. She saw the tendrils writing a new agreement in scar material on Zonka's skin, but she could not make them out. It did not matter. They had to leave.

Indaria looked northwest, straight across the country to her home beyond the mountains. Every living thing for a hundred yards, even to the blades of grass, moved to the side to make way for the massive, spreading oak she sat in. A simple nod of her head, and the tree pulled its roots from the ground and moved - faster than Koksal's steam wagon - across the cleared way.

Only after they passed did some of the plants and animals return to their spot. The scar this passing left might persist for years. *And now the scars on old Black Zonka will persist, too. I'm terrified to find out what they say.*

THE HARKENTALE SAGA

HOLTGART

PICKLED MARBLE

DREAMVINE

Up next…

IVON NOVA

BARD CORPS

FELDWOOD

Connect with the author, find more about the story, or learn about upcoming books and events at

JeremyJamesSmith.com

or on social media

@Harkentale

Made in the USA
Columbia, SC
08 July 2025

60515428R00143